Praise for Alison Paige's
Tame Horses Wild Hearts

"The two main characters in this story are just wonderfully written. Each with their own insecurities and hang ups they really are perfect for each other. Some scenes in this book will make you giggle and even outright laugh, other scenes are so hot they will make you melt."

~ *Roni, Romance Book Review*

"A wonderful story of two damaged people finding love in the midst of danger. Alison Paige has done a fantastic job of writing about a mysterious, mentally ill person, who believes himself in love with a woman who has no knowledge of what is going on. ...This was a great book to read and I look forward to reading more from this author."

~ *Goddess Minx, Literary Nymphs Reviews*

Look for these titles by
Alison Paige

Now Available:

Writing as Paige Cuccaro
Obey Me

Print Anthology
Gifted

Tame Horses Wild Hearts

Alison Paige

A SAMHAIN PUBLISHING, LTD. publication.

Samhain Publishing, Ltd.
577 Mulberry Street, Suite 1520
Macon, GA 31201
www.samhainpublishing.com

Tame Horses Wild Hearts
Copyright © 2010 by Alison Paige
Print ISBN: 978-1-60504-562-7
Digital ISBN: 978-1-60504-534-4

Editing by Anne Scott
Cover by Tuesday Dube

First Samhain Publishing, Ltd. electronic publication: May 2009
First Samhain Publishing, Ltd. print publication: March 2010

Dedication

A big thank-you to my family for being my biggest fans. As always I'm grateful to my wonderful editor Anne Scott and to the hard-working people at Samhain. And a special "Hell-yeah!" to Tuesday Dube for her amazing artistic talent in designing the cover.

Chapter One

Kate had to admit she felt a twinge of sympathy watching Joseph's scowling face wince each time his family jewels slammed against the hard Western saddle. The man would be impotent inside a week if he didn't do something to protect his goodie bag. *Damn shame too.*

Who comes to a horse camp wearing leather dress shoes, beige Dockers, a suit jacket and dress shirt? The guy was asking for problems. Then again, being the sneaky, no-good liar she knew he was, maybe he deserved a few problems.

"Keep those legs still, Joey." Her voice carried across the riding ring. Joseph's wince at the nickname was a little more amusing. "Keep flapping like that and you'll take flight. Squeeze your knees. Try not to flop around so much."

Joseph's dark eyes met hers beneath his curtain of thick lashes. His chin down, his hands gripping saddle and reins, he managed to look sexy, annoyed and pained all at once. "Right. Thanks."

"Not like the movies, huh?" She'd bet dollars-to-hoofs a man like Joseph never needed to try hard for anything. He was a city boy out here playing cowboy. There couldn't be a worse fit.

"Can't just hop on a horse and ride off into the sunset like they do in the Westerns," she said. "Need to build the *right* kinds of muscle. Learn balance. Learn to read the animal. Get a feel for its needs and fears."

Sunshine trotted in line behind the other horses along the white wooden fence that formed the riding ring. Standing dead center for the best view of all her students, Kate didn't turn when Joseph, flopping like a rag doll atop Sunshine, passed behind her.

"Not lookin' for a relationship," he said. "Just a ride."

Not the first time he's said that, I bet.

Not the first time she'd heard it either. She grimaced at the thought and pointedly pushed her mind from the topic.

Kate focused on her other students. The ones who hadn't lied on their camper's applications and weren't annoyingly attractive to a single, sexually ravenous woman.

"Looking good, Nisha! You could take a cue from her, Joey." The nine-year-old girl perked, flashing white teeth against dark mahogany skin with her proud smile. She threw a glance over her shoulder at the grown man who'd joined their class, her stiff black braids brushing her shoulders from beneath her hard riding hat.

Kate followed the glance to Joseph as he came around, his scowl growing deeper by the second. His wrinkled inky brows matched his hair that brushed over his forehead and hung in long waves to hide his collar. He had a squarish face, held tight in annoyance and pain, a thick jaw and a crooked nose. The man had been in a fight or two. A little scar at the corner of his upper lip and another breaking the dark shadow of beard stubble on his right cheek made it an easy guess.

His discomfort was his own doing. He was too stiff. His broad shoulders, straight as an ironing board, fought the move of the horse and made the ride rougher than it needed to be. The rest of his body struggled the same way, thick arms, big hands, and muscled legs all held tense as though he could bully the natural jarring gate of his horse to his will. No doubt something he was used to doing.

Kate imagined there wasn't much a prime stud like Joseph Garity couldn't bend to his will. If he couldn't outmuscle it, that dark gaze of his was hot enough to melt iron and the female libido, whichever the circumstances demanded. A hard-as-stone resolve with a harder-than-steel body, definitely a tasty combo for any red-blooded female. Why'd he have to be a cheating liar? *What a waste.*

She flicked her eyes to his and met that molten gaze head on. His scowl was just as deep, but it wasn't anger flaring in those dark eyes. He looked like he was picturing her naked. And he looked like he wanted to be the one to get her that way.

Heat flooded her insides from head to toe. Her body tingled in that delicious way when everything is new and mysterious between a man and a woman. She glanced away, her exhale shallow. Her ears went hot in a heartbeat. *Shoot.* They were red. She knew it without looking. Her body's bizarre version of a blush brought on when her lower regions were simmering to a boil.

She shifted her weight against the moist heat between her thighs and crossed her arms over her belly. The attraction had her all too aware of her breasts, warm and heavy, the feel of her bra and shirt against her sensitive nipples.

Reflex had her fingers reaching up to fiddle with the high cartilage piercing on her ear—a silver hoop with a tiny dangling cross. Her gaze flicked to Joseph long enough to see his scowl had mutated to a smug grin. *Dang it.* A man knows when a woman's nervous fidget is his doing. *So what?* It didn't mean anything.

Kate forced her hand from her ear, tucking it back in a knot over her belly. She cleared her throat and her hormone-fogged brain. "Heels down, Tony. Let go of the saddle horn, Delmar. You too, Joey. C'mon, sit straight. Hold on with your legs. Show me good seats, girls and boys, and we'll take turns over the jump."

"Are you friggin' kidding me?" Joseph threw his body backward, legs going up, pulling poor Sunshine's mouth so sharply the horse had no choice but to stop after a few rough steps. She thrashed her head until he'd loosened the reins. "Bad enough you've got us running around in circles. You want me to head this crazy beast over a jump?"

"Joey—"

"Stop. It's Joe. Joseph if you have to. But never—*ever*—Joey."

She tipped her chin to the white sticker on his breast pocket. "Your name tag says Joey."

"Noticed that."

"Your camp application said Joey too."

"Yeah. I—"

"Said you were ten."

"I'm not."

"I noticed that," she said. Three breaths of silence passed with them staring at each other, waiting. "Y'know, if you wanted to beat the cost of the farm's regular class rates—"

"No. That's not it." He grabbed a rein in each hand, and muscled Sunshine's head and body around toward Kate. He rocked in the saddle, trying to nudge the horse into motion by shifting his weight back and forth.

"Kick her." Kate had seen it before. *Beginners.*

"Don't wanna hurt it."

"You won't," she said.

He flicked a scoffing smirk her way then went back to his rocking. Sunshine took a step and then another, more because he'd thrown her off balance than she understood what he wanted her to do. Joe clucked and rocked and rocked and clucked, trying everything except kicking to get the horse to move. He looked like an overgrown kid on a playground spring ride. Lucky for him the speckled gray mare was used to the antics of beginner riders and finally meandered over to Kate. *Good horse.*

He pulled Sunshine to a stop beside her. "I just wanted basic riding lessons. Forward, backward, right and left, stop and go. That's it. Simple."

"Not simple. These kids have been here two weeks. You took the spot of a deserving, needy kid and you're late arriving. You expect everyone to sit around and wait for you? Some of these kids have never seen a horse, let alone ridden one. This is their only chance. They've never been camping, never been out of the city—"

"Sorry," he said, his voice sharp enough to stop her rant. "Listen, it was a last-minute thing. You weren't offering classes. I guess because of this City Camp stuff. So my secretary signed me up for the camp. I didn't know. But I'm here now. It's too late. I'll pay whatever the going rate is, but I am not taking this thick-headed fur ball over any jumps just so you can enjoy some sick revenge."

She stopped herself from laughing by biting the corner of her bottom lip and looked to the kids still trotting along the rail, all wide-eyed and listening. He thought this was the best revenge she could come up with? *Silly man.*

"Okay, fine. You're here. It's too late. But just so you know, I'm not into revenge," Kate said. "Trust me. Sunshine's our most sedate horse. She's practically dead. And the jump's only a foot high. She could step over it. This is a beginner's class, but like anything else, if you want to learn you've got to do as the teacher says."

His dark eyes narrowed on her and made her belly flutter, his stern face hardening, voice low. "Yeah. I'd love to be your *teacher's pet*, but this animal's brain is the size of a pea. I don't trust it to remember its way around the ring let alone get the both of us over a jump."

The teacher's-pet remark sent all kinds of dirty little ideas racing through her head. Maybe she should keep him after class for a good spanking. Her gaze dropped to the firm round of his ass, cradled in the leather saddle. Her hand itched at the thought of smacking her palm against the hard male flesh, digging her fingers in, feeling the coarse hairs bristle against her skin. A fresh flood of warmth gushed through her body, tingled low between her thighs. She exhaled.

"If you've got something else you'd like to suggest, dollface," he said. "I'm all ears."

Kate flinched out of her private imaginings and shot her gaze to his. The decidedly carnal direction of her thoughts must have shown on her face. Her ears went hot in a flash, right along with the wet folds between her thighs.

She wasn't embarrassed. She'd always been a very sexual person, oversexed some said. She'd learned to control those impulses over the years living on the Thorndike farm. But it was more than a little disconcerting to have them flaring up here, now, when riding horses was the one thing that stirred her more than sex.

No worries. She could handle it. "You're right. If you're scared you shouldn't do it. A frightened rider will never get the horse to respond. So, uh, why don't you see me after class for a refund and we'll call it even?"

That made him straighten in his seat. Joe's scowl clouded over his face like a heavy curtain, but the angry expression didn't reach his eyes. If anything he seemed secretly amused, fighting a smile even as he tugged on Sunshine's rein, heading her back to the rail.

"I don't think so." He mumbled something about not taking jobs with animals. She tracked his progress. There was something undeniably sexy about a man on a horse—confident, powerful, man over beast—very primal. Of course the effect was totally ruined once Sunshine broke into a jog and Joe's big muscled body started flopping around on her back like a sack of potatoes.

Kate made a point not to laugh and turned her attention back to those students who deserved it. "That's it, Carmen, squeeze your legs. Savion, keep Willow against the rail. No passing, guys."

She walked to the two upright wood posts at one end of the

ring, with the low cross rails X-ing between them. Constantly glancing at the progress of her students, she toed the long post lying in the dirt before the jump, scuffing her already dirty leather riding boots in the process.

With the launch post straightened, Kate backed a few feet away. Close enough to help if there was trouble but not so close she'd distract the horses. "Okay, starting with Nisha. Straight down the center of the ring and over the jump."

The young girl's eyes widened, the whites all the brighter against her dark skin. She gave a nod, her round hardhat nudging forward and back.

"Okay." Nisha's timid voice belied her brave expression. At the far end of the ring she turned the liver-spotted Sylvester toward the jump, a slow jog bringing them straight down the middle. Her smile flickered, fear stealing a moment on her face, chased quickly away by sheer determination.

"That's it," Kate said. "Push up in the stirrups when your horse reaches the launch post...now." A single stride before Sylvester leapt over the small jump, the little girl stood in her stirrups. Nisha gasped at the small hop, both hands white-knuckling the saddle, reins slack and ineffective against the horse's neck.

"Beautiful job, Nisha." Sylvester did his part, unconcerned with his young passenger, so used to the routine he really didn't need encouragement or direction. But Nisha didn't know that and the accomplishment would likely change her world. These kids needed successes. Their lives were already too full of disappointments. Man over beast, it was a natural primal drive and something that had helped her overcome her demons years ago just like it would these kids.

"Okay, next. Garon, Paul, Tony, Delmar. Right in order, guys." She swung her attention to Joe as he and Sunshine trotted around from behind her, his dark eyes fixed on little Nisha, astonished. Couldn't be easy watching a child accomplish something you didn't have the guts to try.

15

"Joey, you're last. Gives you plenty of time to work up some courage." She knew the nickname bugged him, but that was pretty much the point. Besides, he'd screwed with her City Camp days. He had it coming. "Where's your hardhat?"

Joe swung his gaze to her, narrowing his eyes. She figured he was trying for a steely stare. His floppy rag-doll impression ruined the effort. Kate tilted her head and gave her sweetest butter-wouldn't-melt-in-my-mouth smile, blinking madly for effect. Joe obviously saw straight through the act and winked at her, ruining her effort as well.

"Not wearin' it. Musses my hair." His cocky sarcasm twanged through his voice and glinted in his devilish smile. He didn't respect her.

Right. "Then you don't take the jump. You shouldn't be riding without it at all." She hadn't noticed. *Shoot.* He turned her brain to mush.

With no wiseacre retort flying back at her, Kate figured he'd finally accepted who was boss around here. After the last camper had sailed effortlessly over the low jump all eyes turned to Joe and Sunshine standing alone at the far end of the ring.

"C'mon, Joe, you can do it," Tony said. He'd been giving Joe riding tips all day. Kate saw a big-brother thing happening there and hoped Joe was the kind of man a kid could look up to.

"Thanks, kid." Joe rolled his shoulders then his head, cracking cartilage bubbles loud enough the sound echoed off the nearby stables. He looked as though he was about to take on a prize fighter. Sunshine needed no such preparation. She stood with her head low, weight shifted to one side, eyes drifting closed.

"Okay. You can try it, but wait until I get you a riding hat." Kate shifted her weight to move but stopped when Joe's clucks echoed across the ring. His wild rocking motion spurred Sunshine into motion. The flurry of action and noise had woken the horse with a start. Her ears flattened back, head jerked high, eyes wide, big nostrils flaring.

"Hey, I said to wait. Joe." He ignored her. Kate's sixth sense prickled at the back of her neck. Something wasn't right with Sunshine, the look in the horse's eyes, the way Joe flopped side to side, legs winging. The way he waved the reins and strangled the saddle horn—everything.

She edged closer to the jump. "Stop clucking. You're making her go faster. Joe. Too fast. Stop. Pull back on the reins. Joe. I said stop. Don't. Joe. Joe. Joe!"

Sunshine's last five strides were long and powerful, pounding the ground, propelling horse and rider toward a jump that needed less than a quarter of the speed. When her lead hoof clanked against the launch post, Joe stood in his stirrups and Sunshine planted her feet, stopping all forward momentum instantly.

The big horse slid to an abrupt halt.

Joe didn't.

He sailed head first over horse and jump, landing hard on the other side. Tumbling ass over feet several times, he finally came to a stop face down, arms and legs spread-eagle.

"Oh shit," Kate said under her breath. She rushed over, praying he was okay, that she hadn't gotten his neck broken...or anything else for that matter.

He started moving before she reached him. *Not paralyzed— good.* But he was still on his belly, his elbows propping him up, head hanging between his shoulders.

"You okay?" She dropped to her knees beside him, rested her hand between his shoulder blades without thinking. He felt big and solid against her palm, her hand small in comparison. His dark hair tickled her fingertips.

She heard him spit. "Ate some dirt." He spit again. "I'm good. No blood. Nothin's broken. Knocked the wind out of me."

Thank God. She exhaled, relieved. Should she tell him the dirt was mixed with a high percentage of horse dung? *Naw, save it for a rainy day.*

17

"We need to call Doc, Kate?" At Clayton's question she glanced over her shoulder and saw him standing outside the ring, leaning his forearms on the railing, an adult-sized hardhat in one hand. He adjusted his worn cowboy hat, his blue eyes fixed on Joe.

She shook her head. "He's okay. Doc can't fix a bruised pride."

Kate felt Joe moving under her hand and looked back to watch him sit. He brought his knee up, grimacing, and hooked his right arm around it. His other hand raked the tumble-mussed waves of his hair, then dropped to twist a fat gold band on his right ring finger.

"Well that was damn humbling." He didn't seem to realize he was fiddling with the ring and Kate took a second to notice dark etchings on the flat disc section where a gem might have been. She couldn't make out the engraving and didn't get a chance to ask.

"You gonna make him get back on and try again?" Paul asked from atop his dark mare, Phantom. "You make us keep trying."

He brushed his sandy blond bangs to the side under his hardhat, and blinked his pretty, toffee-brown eyes. Paul was hung up on all things being fair and equal—likely because so many things in his young life seldom were. But he was right. Normally she'd insist Joe climb back on Sunshine and try again. Not just to show the horse who's boss, but to avoid a seed of fear that could grow out of control quick if not faced head-on from the start.

But this situation was far from normal and Joe didn't strike her as the kind of man she could *make* do anything. "I don't think—"

"You bet I'm tryin' again," Joe said.

The last thing he wanted to do was climb back on top of that dimwitted beast, but Kate wasn't wrong when she mentioned his bruised pride. The woman had a keen eye and a way of making a man want to be a man just by turning those pretty green peepers his way.

Eating ring dirt in front of a bunch of kids and half the farm staff may have had a subtle influence on his decision too. Christ, he hated anything getting the better of him. But what the hell did he know about riding horses? He wasn't the outdoor, backwoods *Deliverance* type. He grew up in civilization, if the streets and alleys of Pittsburgh can be called civilized.

At least they frowned on cousins and siblings marrying where he came from. Although Kate seemed normal enough except for the piercings—a ring high on the rim of her right ear and five more on each lobe. In his neck of the woods, the piercings actually made her more normal, but then he knew for a fact she hadn't grown up out here in the middle of Bumfucked, USA.

The little kid, Tony, came around on his horse, leading the devil Sunshine behind him. Joe pushed to his feet, ignoring the stitch in his ribs and a quick spin of dizziness. Man, he was gonna be sore tomorrow. Mathers hadn't paid him near enough to endure this kind of shit.

If he was still on the force...but he wasn't. Damn car wreck had closed the door on that possibility years ago. Nearly closed the door on him. Fuckin' police insurance wouldn't clear him for the streets. *Unacceptable risk of seizures* or some such shit. He hadn't had a seizure in years. Yeah he got dizzy more than he probably should, like now, but the difference between light headed and lying on the ground twitchin' with your eyes rolled to the back of your head is...well, not enough to keep a dedicated cop from becoming a bodyguard.

Joe pushed the past from his head and brushed off his pants and jacket. He spit some more dirt from his mouth and took the reins Tony held out to him. "Thanks, kid."

Tony beamed. "Sure thing, Joe. Good luck."

The little ankle-biter was starved for acknowledgement.

Probably felt invisible at home. Joe knew what that was like. No skin off his nose to throw the twerp some attention. Besides, the kid was all right, coal-dark eyes, tan round face and shiny tight curls. Looked half Hispanic, half African American. He was small but lean-muscled, a scrapper just like Joe at that age.

Yeah, he could give the kid a nod now and then while he was here. "You ever fallen off?" Joe asked him.

The boy shook his head. "Nope. But it was neat watchin' you. You were all..." The boy flopped and wiggled his body and limbs mocking Joe's tumble. "Yellin', whoa, whoa, umph, ouch, bonk."

"Ya liked that, huh?" Joe gave him a tense squint-eyed smile.

Tony shot the same smile back at him with a nod. "Yep."

Twerp.

"You sure you're okay?" Kate asked from behind him. Joe turned to face her and noticed she was holding the hardhat. She must've gotten it from Clayton while he was struggling to his feet. *Perfect.*

Damn if she didn't actually look concerned. Three tiny little lines puckered between her drawn brows, the skin edging her pursed lips turning white with her frown. She shifted her weight from one knee-high booted foot to the other as she waited for his response. Her stretch riding breeches shaped over her hips and thighs and down into her boots. And her green sleeveless blouse made her eyes look even greener, almost unreal. *Trouble.*

He forced a smile. "I'm fine, dollface. Thanks for worrying."

Her cheeks flushed and she glanced away then back. "Actually, I was thinking of Sunshine. I mean, I don't want you taking your frustrations out on the horse."

"Right." The woman couldn't lie for squat.

"You're calm?" she asked.

He snorted. "Yeah. I'm good."

Am I calm? He was about to climb back onto the crazy

animal that had nearly killed him and she was worried about his emotional state? Christ, someone should be measuring him for a straightjacket. What the hell was he doing here?

He turned back to Sunshine and caught her napping. Yeah. Like he'd fall for that act again.

"You're wearing this or you're not getting back on." Kate held out the brown velvet-covered hat.

Damn, the little lady was serious. Joe sighed and took the hat, pressing it down on his head, then snapped the chin strap. It was a snug fit, but he figured that was a good thing.

He gathered the knotted reins at Sunshine's shoulders, put his left foot in the stirrup and grabbed the front and back of the saddle. Two hops and one smooth muscled pull and he was back atop the most likely conveyance of his death. *Stupid. Stupid. Stupid.*

He dropped his gaze to his ruined shoes. Three hundred and fifty bucks shot to hell. He'd driven out to the farm straight from the city. How the hell could he have known he wouldn't get a chance to change? *Damn.* He liked these shoes too.

"Ready?" Kate said.

He flicked his gaze to her. She hadn't moved or changed her stance. She looked tense, all wound tight and edgy. Even her hair looked taut, pulled back in one of those braids that started at her front hairline and shaped over her head and down to a thick tail past her shoulders.

Her hair was dark brown, mostly. Although when the sun hit it, he noticed flecks of red, so it looked almost wine colored or maybe a dark cinnamon. He bet it would look great loose and wavy over her bare shoulders. Even better all damp and clingy from sex, molding over her chest, pointy strands clinging to her breasts...

Shit. Knock it off. That's not why he was here. That's the last reason he was here. Joe pulled his mind out of the gutter and tried to remember what she'd asked. He caught her fidgeting with that top earring again, and she was blushing. Aw, hell. She wanted him. Life just wasn't fair.

He'd bet hard cash if she weren't his principal she wouldn't give him the time of day. 'Course she didn't know he was there to protect her. One of life's little bitch-slaps. What'd they call it? Murphy's Law? Yeah, well Murphy could kiss his ass.

"Ready enough." He tugged the left rein to turn the horse around. Joe flapped his legs, jarring Sunshine's sides with his calves, but the crazy horse just stood there with its ears pinned back.

"Kick her with your heels," Kate said.

Thought she was worried about me hurting the thing.

"You look like you're trying to fly."

That tears it. Joe jabbed the heels of his dress shoes into the poor beast's ribs. Sunshine flinched and started walking. *I'll be damned.*

When they reached the far end of the ring he turned the horse toward the jump and gave her one quick kick. Two minutes later he was pulling Sunshine to a stop on the other side of the jump.

Fuckin'eh. His smile was unstoppable. Who knew what a rush riding these things could be?

The little rug rats cheered. "Yay, Joe. Atta' way, Joe. Ya did great."

Even Kate looked pleased. And a pleased Kate was a mighty fine thing to behold. Lord, her smile turned his blood hot and his muscles hard. The woman was lethal to his work ethic.

Her smile softened the features of her face, sparked her eyes and made her seem more feminine. More like the daddy's little angel his client, Edward Mathers, described and less like the sultry no-nonsense equestrian she'd been acting since he'd arrived. Maybe the truth of her was somewhere in between. *Yeah.* He liked that thought.

No doubt the piercings helped form his initial opinion, though the dark cinnamon hair, sun-kissed skin, rose red lips and soft Latino curves spoke more of her sultry side than the angelic. Made him feel like there might be a wild woman trapped behind those guarded jade green eyes, a hellcat inside that reserved little body. Or maybe he was just horny.

Two months since Felicia walked out on him. Two months and eight days since he'd last had sex. Not that he was counting. He'd be more broken up about it if they'd been together longer than a baseball season. But as usual he'd managed to screw things up before the guys he shared the season tickets with even learned her name.

It was his fault. He could admit it. He should've known Felicia would be pissed when he told her he'd rather pull out his teeth then go to her sister's wedding. But jeezus, it was a game day and she'd wanted him to rent a tux. That's insane. He didn't even know the woman and Felicia expected him to be in the wedding party? *No thanks.*

She'd tried that if-you-loved-me-you-would bullshit. Maybe it was true. How would he know? He'd never met a woman who made him willing to do stupid shit he wouldn't agree to do otherwise.

Okay, riding a horse over a jump didn't count. It was part of the job, part of his cover. A cover he wouldn't need if he'd stuck to his guns and refused to guard a client who didn't know who he was or why he was there.

Even after her father showed him the letters he'd received from Kate's stalker, the photographs the creep had taken without her knowledge, Joe had refused to take the job. Edward Mathers swore his daughter, Katharine, wouldn't accept the protection if she knew he'd been the one to arrange it—some crap about teenage rebellion. Didn't matter. The answer was still no.

And then he showed Joe a picture of Kate with these kids. Damn, he should've walked away when he had the chance. *Sucker.* When it came to relationships Joe could be a complete ass, but kids—well, hell, he wasn't heartless. Besides, Kate was pretty hot in that camp group photo, sexy in a tomboy kind of way—and now totally off limits.

His no-fucking-the-principal rule wasn't etched in stone or anything. But it made for a clearer head on his part, which was generally better for the principal in the long run. It'd served him well for the last five years. Joe didn't see a reason to ignore it now—much.

One of those big brass bells clanged a steady toll from somewhere on the other side of the stables. His young camping mates headed their horses toward the gate, jabbering away about his fall and then subsequent jump and other things he couldn't wrap his brain around. *Kids.*

"You heard it. Twenty minutes to get your horses in their stalls and get washed up for dinner." Kate reached the gate before the riders and held it open as they passed.

The long end of the stables was ten feet beyond the gate and each kid dismounted before leading their horse inside. Joe and Sunshine were at the end of the line.

When his feet hit the ground every muscle in Joe's body screamed. He hadn't felt this sore since his police academy days.

"You impressed me today, Joe," Kate said after closing the gate and stepping up beside him.

Joe put a hand to the small of his back and straightened. "Yeah? And fallin' off horses isn't even what I do *second* best." He smiled and put all the sexual innuendo he could into his voice. Why? He didn't know. His friggin' libido had a mind of its own.

"Really?" a man said. Joe couldn't see him yet. He was just then coming around from the other side of Sunshine. "And here I pegged you as a master. Guess you're a natural at making a fool of yourself."

When he saw him, Joe recognized the guy as the one who'd met him at the stable office and told him he didn't have time to change before climbing onto a four-legged, dimwitted beast from hell. Of course he thought better of Sunshine now. Couldn't say as much for the guy.

"Clayton." Kate used his name like a warning. She turned back to Joe. "He's teasing."

He's jealous.

"Have you met my brother? This is Clayton Thorndike," she said.

"Brother?" Joe shot a glance at the blue-jean-and-checkered-shirt cowboy. "I didn't know the Thorndikes had a daughter."

Kate shrugged. "Stepbrother."

"Legally?"

"Doesn't matter," she said. Which told him the answer was no. But he knew that already. "We're as close as any siblings. Right, Clay?"

She smiled at Clayton who'd planted his dirty cowboy boots wide, nudged his hat low over his brow and crossed his thick farm-boy arms over his chest. Joe didn't give a damn what Kate said. This was not the stance of a man who thought of her as a sister.

His cold blue eyes drifted to Kate and warmed a bit. He dipped his chin. "That's right." He looked back to Joe. "And we Thorndikes protect our own."

Joe didn't catch the windup but saw the solid punch Kate landed to Clayton's biceps. Hard enough to stagger him back a step, her slug shot his tough-guy routine all to hell.

"Hey." Clayton rubbed the spot. "What's that for?"

"You're being an ass. Knock it off and help our *guest* stall his horse." Kate reached over and snagged Sunshine's reins from Joe's hand. The sudden move made the horse flinch, but no one else seemed to care.

She shoved the leather straps at Clayton. "On second thought, you stall Sunshine and I'll show Mr. Garity to one of the boys cabins."

Clayton looked at Joe and jabbed the brim of his cowboy hat up with his middle finger—*subtle*. The hat nudged higher on his head and showed a patch of cornflower blond hair.

"Fine." He swung his gaze back to Kate. "But you holler if you need me."

He took the reins and led Sunshine away down the long aisle of the stables.

Yeah, this was going to be a fun couple of weeks.

Chapter Two

Horse stalls lined both sides of the stable all the way down to the center of the building where it opened on either side, wide enough for a horse trailer to drive through. Beyond that was another long aisle with more stalls. Big footlockers, buckets and other horse-type gear littered along the sides from one end to the other.

Joe followed behind Kate, dodging horse ends and stray grooming tools. The kids had tied their horses to stall doors while they removed the riding tack and brushed the animals down. As they finished they led their horses into their stalls, fresh yellow straw cushioning the floor, full feed tubs and water buckets waiting.

"What'd you mean boys cabin?" Joe said when they reached the center throughway opening.

To the right, beyond the white gravel parking area and drive, he could see the huge antebellum-style farmhouse in the distance. The landscaping was richly manicured. The elaborate home sported gabled roofs, tall Greek columns on a covered porch, intricate friezes and several small balconies. It looked like the typical Southern plantation with its circular driveway in front and the long stretch of white gravel between twin rows of oaks out to the main road.

Through the left opening of the stables, ten feet out, was the indoor arena, beyond that more riding rings and pastures. There was another large outbuilding on the other side of the indoor arena where he'd parked. He guessed it was some sort of group housing—a bunkhouse.

Kate stopped and looked back at him. "Your gear in your car?"

"Yeah."

"Where'd you park?"

He gave a nod to the left and she turned on a heel, heading out in the direction of the indoor arena.

"Hey, you going to answer the question?" He hurried to catch up.

"You registered as a camper," she said over her shoulder, not bothering to slow her pace. "The boys and girls cabins are where the campers stay."

He laughed without an ounce of humor. "I'm not payin' to bunk with a bunch of kids, dollface."

"You don't really have a choice. It's either the boys cabin or—" She stopped dead three steps past the corner of the arena facing the bunkhouse. "That's your car?"

Joe glanced at his convertible, Alfa Romeo Spider—his best girl, parked in the last spot at the end of the bunkhouse's covered porch. "Yeah. Listen, I'll take the 'or'. Whatever it is. I don't bunk with kids. They...wet their beds and...cry."

Just because he didn't want the little ankle-biters getting caught in the crossfire of some freak stalker didn't mean he actually liked kids. Not that he didn't like them, but they were...well, *kids.*

Kate looked askance at him and smiled. "They don't wet their beds." Her brow creased in reflection and she looked away. "Probably. I think."

She closed the distance to his little black car. He'd left the cloth top down. His duffle bag and gun case were in the trunk. Nothing else fit.

"Nice." The way she said it told him she appreciated more than the aesthetic value. She braced both hands on the passenger door, leaning over, eyeing the interior.

"Thanks." Male reflex had his gaze appreciating an eyeful of her. Damn, those stretch breeches did fine things for her ass, smooth and round, high with a firm curve at the base before flowing down over her thighs. Either she was wearing a thong or nothing underneath. *Nice.*

"You restore her yourself?"

"Yeah. You like cars?" he asked.

"I like this car. What is it, nineteen sixty-nine, seventy, Veloce? Not the original paint. Restored leather. Original dash. Love the wood steering wheel. She's beautiful. How's she under the hood?"

"1779cc. Purrs like a kitten."

"I bet." Kate looked up at him, a smile sparking her green eyes like gems. "Take me for a ride."

His libido roared *hell yeah* and shot a hot rush of blood to his cock. Hot women, hot cars, might as well be crack to an addict. Made a man go stupid quick. "Where to?"

Kate opened the door and slid in. "To the boys cabin. Where'd you think?"

Joe dug his keys from his pocket, relieved to find he hadn't lost them in his spill. He got in and started the car, shifting to reverse. "First, show me the 'or' you mentioned."

"No point." She looked too friggin' good in his car. "I shouldn't have said anything. The cottage hasn't been used in years. It needs to be cleaned and aired out, probably a new mattress too. It'd take days to be ready."

"Right. Point the way."

Those cute little lines creased between her brows again, but she wagged a finger out toward the service road he'd driven in on, away from the stables. After a quick little maneuver that had her grabbing the door handle with one hand and digging her nails into his biceps with the other, Joe headed out between the arena and bunkhouse.

When they reached the service road, pastures on either side, he stopped to check which way to turn. Left would take them back out to main road. Kate nodded to the right.

The road was the same white gravel he'd seen on the other side of the stables and along the main drive to the house. But here the road led into a thick forest of trees blocking the view on all sides. If he didn't know better he'd think they'd left the farm and entered the dark wilds of the Adirondacks.

"That's the restroom and showers for the campers," Kate said when a gray cinderblock building came into view on the left.

The road curved to the right just beyond it and Joe gave a grumble and nod as they passed. *Mathers didn't say shit about group showers.*

Up ahead he spotted the large cabins, two on the left and two on the right, all four surrounded by seventy-foot pine trees. Any minute he expected to see a moose or a big lumbering bear stroll across the road.

"Those are the boys cabins on the left. The girls are on the right. Six bunk beds, a working fire place, personal shelves and a small bathroom in each," she said. "You'd be comfortable."

He gave a noncommittal nod, downshifted and kept driving. His hand on the gearshift brushed her knee. She flinched, dropping her gaze to his hand and moved her leg. The car was a tight fit, built that way. An accidental touch now and then was inevitable.

"Sorry," they both said at once. Nervous laughs melted into silence.

Stupid. They were adults and she was wearing thick riding breeches—skintight, sexy-as-hell riding breeches. He couldn't even feel the heat of her skin through the things. So why were they both acting like they'd brushed each other's naked flesh?

And then it happened again, only this time she didn't flinch, and he didn't say he was sorry. They drove down the gravel road, hidden from the world by thick towering trees on both sides. He could stop the car right there and they could do...anything, and not a soul would see.

An illusion, he knew. The farm buildings were just beyond the wall of trees. Still, the thought made his chest tight and his throat dry.

He swallowed and did his level best not to look down at her knee, now resting heavy against his hand on the gearshift. It was just her knee, but dammit if he didn't like the connection. Didn't want to risk her pulling away. *Stupid.*

Joe shifted again as they came up beside another long building on the left. His knuckles chafed along her thigh and back up. They both pretended not to notice. His inner thigh muscles pulled tight though. His balls warmed and his cock gave a hard twitch. His arousal would show when he stood. He tried not to think about it. Embarrassing enough he'd gotten a boner from brushing her leg.

"That's the mess hall." Her voice was raspy, softer then it should've been. She cleared her throat. "They're serving dinner now. We've got a little time before they close up."

"Umm," he said, not wanting her to hear the rasp in his voice as well. He glanced at the line of kids going in and caught a peek at the tall open space inside. Brightly lit, alive with people.

Toward the end of the mess hall, on the opposite side of the road, the thick wall of trees broke for the wide entrance to the long end of the stables. Joe stopped the car for a better look.

"The riding ring we were using is on the opposite end?" He asked.

Kate nodded. "Uh-huh. My office is right there on this end and the tack room is across from it. This service road loops all the way around the stables and connects with the main drive."

Joe looked ahead along the road and realized he could see the garage of the main house through the trees. And as he drove to the front of the stables, the grand farmhouse, with two smaller cottages beside it, came into view.

He stopped the car between the stables and cottages. "This it?"

Kate caught her bottom lip in her teeth. She nodded. The woman didn't look pleased with the turn of events. Joe almost felt bad about being a pain in the ass, but then he wasn't here to make friends.

Bunkin' with kids while on a job was a bad, *bad* idea. The whole point was to get between his principal and some wacko. Not a smart move with kids crowding around.

Best-case scenario, he'd have his own space with room to store his stuff, and privacy to come and go as he needed. Better still if that space was close to the principal and apart from other innocents.

"That's my house." She pointed to the small, one-story cottage nearest the main house. "The one next to it is empty."

Better still. "I'll take it."

Kate shoved open the passenger door and got out. She didn't bother waiting for Joe before she went to the footpath that followed along in front of the two cottages.

It shouldn't be a big deal, but there was a reason she'd asked to move into the cottage from the main house five years ago. She liked her privacy. Honestly though, she knew that wasn't the only reason behind the fluttering in her belly and the warm tingle all over her body.

Gawd, he smelled good, like leather and sweet liquor with a dash of raw masculinity underneath. Watching him slide into the driver's seat of that hot little car, his big hands on the wheel, the finely tuned machine utterly under his control... Yeah, she'd never been jealous of a car before.

"Y'know, if you hadn't lied on your application none of this would be an issue." She stomped up the three short steps to the porch, throwing a quick glance at the identical porch on her cottage just a few measly feet away. Was it too close or not close enough?

"Your staff wouldn't have let me come this week otherwise." He must have jogged to catch up, speaking from the base of the steps.

She looked back at him, narrowing her eyes. "Exactly."

"Sorry, dollface. That wasn't an option."

Kate opened the screen door and tried the knob on the green-painted wooden door. Unlocked, just as she figured. "Why? What's the rush? Got a date to play urban cowboy with your buddies?"

It took two tries throwing her shoulder into the windowed wooden door before it opened.

"Something like that." He followed her, flicking the switch inside the door. A stout corner table lamp blazed, casting a hazy yellow glow across the small, furniture-poor living room.

Just like her cottage, the wall to the left was covered in river stone, floor to ceiling, end to end, with a small hearth and fireplace in the center. Straight ahead was a narrow hallway, right led to the bathroom and left led to the kitchen. Though she suspected the fridge was unplugged and the propane tank empty. The bedroom was off to the right. The door stood open revealing a room half the size of the living room.

There was a bed and a chest of drawers. The main room had a brown loveseat, a coffee table, an end table holding the only lamp, a wooden chair made of saplings and a small TV stand with a thirteen-inch black-and-white TV on top. Not exactly the Ritz. And definitely not her problem.

The air was thick and warm after a season or so being trapped in the closed cottage. She turned to the nearest front window and tugged the spring-roll blind so it shot to the top with a *thwap-thwap-thwap*.

"You could stay at a hotel," she said.

"I prefer staying on the farm. Maximize my training time."

The place smelled musty, like old dirt and wood. It tickled her nose and made her chest heavy. She jerked the bottom of the window, then again with both hands. Nothing. It was stuck.

"Maximize, huh?" She gave the window another hard tug. "I'm curious what *exactly* is so important you felt justified stealing two weeks of fun from a needy kid?"

Suddenly Joe was beside her, nudging her out of the way with his elbow, making the oppressive hard-to-breathe sensation even worse—but for a whole different reason.

He flicked the lock and yanked open the lower pane. "Business," he said. "Client loves horses. Wants to meet on his ranch in Arizona. What the client wants, he gets. I'd prefer not to look like a fool in the process. And like I said, I didn't know about the City Camp thing. So how 'bout we get past it?"

Past it? Ha. Tell that to the kid sitting on his stoop back in the city. She moved to the other window and opened the blind, unlocked the window—*duh*—and jerked it up.

She brushed her palms together. "What kind of business?"

"What's that?" He propped his hands on his hips, his wrist holding back the edges of his jacket.

"Your business. What do you do?"

"Oh, I..." His dark gaze darted around the room. His face was tight, and his brow sank low over his eyes. He scrubbed his hand down his nose, mouth and chin, then scratched the beard stubble on his neck.

He dropped his right hand to his side, his thumb flicking the gold ring around and around on his ring finger. Either the man didn't know what he did for a living or he didn't want to tell her.

"It's, umm, complicated."

Or he thought she was stupid. "Try me."

"Airplanes," he said in a rush. "Engines. Jet engines. Parts, actually. Yeah. I buy them, he sells them. Someone else puts them together. You wouldn't be interested. It's boring."

And not that complicated. "So you travel a lot...buying engine parts?"

She caught his nod, his gaze tracking her as she went into

the bedroom and opened the window. "Some. Yeah."

She came back into the living room. "How's your wife handle you being gone so much?"

"Not married."

"Divorced?"

He shook his head.

She glanced at the thick gold ring on his right hand, his thumb still flicking it. He'd slipped his left hand into his pants pocket. *Not an old wedding band.* "Girlfriend?"

He chuckled and dropped his chin, then looked up at her through those yummy long lashes, a coy smile lifting his shadowed cheeks. "Nope. No girlfriend."

What was that look for? *Uhck.* He thought she was fishing for his stats? *Puhleeze.* Or wait. Was she? *Crap.* She turned on her heel and went through the hall into the kitchen.

Kate had to stand on tiptoe to reach the window over the sink. She unlocked it and felt Joe beside her, nudging her out of the way with his hip. Her eyes closed and she took a deep breath before moving. Lord, he smelled good. She let the scent of him ooze through her body, warming her insides like a fine brandy. *A girl could get drunk on the smell of this man.*

"What about you?" He glanced over his shoulder at her while he pushed up the window and watched her unlock and open the back door. She could almost feel his gaze fondling her body. She held her tummy in, shifted her shoulders back.

"Me?"

"Yeah. You and Clayton." He turned and leaned his backside against the sink, twisting the ring with his other hand. He stopped after a few seconds and slipped both hands into his pants pockets.

"There is no me and Clayton." She crossed her arms under her chest and leaned her shoulder against the fridge. *Warm.* Unplugged like she figured and so *not* her problem. "I told you, we're like brother and sister."

"Y'know that only works when you both feel that way. Wasn't exactly getting a brotherly vibe from him before."

She shook her head. "He's just worried about me. Clay can be a little overprotective. We've known each other for like fourteen years. I'm the closest thing to a sister he's got."

Joe snorted. "Right. So what's he worried about?"

"Nothing, really. It's silly. Just some kid with a crush sending me..." *Shoot.* It was none of his business. What was she doing spilling her guts to him? Geez, it's a good thing he didn't ask for her social security number.

"It's nothing. Never mind." The way Clay was overreacting about the stupid secret admirer love notes and poems and stuff was embarrassing enough. If Joe found out how the Thorndikes were blowing it all out of proportion he'd laugh his ass off.

The Thorndikes treated her like a princess. She was the daughter they no longer had. They made a production out of everything she did, throwing big parties when she showed at district competitions, a ball when she made it to nationals.

Clay and his parents, Bill and Wanda Thorndike, showered her with attention. She loved it. They were the family she'd wished for all her life. They gave her what her real family, her father, wouldn't. Attention, overt love.

To the outsider though, their adoration, especially Clayton's, might seem a little over the top.

Joe shrugged. "Whatever you say."

The movement drew her eyes to his shirt collar and the dark...something, sticking out of it. She moved toward him but hesitated when he tensed.

She smiled, almost laughed. "Relax. You've got something..." She closed the remaining distance between them and reached her hand under his dark fall of hair. The side of her hand brushed against his warm neck. His scent filled her every breath.

He didn't move, and she didn't look, but she knew his gaze was on her. She could feel the heat of his attention on her face, washing hot down her chest, tingling her skin. His suit jacket brushed her breast. Her nipples tingled at its touch as she pulled the little clump of dirt and grass from inside his collar.

Her belly quivered. Liquid heat washed through her body, warming between her thighs. She swallowed and forced a shaky smile showing him what she'd found. "You weren't planning on saving this, were you?"

His dark eyes locked on hers. His mouth stayed as it was, soft, relaxed, full lips lightly closed. The small scar at the corner of his top lip drew her gaze. How had he gotten it? Would she feel it on her lips if they kissed?

She dropped the clump into the sink behind him and meant to hook her thumbs on the tiny coin pockets of her breeches.

He caught her wrist, moving so fast she jumped. His other hand slipped over her hip, fitting her in the palm of his hand. His fingers tightened around her, nudged her closer. A deep breath would make their bodies touch. She stared into those dark, onyx eyes.

"So Clayton wouldn't mind if I...kissed you?"

She licked her lips, couldn't help it, and his gaze tracked the movement. She swallowed, sweet anticipation humming through her body. "No."

"Would you?" His voice was low and intimate, the smooth sound doing delicious things to her body.

"No," she said, just as soft, just as intimate.

He tugged her closer, her belly brushing his groin. Though they weren't pressed together, she could feel the harder line of his cock straining his slacks toward her. Her body answered, warming further, muscles pulsing, trembling.

He brought her hand to his chest, below his shoulder. Her other hand held his biceps, her fingers too small to span the full breadth of his muscle.

"Do you want me to kiss you, Kate?" he asked.

She pushed to her tiptoes, her gaze focused on his soft full lips, on the tiny scar she wanted to taste. "Ye—" Her cell phone rang. *Crap.*

Kate stumbled back and Joe made no attempt to stop her. "Sorry." She fumbled in the breast pocket of her shirt for the credit-card-thin phone.

She brought it between them and flipped it open, too frazzled to notice the number. "Hello."

"Where are you?" a man asked.

"Clayton." She flicked her gaze to Joe's. He smiled, dropped his chin and chuckled silently, shaking his head.

Kate stepped back, and Joe braced his hands on the sink behind him. His tan jacket gaped open, and the buttons of his white stretch shirt strained over his chest. Lord, she could make out every muscle, every hard line all the way down to his stomach. From this angle she could also see the obvious bulge beneath his pant's zipper.

She'd barely gotten a peek before Joe shifted, crossing his arms over his chest, which drew the edges of his jacket closed across his groin. She looked to his face and he gave her an impatient expression, one brow high on his forehead, his mouth a crooked slash halfway between a smile and nothing.

"Kate?" Clayton said through the phone.

"Yeah. Hi. I'm here." She turned toward the backdoor, giving Joe her side. It was the only way she could be sure her gaze didn't drift back to his crotch.

"Where's here?"

"I'm showing Joe, Mr. Garity, the cottage—the empty one."

"Why?"

"He doesn't want to sleep in the kids cabin."

"No," Clayton said. "He is not staying in that cottage. Christ, your beds will only be four feet apart."

"Okay, first, that's an exaggeration. It's a whole different building. There are walls and doors and the great outdoors between our..." She glanced over to see Joe blatantly listening.

She looked away. "Whatever. And second, it's none of your business. The man's going to pay full price. Normally that'd get him one of the camper's cabins to himself. But since the kids are here, this is the only option. It's my call, Clay. City Camp is my project."

Except for his soft frustrated breaths, Clayton was silent for several seconds. "We don't even know who this guy is, Kate. For all you know he could be—"

"No," she said before he could finish the thought. She knew where he was going. He was going to say something about her secret admirer or stalker as Clayton had come to describe him. It was becoming a catchall excuse when he wanted her to do something...or not do something.

"He's not the one who's been..." She let the sentence die unfinished, remembering the additional ears in the room. "It's not him and you know it."

"Fine. You're a grown woman. Do what you want. But if you don't get your butt over to the mess hall, you're gonna miss dinner. Don't expect me to ask the staff to wait."

The line went silent. One good thing about cell phones, he couldn't slam the line closed on her like she had a feeling he'd wanted to. She flipped hers shut and turned to Joe. He didn't bother pretending he hadn't been listening.

"Big brother," he said. "Right."

Kate rolled her eyes and left him standing in the kitchen as she headed for the front door. She didn't have to explain anything to this guy. He didn't know her. He didn't know what her relationship with Clayton was like, what her relationship with the Thorndikes was like. Joe couldn't judge her. Hell, he didn't know anything more about her than she knew about him.

And yet two seconds ago she'd been ready to climb him like a tree. Clayton was right. What on earth was she doing setting him up so close to her home?

I'm being my normal oversexed self, that's what. It wasn't her fault. Most little girls had their mommy to tell them cutesy little metaphors about cows and free milk and there being no reason to buy. Kate's mom had abandoned her to a father who was too busy getting free milk for himself to warn her of the pitfalls.

Not that warnings would've done any good. She liked sex and because of that fact, or despite it, she'd never been the kind of cow men wanted to buy. Damn insulting metaphor. *Whatever.*

Joe Garity had gotten admitted to the camp under false pretenses and that pissed her off. He'd taken the place of a needy, deserving kid, and that pissed her off. It was his fault there was no place left for him to stay except the cottage right smack next to hers. But something about the entire situation, about Joe, gave her a warm tingling thrill down deep inside her, and that unnerved her most of all.

"You plan on sleeping here tonight?" she said over her shoulder, one hand on the front door knob.

Joe had followed as far as the entrance to the hall at the living room, where he'd stopped to lean a shoulder. "Yeah."

She gave a nod. She'd figured. "I'll have some sheets and blankets and towels brought over. I think Clayton's cousin, Rich, is the only one who's used the mattress, but maybe there's a fresher one in the main house we can switch out with it."

"Mattress is fine. No worse than a hotel's."

"Good." She wanted to get out of there. Looking at him, at his silky black hair, his warm dark eyes, his soft lips with the little scar at the corner, only made her want to stay. He made her want to revel in the sheer pleasure his body could give hers. And for the first time in her life that wasn't a good enough. Kate wanted more.

"Dinner's over in fifteen minutes." She walked out.

Chapter Three

"Slap a Campbell's label on him 'cause he looks *mm-mm good.*" Ginny edged forward.

Kate snorted and followed Ginny's gaze back toward the end of the line. Surrounded by giddy adolescents, Joe looked perfectly at ease. His hands in his pants pockets, his chin lowered, he listened and nodded at the excited exchanges going on around him.

Without warning or raising his head, Joe's dark gaze met hers. The corners of his mouth rose, his smile crooked, more self-satisfied than pleasantly surprised.

She saw more than heard him say, "Uh-huh, real jet engines," before his attention shifted back to his pint-sized rapt audience. Kate turned her back on the scene and took her tray.

"Technically, he's a camper." She followed behind Ginny to the milk cooler. "Shouldn't there be some kind of moral issue tangled up with lusting after him?"

"Seriously?" Ginny grabbed a carton of chocolate milk and shifted her weight to one slender hip. "Kate, he's a grown man. A *hot* grown man. You're the boss, but if you ask me it sounds like you're fishing for excuses. Which, coming from you is, y'know, freaky."

"I don't go after every man I meet. Sheesh. I do have some self-control." Kate grabbed a carton of two-percent and tried to catch up to Ginny on her way to the counselors table at the far end of the hall.

"I know, but what more do you want?" Ginny rounded to the other side of the table. "He's hot, he's here and he even lied about his age just so *you* could give him riding lessons."

Kate sank into the chair beside Ginny, both of them facing the room, backs to the wall. "He lied to get into the camp. I doubt my teaching had anything to do with it."

"Okay, fine. But he's still a healthy, heterosexual, *of age* man who's been trying to keep his eyes off you since he walked in the door." Ginny nodded to the dinner line.

Kate shifted her gaze to see Joe adding a few final items on his tray—there was little room left. He turned and Kate looked away. She grabbed her ketchup packet, pinched the end, then tore off the corner.

"He's a guy. He can't help looking at every woman in the room." She squeezed the packet over her hotdog.

"Ya think?" Ginny said. "Good. 'Cause if you don't want him, I'd like to see how he rides. Save a horse, ride a cowboy."

The comment riveted Kate's attention to Ginny. She stared in Joe's direction, sitting tall in her chair, shoulders back, chest thrust forward, an eager smile coloring her cheeks.

Better than a seasoned ventriloquist, Ginny's lips stayed frozen in her smile when she spoke. "C'mon, Kate, help a girl out."

Kate followed the direction of Ginny's willing grin and met Joe's interested expression. She looked back to Ginny. "How?"

"Just don't...don't look so experienced."

How the heck was she supposed to do that? Ginny was twenty, Kate would be thirty in two weeks. Kate had indulged in her first sexual exploit at age thirteen. Ginny had lost her virginity last year to a fellow counselor during City Camp and never looked back. Experience defined them. But it was nice knowing she thought Kate might be a distraction for whatever reason.

Kate swung her gaze to Joe strolling toward them, dinner tray loaded. He glanced at one of the camper tables when Tony yelled for Joe to join him.

"Next time, kid." Joe winked with a nod to Ginny. Or was he gesturing to Kate?

The young boy gave him a knowing nod and two thumbs up for his effort. A twinge of competitiveness bristled at the base of Kate's spine, then she considered the competition.

At twenty, Ginny was fresh and new. Everything was where it was supposed to be, high breasts, firm ass, narrow waist, smooth face. She had a naughty-schoolgirl look going for her, enhanced by her ice-blonde hair braided on either side of her head down to the tops of her shoulders.

Bright sea-blue eyes, thin shapely brows, impossibly long lashes, a delicate bone structure and straight white teeth; Kate wondered why she didn't hate the young vixen. Kate was no slouch, but she wasn't twenty.

Joe gestured toward the chair across from both her and Ginny with a tip of his chin. "This seat open?"

"Yes." Ginny dropped her hands to her lap. She squeezed her breasts between her arms so they ballooned along the edge of her scooped-neck T-shirt. "My, I do love a man with a good appetite."

"Good appetite?" Kate snorted before she could stop herself. "Y'know, the camp's all-you-can-eat buffet isn't meant as a challenge."

Joe tore his gaze from Ginny's overflowing cleavage to give Kate a smile, then ate his first hotdog in three bites without a word. He still had three hotdogs left, two bags of chips, two brownies, an apple and three little cartons of two-percent milk.

Lord, she wondered if that appetite extended to things other than food. Kate shifted in her chair and started on her own hotdog. Ginny was right. There was no reason two consenting adults couldn't enjoy the pleasures of each other's bodies.

And that weird feeling fluttering around in her belly, the one that made her mind drift to yearnings she'd learned long ago weren't meant for a woman like her? That could be controlled—ignored. Kate flicked her gaze to Joe in time to see him down a carton of milk. *Definitely worth the effort.*

The sounds of the crowded cafeteria ebbed and rose and ebbed again as campers and counselors slowly finished their meals and went about their day. The kitchen staff closed the buffet and began cleaning the tables as they emptied. The sounds of sliding chairs and clanking pots melted seamlessly into the white noise and hum of conversation all around them, but Ginny's attention remained fixed on Joe despite his often wordless responses.

"You looked really great out there today," Ginny said, picking through the last shards in her chip bag. "Well, not the falling part. That was wicked. I mean, I was totally wiggin' that you'd broken a hip or something."

Joe coughed around a mouthful of his last hotdog and downed a large swallow of milk. It was a good thing Ginny was so attractive. Kate figured it made up for her utter lack of tact. She suddenly remembered why she didn't hate the inept little flirt.

Ginny shook her head as though she needed the physical act to switch the direction of her thoughts. "Anyway, I think it's really great that you're trying new things. Y'know, at your age. Not that you're old or anything. I mean, even I get sore sometimes. There are days I'd kill for a full-body rubdown."

"Umm." Joe swallowed a mouthful of chips and crumpled the bag. He polished off his brownie, washing it down with the last bit of his milk.

Ginny's smile cranked up a watt. She leaned toward him, her breasts shelved on the table. "I give *great* full-body, hot-oil rubdowns."

His dark eyes met hers, male interest tweaked. "That right?"

"Uh-huh." Her expression flickered. "Or I could use Bengay if you need it. I don't mind. I'll borrow some from Clayton. He's gotta be as old as you. I bet he has some. Old guys...uh, I mean older gentlemen always have some sort of achy-muscle stuff lying around. Oh, duh. What am I saying? You probably brought your own, huh?"

Kate snorted so hard she had to cover her mouth to keep her swallow of milk down and shot her gaze to Joe. He'd frozen in the middle of biting his apple. His dark eyes fixed on the clueless but hopeful Ginny.

He finished his bite and dropped his gaze, a smile fighting at the corners of his lips as he chewed. Those inky black eyes of his flicked up to Kate through his long lashes and the two of them shared a moment of complete understanding.

Kids.

"What?" Ginny looked from him to Kate and back again. "Did I say something funny? You need me to borrow some from Clayton?"

Ginny was so eager to ride her cowboy she didn't seem to care what the matter was. It'd take next to nothing on Joe's part to have her follow him back to his cabin and play buckin' bronco all night.

"Thanks, darlin', but I'm here on business. Gotta keep my head on task." Not waiting for her response and possible argument, he looked to Kate. "Heard you say on the phone this City Camp thing's your project."

Kate wiped her mouth then crumpled the napkin onto her paper plate. "Yep. Four years running."

"Impressive." He pushed his tray to the side and leaned his elbows and forearms on the table. "Can't be easy. Coordinating everything. Workin' with troubled kids."

Kate shrugged. "I've got a good staff. Plus Clayton helps out."

"Your *brother*," he said.

Kate met his gaze and his smirking crooked grin. "Stepbrother. Yes."

"Right."

Kate refused to take the bait. Whatever was going on in Clayton's head about her, or whatever Joe thought was going on, didn't matter. She loved him like a brother and nothing would change that. She was certainly under no obligation to explain or defend her relationship with him to Joe.

"Ever have any trouble?" he asked.

"Trouble?"

"Campers getting out of line, disgruntled employees. With you being a woman I'd imagine stuff like that could be rough to handle."

"No harder than it would be for a man to handle." Pride pulled her spine straighter. "And no. No trouble. The kids are chosen by their good behavior in school. A reward sort of thing. And the employees are mostly regular farm staff except for the counselors.

"There's a waiting list at the local college. Working the camp counts toward course credit. Most know they're lucky to be here and work hard to stay."

"Most?"

"She's thinking about Frank," Ginny said. "Ass. He was in one of my psych courses. He sat in the back of the class and slept. Snored so loud the professor threw him out a couple of times. That is when he bothered to show up at all."

Joe's gaze swung back to Kate. "What happened with Frank?"

"Nothing, really." Kate meant to leave it at that, but some strange impulse possessed her mouth and she couldn't stop herself from adding, "He was a little obsessed with me. That's all."

"Obsessed?" Joe's dark eyes sparked, interest leaning him a hairsbreadth closer.

It was like a woman's version of the fish-that-got-away story. The fish gets grander with each telling. Not that Frank was a fish she'd ever want to keep. She rolled her shoulders and nudged her empty milk carton with the prongs of her plastic spork.

"He asked me out a few times." He'd asked her out once. "I had to keep telling him no. I don't date the counselors." But she had slept with one or two who were over twenty-one and too buff to refuse. She'd needed the release.

"He was pretty torn up about it. Started affecting his work." His laziness had been affecting his work from the start. Her refusal only made his poor work ethic worse. "It got so bad Clayton finally fired him."

"*Clayton* fired him?" His right brow shot to his hairline. "Because he was a lousy employee or because he kept asking you out?"

"Well, both. But he wasn't jealous." She could tell that's what he was thinking.

"'Course not." A ghost of a smile flickered across his lips then vanished. "Ever hear from him again?"

"No."

"Ya-huh." Ginny elbowed her arm hard enough to make her topple the milk carton. "Doesn't he work at Sherman's Feed Store now?"

"Oh. Yeah." She'd forgotten. He never spoke to her, barely acknowledged her presence the few times he'd seen her. Not that she cared. She didn't make any special effort toward him either. Why would she?

"But I hardly see him. Probably stays in the back to avoid me. Broken heart. You know." More like he's lounging somewhere trying to sleep through his shift with no reason to rouse himself for a woman who'd already turned him down.

"How often do you go to this feed store?"

"About every other week. Wednesdays, usually."

"Today's Sunday, right? You going this Wednesday?"

"Uhm, yeah." What was with the interest in her schedule?

He gave a nod and settled back in his chair. "I'll go with you."

"What? Why?" He didn't seriously think she needed his protection, did he? The idea was really sweet, but he barely knew her. It was a little soon to be getting all possessive and protective of her. Not that she knew when that sort of impulse normally kicked in. A byproduct of relationships, which made it a foreign concept. Kate didn't have relationships. She had interludes. Relationships were for the cows men wanted to buy. Gawd, she hated that damn metaphor.

"It's in town, right? Figured I'd take a look around. Never been this far out before. I was a city kid myself."

"Oh." Geez, what was it about this guy that made her brain go straight to damsels-in-distress scenarios and her heart to happily-ever-afters? She was so *not* that girl. "Sure. Why not? It's right before town actually. But I'll give you the grand tour of Hickory, Pennsylvania. Then you can figure out what you'll do with the other twenty-three hours and forty-five minutes of your day."

It had taken him less than a day to get a solid lead on who was stalking Mathers' daughter. Not bad. Now he just needed to survive the City Camp activities and riding lessons with taskmaster Kate long enough to get some proof.

"Your legs are flapping again, Joe," Kate yelled from the center of the riding ring. "Heels down. One hand on the reins. You're not plowing a field."

The next day was more of the same. "Grip with your knees, Joe. Keep your butt stuck to the saddle."

Grip with his knees? His knees were Jell-O and his thighs ached so bad he could barely lift his leg high enough to step into his jeans in the morning. And his ass? If the chair didn't have a cushion, he didn't sit.

Jeezus, what was wrong with these people? They did everything on horseback. Okay, he got that City Camp was a horse camp, but games of red light green light, Mother may I, and races balancing eggs on wooden spoons, it was insane. They went on hikes on horseback, picnics on horseback. He'd even caught one kid asleep on the back of his horse. It was possible to have too much of a good thing and these people had passed that mark his first day.

By Tuesday night he could no longer feel vital parts of his body. At least he hadn't fallen off again, but he'd been stepped on twice which only hurt half as much. He'd gone over the jump several times and even figured out how to keep from pinching his balls or having them ram back up inside him every time he hit the saddle.

All things considered he was in a decent mood Tuesday night when he closed Sunshine's stall door and noticed the soft glow from Kate's desk light in her office at the far end of the stables. The office wall facing the stable aisle was windowed along the top half, including the door. So the light, though small, shone clearly at the darkened end of the stables.

Joe draped Sunshine's lead over the hook on her stall and started toward the office. *Kate.* Despite her taskmaster tendencies, she was one of the few things he'd miss about this place.

She was a smart cookie and sexy as hell with that quick wit and those sexy riding breeches. She sure hadn't made sticking close to her easy these last few days without rousing her suspicion.

He didn't exactly have a lot of options. When a man follows a woman everywhere, people don't normally think, *bodyguard.* As far as anyone on the grounds knew, he was hot for the teacher. It worked for him. The only potential for problem was Kate and the reasons *she* thought he was sniffing around so much.

So far she didn't seem to care one way or the other. Oh sure, she wanted him. That was obvious. There'd been a lot of heavy flirting back and forth. But he'd managed to keep it together and his hands to himself. His slip-up the first day helped set his guard. He knew how close he could get before male instinct took over.

What bunched his britches was that Kate didn't seem hung up on what came next. *Weird.* Women he dated were forever asking, "What does this mean? Where are we in our relationship? How do you *feel?*"

Joe shuddered. Christ, his balls shrank just thinking about it. Usually the questions started right about the time he'd screw things up. Not intentionally. He actually liked the women he dated. He definitely liked fucking them. He was just a walking time bomb when it came to relationships. What'd they say—the first step is admitting you have a problem?

But Kate was different. She seemed happy as a kitten in milk the way things were and if their flirting pushed the envelope now and then, she wasn't the one pulling back and taking stock. Not that he wanted her asking those kinds of questions. He wouldn't know what to tell her. But why wasn't she asking?

Joe pushed through the office door, his attention fixed on the small desk lamp directly across from the entrance, the desk's short end against the wall. "Kate?"

"What do you want?" Clayton's voice spun Joe around.

Jeezus, he hadn't even seen him standing there at the wall of file cabinets behind the door. It took him a second to regroup. "Lookin' for Kate."

"I got that." Clayton closed the top file drawer without depositing the manila folder in his hand and moved around Joe to the desk.

He tossed the folder toward the upper corner of the ink blotter then conspicuously moved a nearby clipboard and stack of mail on top of it.

"You're lookin' for Kate a lot these days. Following her around like a damn lovesick puppy." He settled into the cheap desk chair and jabbed the power button on the desktop computer. The small monitor sitting on top flickered to life.

"Right." Joe folded his arms across his stomach and rocked back on his heels. "We got a problem here?"

He didn't give a damn what Kate said. The guy had issues and most of them were tangled up around her.

"Problem?" Clayton shook his head with a wrinkled chin and a shrug of indifference. "Naw, no problem. Not unless you cross the line and then...yeah. We'll have a big problem."

Brother, my ass. She had the guy's head so twisted over her he'd been shooting him daggers from day one. One night he'd even noticed Clayton sitting in his truck in front of the stables, staring at Kate's cottage—watching. Hell, he was as much stalker material as the feed-store guy. Christ, how many other screwed-up guys had the sultry little tomboy left in her wake?

"There something I should know?" Joe asked. "I'm not a man to go fishin' in another man's pond."

Clayton threw him an icy glare, blue eyes narrow beneath the rim of his cowboy hat. "No. Kate does as she pleases."

"Right. So we won't be having this conversation again."

Clayton shifted his gaze back to the glowing monitor. "Right."

Joe waited a beat, scanning the room. The office was littered with all manner of horse paraphernalia. Trophies, ribbons and the odd tack or tool crowded on every inch of the captain's chest behind Clayton.

There were pictures on walls, of Kate and just as many of Clayton, both at different ages over the years, with horses and without.

Except for an overflowing hat rack over the long inside windows, practically every inch of wall space was filled with memories, or little shelves displaying trophies and ribbons.

He could see the night sky through the windows on the other side of the room. A dull indoor-outdoor rug covered the floor. The odd chair here and there, a saddle rack and coat tree helped fill the small room.

It was a nice office, homey, comfortable, welcoming. It was Kate's office and the moment he thought of her, he could smell her there. The aromas in the stable were pungent, naturally, and not altogether unpleasant. But beneath them, like warm smoke over a blazing fire, was the scent of vanilla mixed with the wildflower fragrance of her soap. He breathed it in.

"What the fuck are you doing?"

Joe brought his gaze back to Clayton, training keeping surprise from his face. He threw a nod toward the stack of mail and clipboard. "Stalker send another one?"

Clayton's face went lax and pale. He blinked and the emotion shifted to suspicion. "What do you know about anything?"

"Photo, note or both?" Joe asked. "Does she know?"

Clayton shoved to his feet, sending the desk chair wheeling backward, crashing into the captain's chest. A metal hoof pick clanked to the floor, ribbon tails fluttered and trophies trembled.

Joe didn't so much as flinch—practice not instinct. Clayton was as broad shouldered and muscled as Joe, and only an inch or so shorter. It'd be a fair fight if Joe hadn't had ten years on the force and five years of extra tactical hand-to-hand training on his side.

"You," Clayton said, accusing. "You're the one that's been sending that shit? I shoulda known…"

"Wrong." Joe pulled his leather cardholder from his back pocket. He found his business cards among his thin fold of bills, license and lone credit card. He wasn't big on wallets and even the little pouch was uncomfortable on horseback. But so was the gun strapped to his calf under his jeans. A man makes allowances.

He shoved his business card toward Clayton. "I'm a bodyguard. On the job. Used to be a cop. I know what I'm doing."

Clayton snatched the card from him and scanned it. His hard blue gaze shot back to Joe. "Who hired you?"

"Edward Mathers."

Clayton made a disgusted snort and tossed the card back. It fluttered to the floor. "Get out."

"Your father, Bill Thorndike, knows I'm here. He okayed it."

"You think I won't check that out?"

"I'm counting on it."

Clayton exhaled, his gaze dropping to the folder he couldn't see. He seemed to resign himself to the facts of the situation, propping his hands on his hips. The combativeness took a decidedly lesser edge in his tone. "Kate's not gonna like this."

"Kate doesn't get a vote."

"You know who's been sending this shit?"

"Not yet. Not for sure," Joe said. "Show me what you've got, and I'll find out."

Clayton shook his head. "Edward Mathers never did a damn thing for her. Doesn't make sense. How can I be sure you're not the stalker?"

"Thought the same about you."

Clayton's gaze snapped to Joe's, anger flashing them a brighter blue. "I've known Kate since we were kids. She's a part of the family. I'd never—"

"How long have you been in love with her?"

Clayton's mouth snapped shut. He blinked beneath his wrinkled brow and looked away. "I'd never hurt her. She, she means the world to me. But she doesn't...we aren't like that with each other. Never have been. We never will be."

"Maybe she needs you to be more."

Clayton's shoulders shook once with a silent laugh. "Yeah. I know."

53

Joe knew exactly what was going through his head. Same as any guy. *Lucky—fuckin'—me.* What greater hell than to want to give the woman you love what she needs and what she needs most is your friendship? *Damn.* It's a private torment. The best Joe could do for him was to let Clayton deal with it on his own.

"I was hired to protect her. To help. I don't give a shit about anything else," Joe said. "You an obstacle or an asset?"

Clayton looked at Joe, most of the hostility and abject resentment gone from his eyes. He gave him a nod and pinched the corner of the manila folder. A quick yank and it slipped from under the pile. He offered it to Joe then pulled the desk chair back under him.

"The poem came first," Clayton said. "A week later he sent the first picture. He's alternated poem for picture every week since."

"You put the dates on them?" Joe flipped through mismatched note pages and photos.

"Yeah. After we got the second poem I started keeping track. Police orders."

Joe paused to look at Clayton. "They get any leads?"

"Police haven't done shit. They say he hasn't broken any laws. No threats or anything like that. Didn't even use the U.S. mail. Just left them on her desk or under the door of her cottage or wherever."

"Right." Joe examined the contents of the folder.

Jeezus, how long had this been going on? Two months? Ten weeks? Longer? There were five photos and five notes, plus the ones Kate's father had gotten. He'd have to double-check, but Joe was pretty sure there were a few that predated the earliest one Clayton had collected.

"He was close for some of these." Joe studied the photo of Kate going over a jump. His gaze drifted from the top rail of the riding ring at the bottom of the photo. He'd been standing right next to the ring when he'd taken the picture. She'd seen him. Everyone had.

His gaze slipped back to Kate. She looked every bit the gleaming beauty atop her sleek black steed. Her hair was braided beneath a chocolate brown hunter's helmet. Her body perched over the shoulders of the animal, legs bent, muscles taut in the snug breeches as the horse's powerful body launched upward, front legs already over the tall jump.

Joe exhaled, focused and flipped to the next photo. *Fuck.* His mind processed what he saw, professionally, analytically, but his body responded with a born instinct he couldn't deny. He swallowed, his chest tight. He flicked his gaze to Clayton. "This a cell phone photo?"

"Yeah. Looks that way." Clayton was watching Joe.

He had to have seen the photo, knew it was of Kate wading into a lake, naked, her sun-kissed skin a soft glow in the predawn light, the muscle taut over her nicely round ass as she stepped. A tuft of curly black bush peeked between her legs, the teardrop curve of one breast shown in profile, a teasing glimpse of her puckered nipple.

How long had Clayton stared at it? When was the last time he'd taken the liberty?

"She seen this one?" Joe asked.

Clayton shook his head, dropped his gaze, his fair complexion reddening. "Didn't want to embarrass her. And I... It would freak her out."

"Right." Joe tried to be an understanding guy. But hell, the thought of him staring at her, fantasizing, getting aroused, it twisted his gut. He didn't know why, didn't even wonder.

Joe pushed it from his mind and slipped the photo to the bottom of the folder. Whatever went through Clayton's head when he'd stared at the photo wasn't his business. Protecting Kate's modesty wasn't Joe's responsibility either. That she'd be embarrassed if she'd seen the photo, more so if she knew they'd both seen it, was enough for him to let it go—for now. He'd tell her eventually. Had to. Never mind why.

"Poems are amateurish." He tried to force his mind back to

the job.

"Yeah." Clayton shifted in his seat, sitting straighter, clearly relieved the heavy tension in the air had dissipated. "Kate thinks it's a kid."

Joe slapped the folder closed and dropped it to his side. "Could be right. We'll see. I'll take the stuff back to my bunk and have a better look. See if I can find any patterns, any fuckups that'll tip us off."

"Hell, no." Clayton jumped to his feet, made a reach for the folder. "If Kate knew you were staring at that photo—"

Joe put his arm behind him and held Clayton back with a hand to his shoulder. "It's why I'm here. It's just a picture, man. I have to look if I'm going to do my job."

He could see the reasoning flickering behind Clayton's eyes. The man straightened, took a step back. "Yeah. You're right. *Shit.*"

When he was sure Clayton wasn't going to make another lunge for the folder, Joe turned toward the door and grabbed the knob. "Let me know if you find anything else."

"Yeah." Clayton's tone sounded distracted. "Hey. Listen."

Joe looked back over his shoulder.

"She likes you," Clayton said. "I mean, she's into you. I've known her long enough. I can tell."

Joe shrugged, going for indifference but worried his sudden shortness of breath and hammering heart made him miss the mark. "She's all right. She's…I mean…yeah."

Fuck. She was the job. Had to be. That's it. No emotions. No connections. Otherwise someone got dead. What the hell was he hedging about?

"Right," Clayton said. "You hurt her, I'll kill you."

Joe nodded. "I know."

Chapter Four

"Just tell me how old you were." Joe leaned his back at an angle against the seat and the passenger door. He'd draped one arm over the seatback. The other elbow poked through the open window. He watched Kate behind the driver's wheel, her smile wide and natural.

Countryside whizzed by beyond her, wind whipping wild strands of hair around her head and face. She'd reach up now and again to try to gather the brownish red strands behind her ear only to have them fly free a second later. She didn't seem to mind. The braid held most of her hair in place.

"How old were you?" she asked, her voice light with laughter. She glanced his way and the sun sparked in the gem green of her eyes. When she looked back to the road he couldn't tear his gaze from the silver hoop high on her ear. For some reason the flash of silver made his cock tingle.

"Ten. Did my fifteen-year-old babysitter on top of my Spiderman comforter."

Her mouth opened, the corners flickering between a smile and shock. Her eyes shifted his way then back to the road. "Seriously?"

No. It had been his mom's stoned-out-of-her-head friend. She was in her late twenties. It didn't screw him up mentally or anything—that he could tell. He hadn't exactly been opposed to the idea. It was just weird mostly. He didn't think about it much. The comforter *was* Spiderman though.

"Seriously," he said. "Now tell me yours."

She cocked a thin brow and looked sideways at him. "Uh...no."

The breeches were caramel colored today with dark brown patches on the inside of each knee. Her shirt was the buttoned sleeveless style she seemed to like best, a soft pink, so pale it looked as though it'd been part of a load of whites and a single pair of red panties. The warm colors set off the fiery highlights in her hair and made those green eyes of hers blaze.

"No? Oh. It's like that is it?"

She laughed. Not a girly giggle but a real laugh, deep in her chest, rich and palpable. His muscles tugged. His cock weighed heavier.

"I didn't promise anything," she said.

"Right." He smiled back at her. He couldn't help it. She looked like a goddamn shampoo commercial, smelled like vanilla and wildflowers and actually *got* his sense of humor. Joe didn't know he could be funny, but he liked it. He liked making her laugh—really laugh.

"I told you the first time you asked it was none of your business. Which one of those words confused you?"

He shrugged. "Figured you were being coy."

Her brow wrinkled but the humor stayed bright in her eyes. "What, like flirting coy?"

He raised a brow. "You weren't?"

She laughed again. He felt the heat of it flush his face and wash warm through his body down to his groin. He looked away, smiling, not sure he could keep the arousal from his eyes.

No sense making things harder than they were. Harmless flirting was one thing, even heavy flirting, but the way anticipation sizzled between them, things could turn from fun to feverish in a heartbeat. Joe wasn't convinced he could slam on the breaks that fast. Not with Kate.

"Lemme help you out." Her voice was deeper, hotter somehow. He looked back at her as she watched the road. She licked her lips, lowered her chin and slid her eyes toward him from the side.

Her smile had gone softer, crooked, sexy. "When it comes to flirting and sex, I don't dick around. You won't need to ask."

Joe fisted his hand on the seatback, clenched his jaw. Heat flooded to his cock so fast his chest squeezed from the strain. His muscles snapped tight at once, made him shift in his seat.

He forced a smile and threw her an unaffected nod. "I'll make a note."

He looked back to the road in time to see the blur of a green metal Ford as they swerved to the left and it flew past on his right.

"Watch it." Reflex shot his hand to the dashboard, stomped his feet into the floor.

They were back on the right side of the road before Kate answered. "What? Sheesh, don't yell like that. You scared the heck outta me."

Joe snapped his head around to look out the truck's back window. The little green Tempo was receding fast as they sped down the road. He exhaled and slumped back around.

"Back at ya." He raked a hand through his whiplash-mussed hair. Another deep exhale and his pulse slowly returned to normal. He draped his elbow on the open window again, his thumb flicking his academy ring around his finger. He stopped when he realized he was doing it.

"You look pale." Kate turned her attention back to the road. "I've driven this road a zillion times."

"It's not a road. It's barely a path."

The road was almost two cars wide, no lane lines and worn shoulders where cars edged for extra space. He'd managed to ignore her breakneck speeding along the country lane until then.

"Relax. Everybody passes along here."

"Right."

He saw her glancing at him from the corner of his eye. He wouldn't return her gaze. "Wow. That really freaked you out, didn't it?"

Joe shifted again, settling deeper in his seat. He threw his left arm to the seatback, determined to forget the flash of panic. "I'm good."

She snorted. "Obviously. What, you were in some sort of horrific accident or something and now cars make you wig out?"

He clenched his jaw so hard his teeth squeaked in his head. Joe glanced at Kate, pissed as hell he'd lost it in front of her and allowing the sentiment to show on his face.

"Oh God, Joe, I'm so sorry." Her sincerity squelched his self-reproach and made him regret his reaction altogether.

"Forget it." He shifted his attention out his window.

"No. What happened? I want to know."

Joe looked at her and she held his gaze for a second before shifting her attention back to the road. *Shit.* What could he tell her without blowing his ridiculous cover? Not the truth, that he'd let some joy-riding gangbangers egg him into a high-speed chase, let himself get careless. He was a cop. He should've known better. And now he'd never be a cop again.

He shook his head and gazed out his window. "Bad judgment. That's all."

"It was your fault?"

His thumb flicked his academy ring. He didn't care. "I was flying. Thought I could make the light. I didn't."

He'd made the light. The intersection was emergency red in all directions. The old geezer never did understand why no one was moving. Didn't hear Joe's sirens. Couldn't see his lights around the delivery truck beside him. It was over fast as a bolt of lightning—a crack of thunder. Joe's life changed forever.

"How bad?" Her voice was soft, hesitant as though the

white walls, sanitized sheets, tubes and beeping monitors still surrounded him. As though his life still hung in the balance.

"About a year in the hospital." *Fourteen months, two weeks and three days.* "Couple years of physical therapy." *Two years, five months and twenty-two days.* He'd learned to walk again, learned to feed himself, to wipe his own fuckin' ass. Joe shoved the memories from his head. It was over. He sure as shit didn't want to go back.

He sighed, expelling the dark emotions of those days, and pushed straight in his seat as Kate made the left into a gravel-covered parking lot.

"This the place?"

"This is Sherman's Feed Store," she said, graciously allowing him to escape the discussion.

The cement block building was tan and white, L-shaped, with a red corporate symbol painted along the side. The store stood alone, wide fields on both sides, a farmhouse off in the distance behind. She parked at an angle next to the awning-covered glass entrance.

They reached the doors at the same time, but Joe snagged the handle first and held it open for Kate. A cowbell jangled, clanking against the glass in the corner.

"Thanks," she said.

Joe gave her a nod then followed and stopped two steps in.

Inside was cowboy heaven. Everywhere he looked was tack, buckets, ropes, tools and animal food supplements. There were bridles on one wall, harnesses on another. Hats on pegs, a glass case filled with shiny silver belt buckles and aisles of metal racks filled with dog food, cat food, rabbit food and food for whatever else furred or feathered that ate. It was a country bumpkin's one-stop shopping.

Kate hadn't even hesitated. She wound her way around a center display of wind chimes next to a stack of saltlick blocks, past a pile of bagged goat pellets and a rack of saddle blankets straight to the glass display counter and register at the center of the store.

"Katie girl," the wispy white-haired man behind the counter sang.

"Hey, Donny."

"What can I do ya for?" Donny's round face scrunched and wrinkled with his smile, his happy blue eyes following her approach. He had a belly on him that looked solid, and thick callused hands. He wore a Western-style shirt with the sleeves folded to his elbows. The top snaps at the collar were open, showing his white T-shirt underneath. Cowboy through and through.

"Same as always." Kate leaned her elbows on the glass top. "Oh. I also need a bucket of supplements. The gray's pregnant."

His warm smile brightened, fuzzy white brows jumping to his hairline. "Yeah? Good to hear. Bill and Clay must be dancing the jig. Tell 'em congrats for me, will ya?"

Kate beamed. "You bet."

Donny's gaze flicked from Joe beside the doors to Kate. "Anything else new at Hickory Hills?"

Kate wrinkled her chin, thinking, and shook her head. "Nope. The camp's up and running again. Managed to squeeze in four more kids this year." She glanced back at Joe. "Well...three."

Donny tipped his chin Joe's way. "Who's your friend?"

"Joe Garity," Joe said before Kate could answer. He traced Kate's path through the store to the center counter and offered his hand to the older man.

Donny matched Joe's grip. "Good to meet ya. So are you two...?"

"No," they said in unison, then looked at each other.

Joe knew why he'd answered so quickly. She was his principal. Bodyguards don't fuck their principals. Plus he liked Kate beyond wanting to screw her brains out. And since everyone he screwed wound up hating him for one reason or another, he figured it was all for the best. But what was Kate's excuse?

"He's actually one of the campers this year." She looked at him as though she was wondering the same thing about his quick response.

"Camper?" Donny eyed Joe. "Might consider puttin' an age limit on that application, hon."

Her brows perked. "I did."

Joe winked at her and watched her ears blush. What else could he do? He couldn't tell her the application was her father's doing to get him onto the grounds immediately. Joe hadn't known anything about the camp or that ridiculous application until he arrived.

Donny's belly shook with a silent laugh. "Well, it looks like it's working out for you anyway. Pull the truck to the docks and we'll get you loaded up."

Kate straightened and glanced at Donny. "Yeah. Thanks." She turned to Joe and slugged him in the arm. "C'mon, Joey."

It stung, not bad, but enough. Christ, he hated that nickname. Joe only smiled. "After you, Miss Kate."

With a skill that comes from repetition, Kate maneuvered the truck, ass end in, to the warehouse dock on the lower section of the building. Joe walked around to meet her and reached the dock in time to see her step onto the fat metal bumper and up onto the four-foot-high loading dock.

Joe took the steps at the side. After three days of constant riding, his body was getting used to the rigors. But his legs were aching today in a way that told him he shouldn't push it more than necessary.

The morning sun was bright, casting the innards of the warehouse beyond the gaping doorway in dark shadows. He heard, more than saw, a forklift rolling from the depths before it broke through into the sunlight, a skid of feedbags balanced on its tongs.

Kate waved to the driver, a young man, mid-twenties,

muscled, with oak-brown hair, white tank top, baggy jeans and clunky mud-caked work boots. He gave her a nod, his head bobbing to something piped through his tiny earbud headphones. His jaw worked a piece of gum like cud, his eyes sliding around for a view of her ass as she passed.

The kid had taste. Couldn't fault him that. It was a damn fine view. Joe gave him a nod when he finally tore his attention from the seat of Kate's breeches. A flash of surprise crossed his face, then an appreciatory grin. He shrugged and nodded back. Like art, appreciation of a fine piece is inevitable.

Joe held back, breaking the threshold several steps after Kate. There was a reason he'd come. If things worked out, he'd wrap the case up today. With any luck, this Frank person would be working and Joe would know for sure if he was the one stalking Kate. A few minutes of conversation was all he'd need. It was a gift.

Inside, beyond the reach of the morning sun, high ceiling lights in metal shades protected by wire mesh illuminated the vast space. Joe strolled to the side and leaned a shoulder against an industrial-sized shelving unit, stacked three tiers high with plastic-wrapped bags of feed on big wooden skids. There were rows and rows of the oversized shelves some full, some not.

With his thumbs hooked on the front pockets of his jeans, Joe watched Kate heading straight back from the big doorway toward the far wall and what looked like the open door to an office. Someone was sleeping on a ratty floral-print couch beneath a window beside the office door, cowboy boots propped on the couch arm, hat perched over his face.

"Hey, pony girl," the man stretched out on the couch said as she approached. Clearly, he hadn't been sleeping. Even now he didn't move more than his eyes. "Lookin' good as always."

"Hey, Frank."

Joe perked at the name.

Kate peered in through the office door then back to Frank.

"Where's Greg?"

Frank uncrossed his dirty cowboy boots, rolled to his side, bent his elbow and propped his head. "Off. I'm answering the phones." He nudged his worn Western hat up from his eyes.

"Obviously." She shifted her weight to one hip. "Listen. I wanna ask you something."

"The answer's yes." Frank pushed up and swung his feet to the floor, resting his elbows on his wide knees.

"Knock it off. I'm being serious."

"If it'll get me a whiff of your panties, so am I."

"Ick."

Frank looked close to Kate's age, a little younger, not that Kate looked her age. His ash-blond hair was brutally short, a few weeks past buzz cut, his eyes an average brown.

He had a rounded face, though he wasn't fat by any means. He was lean, muscled, with a wide nose, narrow eyes and pronounced underbite that gave him a dim-witted appearance. But Joe saw beyond that to the leering glint in his eyes that belied the impression.

Tension radiated across Joe's shoulders, pulling his muscles as Frank's grin turned lecherous. He held back, forcing his body to relax. He'd let things play out, see where they went. He was close enough if the situation went south.

"Were you, y'know, *upset* when I told you I wouldn't go out with you?" she asked.

"What answer will get my cock in your pretty little pussy?"

Kate balked, disgust wrinkling her nose, pulling her lips. "None."

Frank snorted and shook his head. "Shoot, then what'ya hawin' about, woman?"

"If I emasculated you—"

"Wha?"

"Made you feel weak, insignificant. You know, less of a man."

Frank shot to his feet. "Hell no. Don't be sayin' that shit about me. You ain't all that."

Kate's eyes shifted to Joe. Frank showed no signs that he noticed or even realized Joe was there.

She licked her lips and focused on Frank again. "Frank, it was obvious you weren't happy I turned you down."

"Maybe, but I weren't no e-man-ulated, er, whatever." He reached down and adjusted his balls through his jeans. He sniffed and strutted toward her still holding himself. "Want me to prove it?"

Kate shuffled back a step, though she didn't look frightened. "Not necessary. My point is that if I hurt you, your feelings, I'm sorry."

"Yeah?" His brows shot up.

"Yes. So, if you've been thinking about me, y'know, wishing things had been different...trying to figure out a way to get me back, or back at me," she mumbled. "I hope you can let it go."

She smiled and slipped the tips of her fingers into the little front pockets of her breeches. "You're a good-looking-enough guy. I'm sure there are plenty of women out there who'd like to... I'm sure there are plenty of women out there."

Frank had stopped groping himself, although his hand remained on his crotch. He listened, his face lax, brows high. "That right?"

"Sure." She shrugged. "I mean, you were always nice to me...sort of. I'd feel bad if I really hurt you. I just wanted to make sure we were okay. Make things...right, between us."

Frank's brows knitted, his eyes shifting. Joe could almost see his mind working.

"Well, what if I say I am hurt? Yeah. What if I am that e-man-thing?"

"Well, like I said, I'm sorry—"

"Naw, that ain't good enough." Frank's gaze raked over her like a lecherous hand. He licked his lips, his hand squeezing his cock, rubbing, massaging up to his chest.

"You're gonna make it up to me," he said. "You owe me."

Frank straightened, his eyes hungry, his body somehow bigger, more menacing. He moved toward her, and Kate understood a heartbeat too late what he meant to do.

"Frank, no." She moved back, leaning away from the hand he thrust toward her. His fingers brushed her arm just as another larger, stronger hand clamped around Frank's wrist.

"Bad choice, cowboy."

Kate looked to Joe, suddenly between them, protecting her. For two full heartbeats she couldn't breathe, couldn't close her mouth, couldn't take her eyes off him.

"Hey." Frank bent over the wrist Joe twisted back. "Hey. That hurts. Le'go. Le'go."

"Sit." Joe shoved Frank backward so he stumbled into the couch and dropped.

Frank rubbed his wrist, his wide face angry and stiff. "Who the fuck are you?"

"Write any poems lately?" Joe's voice was ice cold, eyes dark. "Take any photos?"

"Hey, you can't just come in—" He tried to stand and Joe shoved him back down.

"Sit. Answer."

"What? I don't know what you're talkin' about, you whack job." He got to his feet only to be shoved back down again.

"Restraining order. You understand that? Leave her alone. You hear me?"

"Joe." Kate wasn't sure Frank was the one who'd been sending the poems and photos. She'd made the exchange between them sound worse than it'd been, and Frank wasn't exactly showing his best side today. Joe was jumping the gun, overreacting, and it was her fault.

"Who the fuck *are* you?" Frank stood fast and puffed his

chest into Joe's. "She was hittin' on me. Came sniffin' around lookin' for some cock. For *my* cock, and ain't you or nobody else gonna stop me from givin' it to her."

Joe outweighed him by nearly ninety pounds and Frank was a good four inches shorter. Joe didn't budge.

"I'm gonna shove my cock so far down her throat—"

Bam. Frank's head snapped back a half second before Kate's brain processed seeing Joe's punch. His fist had jabbed out and back. Nothing else on Joe's body had moved.

Frank staggered backward, blood gushing from the twisted ruin of his nose. He collapsed onto the couch, hands cupping over his face.

"Joe!" Kate lunged forward to stop him from doing any more damage, but Joe wasn't moving.

He hissed under his breath. "*Dammit.*" His dark eyes held a shadow of regret, but his voice didn't waver. He looked at Frank. "We understand each other?"

Frank nodded.

Joe glanced back at Kate, not meeting her eyes then turned and headed for the dock. "I'll be in the truck."

"He could be your stalker," Joe said when they'd arrived back at Hickory Hills stables.

"Finally. He speaks." Kate shoved her office door closed behind them. The glass rattled in the frame from the force. "Wanna tell me how you even know about any of it?"

Joe dropped into the brown leather chair opposite her desk. He pinched the bridge of his nose, eyes closed, elbow perched on the chair arm. "Magic."

"Har-har." God, he looked good, the gray Mustang T-shirt snug across his chest, stretched around his muscled arms, the faded jeans bunched at his crotch. Smelled good too, sweet male cologne, horses and the musky scent of the man that made all the rest uniquely him. *Yum.*

But she was pissed, dammit, and annoyed that she had to keep reminding herself. She wanted to hear him say it, even though she knew the answer. *Clayton.* Who else? She'd wring his neck for pulling Joe into the Thorndike melodrama.

Joe hadn't spoken a word since they'd left the feed store. He'd spent the trip scowling out the window, hands balled into fists, jaw clenched. Just what she needed, another macho testosterone factory on overdrive stomping around trying to protect poor little Kate from the big bad world. *Puhleeze.*

"I don't know what all Clayton told you, but trust me, he blew it out of proportion." She dug the receipt from her pocket as she came around her desk and pulled the gray ledger from the bottom drawer and sat.

Joe dropped his arm. "You think it's one of your campers."

"Yeah. I do."

"How many of those kids have camera cell phones?"

"None." She looked up from her tallying. "They're underprivileged. Some are lucky they have shoes, but the ones that might are told to leave any kind of electronic devices at home."

"Right." Joe slouched deeper into the cup-style chair, his arms nearly level with his shoulders on the chair arms. The waves of his black shiny hair brushed his shoulders. His hands dangled over the edges, big and strong, the knuckles of his right hand beginning to bruise from the punch.

He wasn't smiling. He looked dangerous. He looked like an ad for hard liquor with a promise of harder sex. Shadows edged his jaw, his rough beard stubble long overdue for a morning shave. His eyes dark, unflinching, watched her, made her breath catch. She dropped her gaze to his mouth, his top lip a perfect plump bow, a small slash of scar at the corner, his bottom a tempting mate.

He kissed with those lips. Kate couldn't help the thought. He pressed them to his lover's lips and made her moan into his mouth. Those lips had tasted a woman's breast, suckled her tender nipples, parted for his tongue to pass through and drive her mad. All that tightly leashed strength, all that reined emotion, could turn to passion, to heat.

Kate licked her lips and caught his eyes following, drawn to the spot. His dark brows wrinkled. He wasn't pleased, but he didn't look away.

"Why'd you ask about cell phones?" she said.

His gaze flicked from her mouth to her eyes. "The stalker used a cell phone to take one of the photos."

"How do you know?"

"I know."

Kate slapped the ledger closed and shoved it back into the bottom drawer. "Maybe one of the kids snuck a phone in then."

"And a printer?" One of Joe's brows swooped higher than the other. "It's not a camper, Kate. It's not a kid. It's serious."

Kate grabbed the receipt and stood. Joe's gaze made a quick trip down her body and back, as if on reflex. She forced a smile and ignored the flutter in her belly.

"Well, thank you." She walked around her desk past Joe to the file cabinets lining the back wall.

"Kate."

"I appreciate your opinion, Mr. Garity. But this is really a personal matter."

"I'm a cop."

"My family and I are handling it. We don't need a sales—" She turned around, hand on the file cabinet. "You're a what?"

Joe pushed from his chair, his movements sluggish, as though dreading the explanation. He came around, crossing the room to her. "I'm a cop. Retired."

"But you said...why would you..."

"I'm here to help."

The pieces clicked together. "The notes. They hired you because of those stupid love notes and photos," Kate said. "Bill and Clayton, they knew I'd be pissed so they made you lie."

"The stalker might've bolted if he heard cop." Joe propped his hands on his hips. "You ask me, it's a bad idea to keep the target in the dark. You needed to know."

"What, you're some sort of PI now? That's why you're here? That's why you've been following me around?" She laughed, disgusted with herself. "I'm such an idiot."

"Come again?"

"Nothing." She smiled and shook her head, shoving the file drawer closed.

How'd she let herself think things would be different with Joe? She wasn't any different. That comfortable connection she'd thought she felt with him was only Joe sticking close to uncover her secret admirer. She couldn't blame him though.

She wasn't the relationship type. Never had been. But she was okay with that. Men wanted her and she enjoyed what they had to offer. Heck, half the time it was Kate cutting things short, moving on when she'd had her fill of a guy. They got over it fast enough. But Joe somehow made her forget herself, the self she'd learned to accept long ago. What was it about him?

She needed to clear away the silly romantic fantasies he made flitter through her brain. She needed to force herself to think of him the way she did every other guy she'd been hot for.

"You're a cop," she said.

He folded his arms across his chest, muscles stretching the sleeves of the cotton tee. "Was."

"You punch all your suspects in the nose?"

"No. I..." Joe looked away for a moment. His jaw tightened. He exhaled then met her gaze. "No. Never."

"So what happened with Frank?"

Joe hesitated, then said, "Lost my perspective." His voice was lower, softer, twice as intimate. His dark eyes held hers, told her things he hadn't.

He wanted her. Those midnight eyes shimmered with masculine hunger. She could tell his thoughts had gone far

71

past easy flirtation, a casual touch, a kiss. Everything female inside her roused, a primal awareness. He stared at her as though he wanted her naked beneath him and the idea sent a flush of warm shivers through her body.

Her gaze dropped to his mouth, the intriguing slash of his scar. He wanted her. The knowledge filled her with feminine confidence. This was it, what she needed, to see him the same as she did any man. It's who she was, what she was good at. She'd been holding back and it'd messed with her head. She wouldn't hold back anymore.

Strong, male, Joe was all that she needed. Her body wanted his, wanted the hard unyielding feel of him, on her and in her. That's all. Nothing more. No emotions beyond the want of him.

She closed the small distance between them, licked her lips, anticipation thrumming through her veins.

"Kate," he said, a warning so soft and weak it was meant to be ignored.

She flicked her gaze to his, rose to her tiptoes, her hands finding the rough waistband of his jeans for balance. "Remember what I said about me and flirting?"

"You know what you're doing?" he asked, his arms still knotted across his belly, his voice a low rough whisper.

Kate leaned in, her breasts brushing against his chest and flicked her tongue over the scar on his lip. "I know."

As though released from a spell, Joe's stoic body came to life in a fluid rush of movement. His arms opened, his mouth taking hers, covering her lips with his moist heat. One hand slipped around her back, the other fell to her hip, and his whole body pushed her backward to the file cabinets, his hand cushioning her back when they hit.

His hard muscled frame pressed into her, from the firm swell of his chest to the stone line of his sex along her belly. She welcomed him, eager, circling an arm over his shoulder, the other under his arm and around his back. She pulled him closer, tighter, opened her legs to nestle his body where she wanted him most.

His hips rocked the swell of his sex against her, his mouth stealing her breath, drawing her deeper and deeper into his kiss. Heat swirled through her body and mind, pooling like liquid fire between her legs, her heart a thundering clamor in her ears. She breathed him in, the scent of his cologne, the musky aroma of the man. His taste salted her lips, warmed along her tongue and down her throat like an exotic liqueur.

Joe shifted his weight, dropped his mouth to her neck behind her ear. His hand smoothed up from her hip catching under her blouse, palm rough and warm along the flesh of her ribs. His thumb stroked her, the very tip brushing the bottom swell of her breast through her bra.

Her breath caught and Joe crushed against her, imprinting the feel of his stiff cock along her belly. His thumb stroked again, and again, moving higher each time until it teased over the firm tent of her nipple. He pressed his hips into her, his hand taking the full weight of her breast into his palm, squeezing, molding the sensitive flesh.

Kate's breaths came ragged from her lungs, her fingers digging into the hard muscles of his back. His kisses on her neck turned to nibbles, then to bites, not breaking the skin but scraping, tasting, sending jolt after jolt of sensation trembling through her body.

He pulled back, brushing the rough stubble of beard along her cheek and found her lips just as his fingers pinched the tender pucker of her nipple through her bra. She moaned into his mouth, her body liquefying.

"You two almost fuckin' done or you need another minute?"

Clayton. Kate jerked back, gasped.

Joe growled, "Give us twenty."

Chapter Five

"So...what'd he say?" Ginny asked, absently brushing the same spot on Wizard's rump for the last five minutes.

Kate shrugged. "Nothing."

"Nothing? You two practically boink each other right there in your office and he hasn't said anything? I can't believe it."

"Believe it." Kate smoothed a hand down the back of the mare's front leg, pinching the hollow above her fetlock. Wizard's ankle crooked on reflex and Kate leaned into her, lifted, so the horse bent her knee and curled her leg back for Kate to clean out her hoof.

"Wow, guess I was wrong," Ginny said. "Thought he really liked you. Guess he was just taking what was offered. Y'know, like a free candy dish."

Kate glanced up at her.

"Oh. No offense," Ginny said. "I mean, you're great. He'd be lucky to have you. But you'd think if he was interested in anything more he'd have come talk to you, sent out some feelers. Y'know, ask how you're feeling about what happened, what comes next, what you both want out of this. Normal stuff."

Kate let Wizard's foot drop and she straightened. "We really haven't had a chance."

"It's been three days. You avoiding him?"

"I've been busy." Kate shooed Ginny out of the way so she could clean Wizard's back hoof. "We haven't been alone."

"In three days?" Ginny backed up and leaned against the wall on the other side of the stable aisle. She bent her leg, propping her Timberland hiking boot knee high, sole flat against the wall. "Trust me. If he was interested in starting something he'd find a way to get you alone."

The same thought had been swimming around in Kate's head for the last few days. Never mind that she hadn't made any attempts to talk to Joe either. Why should she? She knew how the conversation would go. She'd had it plenty enough times before.

"There's nothing to say. It didn't mean anything. We just got carried away." The words rattled out of Kate like a platitude. It wasn't the first time she'd said them, certainly not the first time she'd heard them. And for some reason she couldn't stomach hearing them from Joe.

So maybe she had been avoiding him. Kate dropped Wizard's back hoof and straightened with a casual glance down the long aisle of the stable. Wheelbarrows dotted the wide corridor. The campers were cleaning stalls.

Sunshine's stall was the farthest down, toward the ring end of the stable, and as Kate watched, Joe stepped out from the stall, pitchfork overflowing with dung and straw. Dumb luck made him glance her way.

Distance and the afternoon sun shining bright cast his features in shadows, but she could see his nod, knew he'd smiled. Her belly fluttered and Kate turned away without so much as a wave.

"I don't know how you do it," Ginny said while Kate lifted Wizard's other back foot. "I've never been good at the catch-and-release thing. Besides, Joe's a pretty hot fish to be throwing back."

"Some fish aren't made for captivity."

"How can you tell?"

He's male. "I don't attract any other kind," Kate said, matter-of-fact, dropping Wizard's foot. She backed up and smoothed her hand down the back of Wizard's front leg to clean her last hoof.

"Uh, Kate..."

Kate looked at Ginny who'd pushed away from the wall. She stood with the tips of her fingers dipped into the front pockets of her cut-off jean shorts, her ice-blonde hair in pigtails beneath a red bandana. Her "hundred-percent genuine cowgirl" T-shirt hugged so tight over her breasts and around her small ribs, reading it seemed an invasion of her privacy.

She was smiling, her head tilted to the side, her hip bouncing just enough to jiggle the parts of her that looked best in motion. Kate knew that look and followed her gaze. Her heart skipped.

Joe was striding down the long corridor toward them, his arms swinging easy at his sides. The sleeves of his black Western shirt were rolled to his elbows, exposing thick muscled forearms brushed with dark hairs to match the wavy silk strands on his head.

The first few pearl-like snaps at the dress collar were open, a small patch of tanned male chest peeking from underneath. The bottoms of his jeans bunched over his sneakers and he sported a three-inch silver belt buckle above his groin. She knew Joe had gone back to Sherman's Feed Store. Apparently it wasn't all business.

"What do you do if the fish jumps back in the boat?" Ginny asked.

Kate dropped Wizard's foot and swallowed the cotton-ball feel at the back of her throat. "I don't know. It's never happened."

"Well, grab a net," Ginny mumbled through her smile-locked teeth. "Hi, Joe."

"Hey, peanut."

Ginny's smile brightened. "You're lookin' good enough to ride in those cowboy clothes."

"That right?" He winked at her, his smile a gentle curve of

his lips. His gaze slid to Kate and his expression warmed. "Kate."

"Hey. Um, nice duds." She cringed at the comment, wishing she'd stuck with "Hey."

Joe looked back to Ginny. "Give us a second, hon?"

"Sure." Ginny glanced at Kate as though double-checking she wanted the privacy and then back to Joe. "Don't forget to lock the door this time."

Joe's face flushed, not much but enough to show he wasn't completely unaffected. He waited until Ginny had sashayed far enough away then turned to Kate.

"You gonna tell me?" He hooked his thumbs on the back pockets of his jeans.

"Tell you what?"

"Your first time."

Seriously? Kate shut her mouth and turned to collect the grooming supplies scattered around Wizard's feet. "What are you, eight? I'm busy, Joe. Go play with the other kids."

She could hear him shuffling along behind her into the tack room. She could feel his presence over every part of her body. And the urge to lean back into his hard chest, let him wrap his arms around her, let him kiss her, touch her...was damn annoying.

She didn't expect a testament to his undying love. But an indication that he didn't think of her as a free candy dish would've been nice. Why did she care? She never had before.

"Gimme a break, dollface. I'm tryin' here."

"My first time? That's the best you could come up with? Forget it." She shoved the brushes into their coffee-can nooks on the wall and dropped the hoof pick into the bucket with the others.

"Right." He exhaled loud, almost a sigh. "Time's up. You had your space, but enough's enough. It's not safe." There was a gruffness in his voice, a frustration that wasn't there a moment ago, as though he'd suddenly lost patience—or hope.

Kate spun on her heel, caught his flinch. "Fine. You wanna know about my first time? I was thirteen." She gathered the tack she'd need for her ride. "He was fourteen. We did it in the backseat of my father's limo on the way to school. I loved him and I thought he loved me. He didn't. He fucked my best friend two days later and told me not to cry about it. After all, didn't I know? I'm the kind of girl boys want, but not to keep."

She pushed past him before he could find words, the saddle and pad cradled over her arms, bridle draped over the velvet seat. Joe had to stumble out of the way to keep from getting the horn jabbed into his gut. Kate didn't care. She hated that she'd told him that story. But more than that, she hated that the story was true.

It'd happened years ago. She was over it. But retelling the story was like a fresh stab to her heart. She didn't want to be that girl anymore. She wanted to be the kind of girl boys kept.

"You going somewhere?" Joe asked as she slung the saddle and pad to Wizard's back.

"Guess."

"Where ya going?" Clayton asked, coming from the office behind her.

"To the beach. Any more stupid questions from the male population on this farm?" God she must be getting close to her period. She felt bitchy.

"Wait for me." Joe headed toward the other end of the stable at a jog.

"Hey. It's not the kiddy trail, buddy," she called after him. Joe didn't answer, didn't stop. *Screw it.* He was on his own.

"You gonna wait for him?" Clayton asked.

Kate slipped the halter off the big mare's head and fitted the bridle in her mouth and over her ears. "Use your powers of observation and tell me what you think."

"Listen, Kate." Clayton took the reins while she tightened

the girth around Wizard's belly. "I'm a founding member of the Garity's-an-ass club, but whoever's been sending you those notes and pictures is a couple crayons short of a box. You shouldn't be alone. Not so far out. Not 'til we know more."

"The safest place for me is on this horse's back." She snagged the reins from his hand. "I can outride anyone. I need to get out of here, Clay. I need to...get away from him."

Tears stung her eyes. She blinked and looked away, doing her best to keep them from falling.

"You got your cell?"

Kate tapped the credit-card thin phone in her breast pocket, then led Wizard the few feet out of the stable.

Clayton followed and waited as she mounted. "There's a storm coming."

"It won't rain on me," she said. "Wouldn't dare."

"Where is she?"

"She needs some space, Garity. Kate knows these woods better than anyone and she can stick to a saddle like nobody's business. She'll be fine." Clayton hadn't even looked up from the computer at Kate's desk.

Joe took another step farther into the office, Sunshine's reins in his hands. If it weren't for the horse standing outside the door he'd be crowding over Clayton, getting what he needed out of him more efficiently. "How do I find her?"

"You can't." Clayton finally spared Joe a glance. "Hey. No horses in the office."

Joe threw a look over his shoulder in time to see Sunshine trying to pass her horse-sized body through the people-sized door. "Whoa. Whoa, girl. Back up."

He got her into the aisle again and asked from the office door, "Is there a trail?"

"Barely."

"Give me a fuckin' direction to head. Which way did she

go?" Joe had grown up on the streets, survived on his wits. He'd found his way around every street, alley and abandoned building in the city. How hard could a bunch of trees be?

Clayton narrowed his eyes on him. After a moment of obvious deliberation he sighed and pushed to his feet. "What do I care if you get lost out there or break your damn neck in a fall?"

"Right." Joe stepped out of the way when Clayton reached the door. He followed him out the stable entrance up the wide gravel drive to where it met the service road in front of the kids cabins and the mess hall.

Clayton swung a finger toward the wall of forest. "That way. Between the mess hall and the boys cabin. See the break in the trees? That's the trail." Then he turned and walked back to the stables.

Thunder crackled overhead, a rumbling warning as the sky darkened and winds tugged at the leaves. Joe steered Sunshine around a ten-foot-by-ten-foot patch of gnarled prickly bushes, weeds and other forest debris. He refused to dwell on how unnervingly familiar the patch looked.

Everything looked the same. Trees. Weeds. Prickly patches. No matter which way he looked it was all the same. There was no trail. He was walking blind, over hills, around fallen trees, under low branches. Rushing out after Kate was a stupid move no matter how he cut it.

Joe checked his watch. "Fifty-five minutes," he mumbled to himself. He'd been looking for almost an hour, had even considered turning back and taking a different tactic, but hell if he knew which way was back.

He ducked, but spindly twigs snagged in his hair as Sunshine cut too close to a tree. "Dammit."

Sunshine kept walking hanging her head to avoid any spindly twigs snagging her hair. Smart horse or dumb rider?

The question vanished from his thoughts the moment the first raindrop plopped on his shoulder.

Joe shot a look toward the sky. Trees towered overhead. Between them, in tiny swaths of clear space, he could see the boil of blue-black clouds and silvery streaks of rain. A cool drop hit his hand and another one hit his leg. It was raining harder above the canopy of trees. The leaves sheltered him. But that wouldn't last.

"Kate! Kate Mathers!" In case there were any other Kates wandering the woods. "Kate!"

Sunshine's head flinched each time Joe yelled. He could feel her body tensing beneath him. "Easy, girl."

Joe clucked to the horse, gave a gentle kick to her ribs and Sunshine walked on. But the rain was falling harder, faster, and within minutes Joe's jeans were a dark blue, his shirt clinging to his shoulders and back.

Sunshine's furry skin twitched. Annoyed with the growing thrum of rain, her ears swiveled back, flattening against her head. Thunder rumbled overhead like the roll of a giant drum and Joe looked up in time to see a bolt of lightning lash across the sky.

He shoved a hand through his sodden hair, blinking against the patter of rain, scanning the cluttered forest. There was something up ahead, a thousand yards, maybe more. Big, black.

"Kate," he yelled but he could barely hear himself over the loud hiss of rain rushing down through the leaves all around him.

"C'mon, girl." He jabbed his heels hard into Sunshine's ribs at the very instant a white-hot lightning bolt blasted the ground to his right.

Thunder exploded in his ears. Sunshine jerked faster than he could follow. He hit the ground hard. The air in his lungs crushed out of him on impact. Blind, deaf, skin tingling with the discharged electricity, he lay on his back, pain screaming through his head and body.

He gasped only to have the rain shower down his throat. His lungs wouldn't expand, his body still clenched tight. Joe rolled to his side, tried to will himself to calm, to breathe.

"Joe, are you hurt? Ohmygod. Joe." Kate's voice sounded distant, like she was talking to him through a child's tin-can phone. But a moment later he felt her knees at his back next to his shoulders, her hand on his arm.

She rolled him over, his head on her lap, and he finally managed to open his eyes.

"Gimme...a...sec." Pins and needles tingled over his skin, even into his scalp. The metallic taste in his mouth—like chewing on tinfoil—was beginning to dissipate.

"What are you doing out here?" She sounded closer now, still muffled, but watching her mouth helped.

"Looking for you."

Kate's thin brows pinched. He thought she was going to say something, but she just shook her head and scanned the forest. "Sunshine bolted. She'll head back to the stables. God, you could've been killed," she said, then mumbled, "*Idiot.*"

"Right." The ringing in his ears dimmed to a soft hum. "You too."

Her gaze snapped to his and he could tell she was wondering if he'd meant her being killed or being an idiot. He didn't offer to solve the mystery.

Joe grunted his way to a sitting position. His brain spun the moment it moved higher than his heart. The forest whirled by so fast he had to catch himself from falling back. Another flash of light streaked across the sky, lighting the black belly of the storm overhead. He cringed, a boom of thunder shaking the ground beneath him.

He reached up and felt the knot forming at the back of his head. Not good for a severe head-injury survivor. He brought his hand around, glanced at his fingers for blood. None. *Good.* But he was soaked through, covered in dirt and forest debris without a clue how to get his bearings.

"Anything broken?" Kate's dark cinnamon braid was soaked black with rain, thin strands plastered over her forehead and down both sides of her face. Clear water formed tiny balls at the tips of her long lashes, dripping lazily to her cheeks when she blinked.

Her powder-blue buttoned blouse had turned see-through, her white lacy bra a thin barrier of modesty. Her skin looked pale beneath the tint of blue, the cotton fabric molding over the large swells of her breasts forming snug against the pebble of her nipples.

Goose bumps covered her bare arms, her hands cupped together in her lap. She was still kneeling, her long leather boots protecting her shins from the sodden ground, her knees dark with dirt and rain. She shivered, her chattering teeth trembling her cheeks.

"You're freezing." He pushed up to his knees. A hard yank at his collar unsnapped the buttons of his new cowboy shirt in quick succession. He shrugged out of it, then wrapped it around her shoulders.

"Thanks."

"It's wet," he said. "Better than nothing."

"I know." Her attention dropped to his chest. His muscles tightened under her stare, his heart slugging a half beat faster. She licked her lips, her pink tongue swiping raindrops. She reached toward him, hesitating a few inches away, pointing.

"Is that new?"

Joe had to lift his left arm to see the dark bruise forming in a misshapen oval toward the back of his ribs. "Must've hit a rock."

"And that?"

He followed her gesture to the thin line of scar tissue tracing his deltoid and pecs where his arm jointed to his chest. "Old. Car accident."

Most of his scars were from the accident. Ironically he'd had a nearly injury-free career before that day. He had the scar on his lip, another on the top of his head, hidden by hair, and one on his right side above his missing kidney. There were a few on his legs and one on his back, but the broken nose and the scar on his cheek were from a fight he'd had in prison—juvee.

Kate pushed to her knees, her small hand drifting closer to the scar. Joe didn't move. He watched her, the way her bottom lip caught between her teeth. She glanced at his eyes just before her fingers touched his flesh as though checking for his permission. He didn't grant or refuse her.

Her touch was cold though it burned through him like fire. Joe clenched his jaw against the hot surge of blood flooding his veins, swelling his cock. He didn't want to be affected by her, not like this, not now. He was pissed she'd behaved so irresponsibly, riding off into the woods alone.

Besides, she'd been a bitch to him earlier. So the opposite sex disappointed her. Welcome to the fuckin' club. Now she wanted to play doctor out in the woods in the middle of a storm? *Not likely, dollface.*

Joe glanced at the sky, fighting the heat galloping through his body. The rain had let up, pattering through the leaves, sounding like popcorn nearly done. He hadn't even noticed.

Her cool fingers traced a chilly path to his shoulder, then fluttered to his face. He flinched before he realized she was reaching to brush a few wet strands of hair from his eyes. His balk had stopped her, so he brushed the hair away himself with a quick rake of his hand. Her green eyes followed the movement.

She sat back on her heels, staring at him, seeing the body not the man. Joe knew that look, hungry, lustful. It made his gut clench and his muscles tight. As surely as if she'd reached out with her hand, his body tingled in the wake of her gaze traveling over him.

Her eyes lowered, boldly admiring the bulge at his crotch.

The openness of her stare sent the hum of arousal vibrating over his skin. His muscles pulled, jerking his cock, a quick involuntary movement beneath his jeans that brought a smile flickering across her face.

She put her hand to her lips, the very tips of her fingers tracing the soft curve as though imagining the feel of his cock there. Joe's chest squeezed at the thought. Emotions he couldn't name flashed through her eyes before she flicked her gaze back to his.

An expression of worry pulled her brows. She sighed and got to her feet, speaking as though her desire were a thing easily ignored. "Promise me you won't do something this stupid again."

Joe blinked up at her, not having near the same control over his lust. "Come again?"

"You could've been killed."

He stood, fighting off the dizzy spin of his brain. "You're joking."

"You're not a good enough rider to be out here alone. Honestly, you can't expect me to rush in and save you every time your ego takes control of your brain."

"Save *me*?" Joe couldn't decide if he should laugh or scream. Was she serious?

Kate knotted her arms under her breasts, shifted her weight to one hip and hiked a brow. "You're welcome."

Christ, she was serious. His hands fisted, itching to shake some sense into her or pull her close and kiss her senseless. The woman could drive a man to madness or murder.

A ghost of a smile trembled at the corner of her lips and suddenly indecision vanished. He reached for her, his hands cupping her face pulling her to him so fast she gasped against his lips. He kissed her hard, drove her back to the thick tree trunk behind her. Kate's mouth opened to his, welcoming the sweep of his tongue.

Lord, he couldn't breathe. Her smell, her taste, her feel, the whole of her engulfed him. Fresh and clean, summer rain mixed with sweet wildflowers, her scent filled his nose, swirled through his lungs.

Her tongue stroked soft and warm against his, the flavor of mint and Kate an intoxicating taste. His fingers tunneled into the thick braid of her hair, fisted, held her captive. His arousal tightened his jeans, the urgent press made worse by the feather-light brush of her hands on his skin.

Cool fingers traced his muscles, tickled over his nipples, shooting a tingling rush of sensation straight to his cock. His abs shuddered against the chilly sweep of her fingers, then tugged as they dipped beneath the waistband of his jeans.

Her fingertips teased the very head of his cock, swollen, straining for release. He gasped, holding her back, his hands framing her face.

"Kate."

"It's okay. I want this." She closed the small distance between them and pressed her lips to his, her body molding snug against him.

Her damp shirt chilled against his chest, her breasts a quick flame of warmth beneath. She snaked an arm around his neck, the other under his arm, her palms cool and flat against his back. Joe's hands dropped to her waist, fingers tightening around the waistband of her breeches, gathering the stretch material into his fists.

Kate wriggled against him, brushing her thigh up the outside of his leg, grinding her sex against the straining bulge of his cock. He groaned into her mouth, his hips rocking forward on reflex. Heat sizzled through his veins, instinct, need, thrumming through his muscles. His body responded to hers, to the soft give of her flesh, the sweet smell, the addictive taste. Lord, he couldn't stop. He wanted more.

His hands opened on her hips, pushed her back, so she pressed hard against the tree. No escape. Their foreheads rested against each other, their breaths quick heated pants.

"You'll make me come in my jeans."

She smiled, lopsided, sexy. "Fight it."

His heart lurched, chest muscles snapped tight, squeezing the breath from his lungs. "Right." He took her mouth, his hand cupping along her jaw.

He drove his tongue into her mouth, tasting the subtle flavor of her, then moved to her cheek. His lips traded kiss for nibble and back again until he reached her ear. He nipped her lobe. Kate's body shuddered in his arms and pulled an answering quake through his.

Joe rocked his hips into her, feeling the soft give of her body stroking the aching hardness of his cock. Need burned through every part of him, the drive to bury himself inside her too much to resist.

His heart beat wild and frantic in his ears, his muscles so stiff he could barely breathe, barely stand. He slipped a hand down her neck, her skin soft and cool from the rain. His fingers worked the buttons of her blouse, his pulse quickening as each popped free.

Seconds passed. Kate's small fingers pressed between his belly and jeans, teasing the head of his sex, flittering over the fasteners of his jeans. Joe pushed the anticipation from his mind and slipped his hand beneath the damp fabric of her bra. The weight of her breast in his palm flooded a wash of heat through his body filling his cock, pinching against the confines of his jeans.

"If you don't get my cock free soon it may cause serious damage. Not good for either of us."

A flick of his wrist spilled the supple mound of her breast out of the cloth cup, her nipple hard against his palm. Kate hurried to undo the button then the zipper fly of his jeans. Puffs of her breath warmed against his chest, growing shallow, quicker, as he bent to take her breast into his mouth.

Her rosy flesh wrinkled like a sweet raisin against his tongue, the urge to bite a near undeniable temptation. He flicked his tongue, swirling it around the hard little nub, teasing the skin. She tasted sweet, like honey clover, and the scent of her skin had him lightheaded, drunk. He drew her in, filling his mouth just as she freed his cock.

Cool air washed over the heated flesh of his sex—made his breath catch. His muscles pulled tight, thighs trembling. His hand squeezed hard around her breast, pressing it to a fat supple point. He scraped his teeth over the erect little nipple, pinching and suckling.

She moaned arching into his grip, her hands cool and hurried against his shaft. Her fingers toyed over his balls, the other hand choking around his cock.

"Fuck, yesss..." His words hissed out of him, his hips following the stroke, heat shooting from his balls to his head. Primal need took hold.

"Enough. I want inside you." He tugged and jerked at the hook of her breeches, then pulled the edges so the zipper ripped open. He didn't know if he'd ruined them or not. He couldn't find the mind to care.

"Take these off," he said.

Kate's chest rose and fell with ragged breaths, her mouth open, green eyes hazed. "I..." She swallowed, licked her lips. "Can't. Boots."

Joe leaned back enough to glance at her feet. The damn knee-high riding boots were more than his brain could tackle. *Fuck it*, he'd work around them. Just then her hand squeezed up quick to the tip of his cock rippling over the sensitive head and Joe forgot his name.

"Christ..."

She flicked her thumb over the tip, spreading a bead of come, suddenly cooling his flesh. Sweet pressure swelled inside him, building from the very depths of his body, swirling faster and faster with each strangling pump of her hand.

"Kate..." His hips rocked even as he shoved and tugged at her breeches. "Stop. Shit."

Her pink panties bunched and rolled into the waistband of her pants. Joe couldn't stop to care. He shoved hard, jerking the tight fabric down her soft cream-coffee thighs.

Her flesh jiggled with his hard yanks and pushes, heating his already fiery need. His cock grew harder in her grip, swelling painfully thick. When the tight breeches reached her knees Joe grabbed her hips and spun her around.

Kate gasped at the sudden move, her hands snagging the tree for balance. She was bare to him, round and soft. He pressed his hips into her ass, squeezing his cock between the warm plump cheeks.

"Jeezus, that feels good," he said, even as he fought to stop. He thrust forward, he couldn't help it, her ass cheeks hugging around his cock as he slipped his hand around to her sex. His fingers pushed through the coarse damp hairs of her mons, found the lips of her pussy, parting them.

"Oh, Kate. Fuck. You're so wet." He rocked in through the hug of her ass again, each stroke churning a fresh rush of tingles humming over his body, zinging through his balls.

Her cream coated his finger. His finger spread her juice to her clit. He rubbed quick little circles over the swollen bud, flicked and pinched, feeling Kate's body shudder beneath him.

"Joe. Yes. Joe." Her voice was breathy, her knees trembling, straining to spread wider against the tangle of breeches and panties at the top of her boots. Her hips thrust back, ramming her ass against his groin. Her cheeks went hot and slick, her orgasm pulsing through her, creaming her ass.

God, he wanted to taste the hot juice he felt gushing over his fingers. His brain wouldn't let the need escape. He knelt, spreading her cheeks with both hands and gazed at the beautiful pink folds of her flesh. Her cream glistened. The opening of her pussy pulsed, her orgasm still drizzling come through her folds. He licked her, the creamy heat trickling over his tongue, salty, deliciously feminine. He pushed into her, wanting to taste her from the inside.

Kate moaned, unashamed. She pressed into his face, driving his tongue deeper, riding his mouth through the last throbs of her come. Her pussy muscles squeezed, a fresh gush of juice wetting the walls, and it was all he could do not to lose control. His balls pulled so tight his cock thumped against his belly, a small spurt wetting his skin.

His muscles jerked, need riding him hard. He'd pushed the limits of his restraint. Joe stood, knees weak. He palmed her hips, his cock arrow straight in front of him.

He stroked himself from root to head and back again, drawing out the glittering thrill of anticipation.

Enough. He nestled his cock between her cheeks, his hand guiding the head, stroking her pussy, pushing until it slipped inside her.

"Fuck, yesss..." he said and Kate gave a matching groan.

Sensation rippled up his cock, knotting tight in his balls, thundering through his heart. Kate pushed into him, her snug pussy squeezing around him, drawing him deeper. Her muscles milked his shaft, molding to him so every move sent a breath-stealing rush through his body. His fingers gripped the top of her legs at the bend of her body. He drew back, rocked her forward, then slammed their bodies together again.

In seconds he was driving himself hard and fast inside her, his bare thighs slapping against hers. Her muscles clamped tighter, sweet friction building and churning, tensing his muscles, drawing him closer and closer to the edge. He couldn't breathe. It didn't matter. His chest was so tight he could feel his pulse pounding against his skin.

Kate's body clenched. "Joe. Yes. There. Don't stop..." Like the quick clench of a wicked vise, her pussy walls hugged harder, tighter around the slip and slide of his cock. She jammed her body backward firmer, faster, meeting his thrust.

All at once he felt her release, everything inside her gushed hot, muscles fluttering, pulsing around his cock. He squeezed his eyes, ground his teeth, fought against the undeniable pull of his own orgasm, drawing out hers as long as he physically could. And then he couldn't last a moment more.

Joe pulled out and strangled his cock in his hand, pumping his shaft under her belly, his hips bucking as though he was still inside her. Release came in a heart-stopping rush.

"Fuck...fuck...fuck...," he panted, his hand slowing as the last spurts squeezed out of him.

Joe straightened and Kate leaned forward against the tree, her thighs wet with her come. The haze of lust dissipated from his brain. Reality settled in.

He'd broken his first rule of bodyguarding. He'd fucked his principal. That was bad. It changed everything. So why the hell couldn't he stop smiling?

Chapter Six

Kate paced the narrow covered porch of Joe's cottage, wringing her hands. He caught glimpses of her as she crossed by one window to the next. Her riding boots scuffed and clomped over the wooden floor.

"Get her in here," Joe said.

The white-haired doctor looked up from his watch, his brows high, wrinkling his forehead more than normal. "If she wanted to, she'd be in here. Trust me. That girl's not one to pussyfoot around."

He dropped Joe's wrist and reached into his black leather bag on the couch beside Joe. "Pulse is good, heart sounds good. You feeling any nausea, dizziness? Any pain?"

Joe shook his head. He knew the drill. He was fine. Bruised some, no concussion, nothing worth mentioning. Not that he could focus on anything besides the sultry young woman wearing a rut on his front porch. *Scuff-clomp. Scuff-clomp.*

Light flashed in his eyes. Joe flinched, shifting his attention from the front windows to the penlight the doc held two inches from his eye. Kate had called the old geezer in to check him over before they'd made it out of the woods. Damn, he never should've told her about the car accident. Women—always trying to mother things. A smile tugged the corner of his mouth at the thought.

"Look right here." The doc flicked the top curve of his enormous ear with his finger, then swung the light in and out of

Joe's eyes. After a moment he stood and sighed. "Nope. No concussion. Take it easy for a day or two, though. Head injuries can be tricky. Especially with your previous damage."

Damage. He liked that. Yeah, he must be damaged to have fucked his principal. In the five years he'd had his business, he'd never lost focus like that. Never forgot they were the job. Not people. The job.

He'd guarded women before, good-looking women, hot women, women who offered to suck him off just to pass the time. He'd turned them down. He did *not* fuck the principal. Ever. Until Kate.

Joe sank deeper into the thin cushioned couch and scrubbed his hands over his face. Jeezus, he'd fucked things up royally.

"Yeah. Thanks. I'm good. Been down this road before." He shoved his fingers through his rain-stiff hair then dropped his hands to his lap, leaning forward, elbows on his thighs, fingers twisting his ring between his legs.

The old man snorted, smoothing a wrinkled hand down the run of buttons on his sea-green dress shirt. He had a small paunch he patted and adjusted the tuck of his shirt behind his belt buckle, straightening an errant fold. "I imagine you have. Well, you know the drill. Call if you experience any symptoms. The Thorndikes have my number."

"You bet. Hey, Doc." Joe nodded toward Kate on the porch. "Send her in, will ya?"

The balding man smiled. He glanced over his shoulder at Kate and back to Joe, his cheeks pinking. "I'll suggest it."

"Right."

A few minutes after the doc left, Kate peeked around the door. "You good?"

"Absolutely. Come." His heart picked up pace. Damn, she was gorgeous. He liked looking at her. Nothing wrong with that. So what if he smiled whenever she walked into a room and his chest pinched? She was a sweetheart most of the time and a pain in the ass other times. But in a good way. Not that it mattered. He felt responsible for her, protective. It was his job. That's all. That's why.

Bullshit.

Kate's smile lit her eyes, though she shied away from meeting his. She closed the door and leaned her shoulder against the wall beside it. Her blouse was dry enough to lose the translucent quality, but her breeches were mud stained and wet. Her hair was still a dark braid down her back except for a few wispy tendrils around her face.

"Listen. I'm...I'm sorry," she said. "I wasn't thinking. I should've made sure you were okay before we... I mean, I knew about your car accident. I just didn't think about your head."

"I'm fine." Joe watched Kate's little ears go blood red. Yeah, he liked that about her too. So what?

"I know. But what happened between us. It was great and everything." She rolled her eyes. "Hell, it was amazing. But I need you to understand that's not me. Well, not really. I mean, I'm more than a decade past virgin, but it's not like me to take risks like that. I wasn't thinking. I can't believe we didn't use a condom and—"

"I'm clean, Kate. Relax. I had it under control. Nothing got in. And don't worry, I still respect you." Lord she was adorable.

"Good." She sighed, relieved. Finally her gaze locked on his. "But it can't happen again."

"What's that?" He blinked. Tried to process the direction the conversation had turned. His gut twisted.

Kate's deep-green eyes flicked to him, her brows shrinking together. "Not just because of your injuries, but... I mean, you're a client, a business associate and technically a camper. Besides, what happened wasn't planned. It was just fun—just sex. A one-time thing, right?"

Was she asking or telling? Joe exhaled, his chest uncomfortably tight. He flicked his academy ring around his finger trying to figure out what the hell was wrong with him.

This was his out.

Just sex? Most women would be picking china patterns already, talking about feelings and morals they hadn't displayed. *"I've never slept with a guy on the first date. You mean so much to me."* Yeah right. Until the guy writes the wrong name on a Valentine card then it's *adiós muchacho*.

But Kate was letting him off the hook—for whatever reason. He had to take the offer. Never mind whether he wanted to or not. Her life might depend on it.

"Agreed."

"Great." It seemed she meant it.

Joe's chest gave another squeeze, his gaze traveling over her body. He could still feel the soft give of her flesh in his palm, the liquid heat of her sex. If he closed his eyes he could remember the feel of her pussy hugging around his cock, smell the wildflower scent of her skin, taste the feminine flavor of her cream.

Heat flared through his veins, muscles tingling. He had to concentrate not to clench his jaw. *Damn.* Not a good sign.

Would one more go 'round really be so bad? His cock nudged at the thought of burying himself balls-deep inside her. What could it hurt? "Kate, what'd ya say we—"

Someone knocked at his door. Saved or foiled? Joe didn't want to think about it.

"What?"

The door creaked open and a head of shiny black curls poked around the edge, a foot above the knob.

"You sick?" Tony's coal black eyes appeared, the rest still hidden behind the door.

"What'd ya need, kid?"

The little rug rat shoved the door wide and strutted in, his posse, Delmar, Savion, Garon and Paul, fast at his heels. "Wanted to see what you were..."

His focus drifted to the left, drawn by Kate's movement

behind the door. Tony jumped, his eyes wide. "Miss Kate."

The rest of the gang gasped and jumped a half beat later, like the wave at a football game.

"Hey, guys. What's up?" She smiled wide, swinging the door closed behind Paul, the last in line.

"Uh… We, uh…" Tony glanced from Kate to Joe and back again.

"Checkin' on Joe. That's all," Savion said, his slouching been-there-done-that stance making him look years older than the twelve Joe knew him to be. The boy tossed his head so the swath of dirty brown bangs swung from his eyes. A second later they curtained back, nearly obscuring his right eye.

Tony blinked at his friend, his ability to form sentences flooding back. "Yeah. That's right. Heard they called the doc on him. Makin' sure he wasn't dead."

Kate checked her watch. "That's very sweet of you boys. But Joe needs his rest and you guys should be saddling your horses by now."

"Yeah, okay." Tony edged farther across the room toward Joe. "We'll be there in a minute. We need to talk to Joe first."

Kate flashed a suspicious smile. "About what?"

"Uh…uh…"

"Guy stuff," Savion said, saving Tony again.

"Yeah. Guy stuff."

"Oh. I see." Kate's sexy gaze slid to Joe. "Then I guess I'll leave the men to their chat. Make it quick, boys."

Kate pinched Paul's skinny arm as she passed, not hard, but enough to make him flinch and rub the spot. She winked at him and he smiled, his pale cheeks pinking as the gang of males, Joe included, watched the door drift shut behind her.

Tony and the posse spun toward Joe, then rushed him. "Did ya get her anything? How old is she? Why was she here? You guys doin' it? Are you comin' to the party? Did you fall off your horse again?"

Joe tried to decipher the flurry of questions. "What party?"

"Miss Kate's." Tony stood beside the couch, hands braced on the upholstered arm, elbows locked. "Next Saturday's her birthday. Ya got her something didn't you?"

No. "Don't worry about it, kid."

Savion poked an elbow into Tony's arm. "Course he did. Everybody knows women get grouchy if you forget stuff like that."

Dating pearls from a twelve-year-old. Joe wondered if he should be taking notes. "Where's the party?"

"We're gonna decorate the indoor arena." Paul plopped his thin frame on the couch next to Joe. "It's a surprise. We've been making gifts for her during craft hour. But you keep skippin' so..."

Macaroni necklaces and twig-framed God's eyes? Yeah, he'd had other things he had to do, like keeping a close eye on Kate. Besides, his gift to her would be keeping her alive to enjoy another birthday.

Birthday. There was something in one of the notes the stalker had sent Kate's father. He'd have to check.

Joe swung his attention to Savion. The kid stood next to Tony, weight on one hip, his small arms crossed over his chest, his freckled face stuck in a perpetual scowl. "You ask if I was doing her?"

The kid shrugged. "I'd do her. Whatever that means. She likes cars. That's tight."

"I know. Get outta here. Alla'ya." Joe fought to keep his smile from taking hold. "I'll catch up in a minute."

"Miss Kate said you had to rest," Paul said, hopping to his feet.

"Yeah, maybe if I was a *girl.* Now, get."

The boys agreed with manly nods and childish giggles, flowing out the door like a swarm of gnats.

Joe went to the bedroom and the chest of drawers where

he'd stored Kate's files—the one from her father and the one he'd confiscated from Clayton. He laid them on top, opened the folder from Mathers. He riffled through the photos and notes until he found the one he was looking for.

Dear Mr. Mathers,

I'm writing to respectfully ask for your daughter's hand in marriage. I bought a ring. It's a real diamond. I'm going to do it right. Don't worry about that. I know she comes from a classy family. I'm going to take good care of her, sir. You can see from the photos I'm with her all the time. I'm going to ask her to marry me on her birthday. I really hope you approve. I love her. I'm going to make her happy. No matter what.

Respectfully,

Your future son-in-law

There it was. The stalker had given himself a deadline, and this Saturday, time was up. He'd probably be feeling the pressure now, anxious for the situation to show a positive progression toward his goal.

Worse, if things weren't moving fast enough, the stalker might be tempted to force the issue. Joe shoved the folders back into the top drawer and headed for the door. He pushed the twinge of anger and the distracting personal concern for Kate from his mind.

Focus on the job. He was all that stood between Kate and the jerk who wanted to own her. It wouldn't happen. The son of a bitch wouldn't get near her.

Sweet anticipation hummed along her skin, more so than usual, as she wiggled each foot out of her flip-flops. Kate scanned the dark forest, not because she actually thought someone might be watching, but more because it's what you do before you get naked out in the open. She dropped her robe and tiptoed to the edge of the dock.

God, she needed this, especially after losing her head and screwing the hunky ex-cop out in the woods yesterday. Her body was a mass of tingling, molten lust and Joe hadn't allowed her a moment's peace since then to shake it off. The cool lake water would clear her head, always did.

A whole day, that's how long it'd taken her to find an opportunity to sneak away from her lousy shadow, a.k.a. Joe Garity. She still wasn't convinced she'd be alone until she heard him snoring through his cottage window at half-past one in the morning. She wasn't worried about the campers. They didn't even know the lake existed. Plus, distance, camp rules, dense woods and the late hour made accidental discovery a virtual impossibility.

Kate sighed, trying to exhale all the tension and hot carnal thoughts from her body. She gazed out over the moonlit lake, big enough for a fishing boat, too small for a Jet Ski, hugged on all sides by the dark woods. A soft, almost-there breeze rippled the black water, ruining the glass look of the lake. She dove in.

Her body sliced through the water with quiet efficiency, her mind focused on the easy mechanics of the freestyle stroke. She swam the long length toward the opposite shoreline, the cool water wrapping around her naked flesh, caressing her in places only she and her lovers had touched. Thoughts of Joe filled her head, his touch, his voice, those dark sexy eyes.

God, why had she told him about Dale? Her first sexual experience had been wonderful and heart-wrenching all at once—and too humiliating to hold focus in her brain for more than a moment. She'd been so naïve, thinking it meant anything more than sex, mistaking lust for love. She'd never made that mistake again. Until Joe.

Kate put her feet down when she knew she could touch and walked a few steps squishing her toes in the soft muddy bottom. She turned around, brushing hair and water back from her face with both hands, preparing for the return swim.

The moon made the faded wood of the dock appear white at the other end of the lake. She could see the small pile of her robe near the edge. The forest looked like a dark wall several yards back, countless trees with pitch-black night in between. Nothing stirred. She didn't expect it to.

Kate turned again and leaned back into the water, pin-wheeling one arm over her head then the other. The backstroke was her favorite for a lazy swim. No thought required. The water lapped at her cheeks, cocooned around her ears, shutting out the world. Her mind wandered.

What was it about Joe that made her forget all she'd learned about herself? Why with him did she want more than she knew she could have? She couldn't blame the sex. These feelings were with her every time he smiled at her, every time he made her feel special, like an intimate friend.

Joe wanted sex. Nothing wrong with that, she liked sex. But his attentiveness, his companionship, so much of the reason she wanted him, was fake. He followed her around, gave her his attention, because the Thorndikes paid him to do a job. She had to remember that. Why was it so hard to remember that?

Familiarity gave her the sense she'd nearly reached the dock and Kate glanced behind her. Someone was there. She turned around, treading water. "Joe?"

"You expecting someone else?"

"You were sleeping."

"'Til someone snooped around my window."

Kate dropped her gaze to see he held her robe balled in his hands. "I'm going to need that."

Joe looked at the robe and back to Kate. "I figured. You want company?"

"I'm naked."

"I figured."

A tremble of awareness rippled through her, warmed her sex. "We call this Bare Lake. And it's got nothing to do with the animal. It's a rule."

"I figured." He dropped her robe closer to the ladder on the right and toed off his sneakers.

Kate's heart skipped, the pace quickening, her stomach pulling tight. Three days earlier the view would've been far less enjoyable. The moon tonight was two days 'til full. The sky was clear and sparkling with stars and Joe's lean body was basked in silvery light.

He gathered the hem of his T-shirt and yanked it over his head stretching all the long muscles of his torso. He dropped the shirt without looking then worked his belt and jeans. The man was definitely in shape, but that body didn't come from hours in a gym.

The planes of his frame were round and thick. His belly flat, with horizontal shadows defining his abs. He wasn't cut or ripped, but he looked powerful, like a man who used his body the way it'd been designed to be used.

Joe's thumbs hooked on the waistband of his jeans and shoved them down past the narrow angular slope of his hips. She couldn't see the dark strip of curls she knew trailed from his navel to his cock, but the moment his sex was free, it sprang up, thick and ready.

Kate swallowed convulsively, her gaze drawn to the spot. Her sex muscles flexed with the memory of that plump velvet head pressing through the outer lips of her pussy, the fat shaft stretching her wide, filling her. When he turned to toss his jeans with his T-shirt, she could almost see the ropey veins that felt so wondrous inside her, his heavy sac nestled between his thighs.

"How deep?"

All the way. "Huh?"

"Can I dive?"

She nodded then realized he might not be able to see the gesture. "Yeah."

He sprang off the end of the dock, piercing the water like a needle through silk. He came up several feet out and began swimming toward the far end of the lake. By the time Kate caught up to him, he stood waist deep along the incline to the shore, arms loose at his sides.

Kate put her feet down, squished her toes along the soft lake floor, knees bent, breasts concealed beneath the surface.

"Shy?" he asked with a raised brow.

She realized he was waiting for her to stand.

So she did. "Not in the least."

His gaze dropped to her breasts. He stared at her, male appreciation showing in the easy expression of his face. The focused attention pulled her nipples tighter, making her acutely aware of their weight, of the cool air tickling over the sensitive flesh.

Her pussy flexed beneath the water, warming despite the chill of the lake. He raked his hair back from his face, black and sleek against his head, the water pulling the waves straight.

The head of his cock broke the surface in front him, his body clearly unaffected by the chill of the water. It was gone a moment later as he moved toward her, the water a few inches deeper where she stood. His hands went to her breasts, fingers tracing the bottom curve of each, feathering up to pinch her nipples.

"You're sexy as hell, Kate. I can't stop thinking about being inside you." He fondled her as he spoke, opening his hands on her breasts so her erect pebbles pressed against his palms, then drawing back so his fingers traced along the sides and back up to pinch her nipples again.

She found herself arching into him each time. "I know what you mean."

Heat flooded through her, arousal shaking her breath, humming along her skin. God, she wanted this. She wanted to feel his thick cock inside her again, stretching her pussy, filling her perfectly.

Yes, she wanted more. She wanted his heart and mind. But right now, with his hands touching the most sensitive parts of her body, his sweet scent misting the air, his body thick and hungry for hers, right now she wanted sex most of all.

He took her hips in his hands, pulled her to him so her breasts pressed against his chest, and his cock squeezed against her belly, warm and hard. She wiggled, enjoying the way his breath caught as his thick shaft rolled between their bodies.

He kissed her hard and fast, his tongue sweeping into her mouth, his lungs stealing her breath. Then he stopped. "You were wrong. I'm not a camper, I'm a fellow employee." He kissed her again, his lips brushing hers when he spoke. "You got rules against employees fucking?"

Kate had to force her eyes open, her mind doped and sluggish on lust. "Uh, no. Not one."

"Right." His knees bent as he scooped her up, lifting her to his waist.

Kate wrapped her legs and arms around him, clinging as he carried her deeper, his cock brushing against her bottom. The moment the watered buoyed her weight he stopped and took her hips in his hands again.

"Can you feel my cock against you?"

Kate nodded. "Yes."

He lifted her, shifting his hips, so the plump head pressed along the lips of her pussy. "I can feel your heat even through the water. I think you're warming the lake."

"That's your doing." She watched his smile stretch, so male, so sexy.

"Right." His fingers gripped firmer and he moved her into perfect alignment. The soft head of his cock parted her lips, cool water lapped at her entrance before he filled her.

She wiggled, her muscles flexing, trying to draw him in, but Joe didn't budge. Her body tightened, anticipation aching through her sex, clenching her chest. "Joe, I want you inside me. I want it now."

"You sure?"

"Fuck, yes. Do it."

Without another moment's hesitation Joe pulled her body down his shaft, driving himself deep inside her. Kate gasped, white-hot pleasure exploding through her body. The water around them warmed with their heat and Joe held her tight, impaled on his cock.

"I want to come inside you," he said before she opened her eyes. "I'm clean. Are you on—"

"The pill? Yeah."

His brow smoothed, not completely but enough that he looked more turned-on than pained. His fingers flexed on her waist, repositioning, and he slowly lifted her, sweet friction sliding her pussy up his shaft. Ropy veins on his cock rippled through the tight squeeze of her walls making her close her eyes, enjoying the draw.

The fat head reached her opening, stretching her more than the shaft. Her muscles pulsed and Joe closed his eyes, his mouth lax. Kate wiggled again and he opened his eyes, smiling wicked and sexy.

Kate readied herself for the ride. She held his arms, her hands small over the tight bulge of his biceps.

He started slow, drawing her body down his cock, rocking his hips in to meet her, then again and again. Each thrust came harder, faster. Within seconds the pace quickened. Kate's nails bit into his skin, his cock filling her, stretching her, ramming so deep and full there wasn't an inch of her sex left wanting.

Her flesh hummed with sensation, each thrust sending a jolt of tingling pleasure along her nerves, traveling to every corner of her being. Their bodies slid easily in and out of each other, the cool water making the passage maddeningly slick, the fat length of Joe's cock more than enough to churn the delicious friction.

She leaned back, holding the backs of his arms, so he drove his cock almost straight into her. Pressure built inside her, each of his thrusts adding to the last, driving her closer, closer. She held her breath, staved off the tempting release, forcing the sweet anticipation to build and build. She was almost there, the force of her need squeezing in around her, tightening her lungs, curling her toes, pulling her belly. Then it broke free.

"Ohgod..." Liquid heat gushed through her body, rapid pulses shuddering through her pussy. The water went hot between them and Kate's mind swam thoughtless in the exquisite satisfaction.

"Kate." Joe's pace didn't falter, his hands driving her body up and down his cock, faster, faster. "God, what you do to me. I can't... I'm, I'm gonna come."

The jarring thrusts churned the water, splashing over her breasts, adding an intense contrast to the rolling waves of her orgasm. A new tightening squeezed through her sex, a fresh tingle that built to a quick roaring need, matching the frantic pace of his thrusts. Her body timed it perfectly, the explosion quaking through her at the very moment his restraint let go.

"Fuck, yes!" Joe's voice echoed off the forest, his hips still pumping into her, milking every ounce of friction. He slowed, rocking to a gradual stop like the final swings of a pendulum.

They stilled and Kate allowed Joe to gather her to his chest, cradling her in his arms as his cock slipped from her sex. She nestled her head under his chin, his chest warm against her cheek, watching the ripple of waves from their actions lap the shore.

She could hear his heartbeat, listened as it found a normal rhythm. God, she could lose herself in the warmth and safety of his arms. The gentleness of his embrace, so tender it warmed her heart. She felt...special. If it could only last a little while longer.

"Kate." His voice was soft, though it rumbled through his chest against her ear. His hand stroked the back of her head, the other snug around her back. "You okay?"

Okay? Okay with being a fuck buddy? Okay with never being the girl they take home to Mom? Okay with wanting more than a late-night booty-call and knowing as great as they are together he'll never see her as anything else?

"I'm okay." Kate let her legs slip down over his hips. Her feet squished into the lake floor and she stepped back. The water was suddenly icy cold. "Yeah. I'm great."

Chapter Seven

"Where we going?"

Kate knew it was Joe on Sunshine trotting up behind her the moment she'd heard the hurried hoof steps.

The man was certainly dedicated to his job. From the second she found him leaning against the newel post at the bottom of her porch steps this morning, he hadn't left her side. Casual and sexy in his sneakers and faded jeans, the waves of his shiny hair brushing the collar of a snug Meatloaf concert T-shirt, he'd been one step behind her all day.

If she didn't know better she might mistake his focused attention for a deeper, more meaningful interest. She didn't want to think about it. If she thought about it her silly fairytale hopes would get away from her.

Why'd he have to be so easy to talk to, so down to earth, so...perfect? She liked him more than she should already. Having him around felt nice, natural and way too easy to get used to. If he'd spent the night like he'd hinted he wanted to when they got back from the lake, she'd have been using words like "boyfriend" and "love" in no time.

"Going to check on a pregnant mare out in the south pasture." Kate didn't stop or even look back at him. "She's at nine months. I like to keep tabs."

"Mind if I tag along?" He slowed Sunshine when her nose was even with Kate's horse, Wizard.

"Do I have a choice?"

"Only if your answer is yes."

She threw him a sideways glance, her smile more heartfelt than she knew was good for her. "Guess it's good I packed lunch for two."

"Kate," someone called from the stables. "Wait up, Kate."

She looked over her shoulder.

Eddy reminded her of Jack in *The Nightmare Before Christmas*, spindly arms and legs, lean body, even more so the way he was flailing his boney arms to get her attention. His long stride shrank the distance between them in seconds.

"What's up, Eddy?" She stopped Wizard and Joe turned Sunshine around, his dark eyes narrowing on the young man.

"You...you..." Eddy dropped his hands to his knees, panting. After a moment he stood, holding his side, grimacing. He swallowed. "You said we'd do the camper evaluations today."

He jabbed at the bridge of his gold, wire-framed glasses, shoving them farther up his nose only to have them slip right back to where they'd been. His long bangs, the color of dirty mop water, clung to his eyelashes behind his lenses making him blink, though he did nothing to brush them from his eyes.

His pockmarked face was flush from his run, and his mouth gaped open trying to catch his breath. Saliva made his thin lips shiny.

"Can it wait one more day?" Kate asked. Eddy was one of the first campers to come through Hickory Hills City Camp years ago. And now that he'd gone on to college Kate made special exceptions for his needy nature.

"That's what you said last time. I have to have this project for my psych class." Eddy glanced at Joe. "Haven't you spent enough time with him?"

"I'm going out to check on Foxy. Joe's keeping me company." She wasn't sure why she felt compelled to explain to Eddy, but there was nothing to hide and it seemed to relax the tight line of his shoulders.

"Well, if I don't get the evaluations done before the end of the week, it'll screw up the whole project."

"Maybe Clayton could—"

"No." Eddy propped his hands on his narrow hips, his tone sharp. "Clayton doesn't notice things the way you do. He's not as...smart, or sensitive, or understanding. No. It has to be you. You helped me do the initial evaluations. You have to help me do the follow-up. Do you want me to fail?"

"Of course not. But I—"

"I'll check on the horse," Joe said. "Go help Whining Willy there. You can pay me back with dinner. Just the two of us."

Kate turned to Joe. The thin scar over his lip was nearly invisible in his crooked smile, the look in his dark eyes, intimate. A warm tingle shimmied down her spine and pooled hot between her legs, making her panties suddenly moist.

Judging by that look the only thing Joe would want on their private dinner menu was her. *Even better.*

"Aw, geez-o-pete's. Never mind," Eddy said. "If it's that big'a deal forget it. I don't want you to owe him because of me. But we gotta do it soon or it'll blow my whole project."

"You sure?" Kate said.

Eddy nodded, his head low. He kicked the gravel as he turned and headed back to the stables.

"Thanks, Eddy," she called after him. "You're a sweetie."

He gave a halfhearted wave but didn't stop his dejected retreat.

She looked to Joe who was watching Eddy. "Guess I won't owe you dinner after all."

Those dark eyes swung to her and a fresh wash of heat flooded through her body.

He winked. "For now."

The south pasture was a mile out and the herd of six took time to find. Foxy's pregnancy seemed to be progressing normally. Kate and Joe checked a few breaks in the fence she'd sent workers out to fix recently and then finally stopped for lunch. The apple tree Kate chose next to the pasture fence was the same one she'd eaten lunch under with Clayton and his dad a hundred times before. But it had never seemed so isolated, so perfectly romantic.

She tied Wizard to the thick wood rail and Joe tied Sunshine beside her. The forty-foot span of leafy tree limbs threw plenty of shade for both man and beast. Kate's belly somersaulted. This was the first they'd been totally alone since last night and the possibilities sent her nerves jittering. She had to think of something else. Anything else.

"Did you always want to be a cop?" She yanked the two paper-sack lunches and canteens of water from the saddlebag. She handed one of each to Joe and settled under the shady tree next to him.

"No. That was Riley's doing." Joe leaned back against the tree, his T-shirt molding to the solid muscles of his chest and stomach.

"Riley?"

"Yeah. The cop who busted me for jackin' cars when I was a kid."

Kate choked on her swig of water and wiped her mouth with the back of her hand. "You were a car thief?"

He looked askance at her, his brow tight. "Yeah."

Joe took a bite of his PB&J sandwich and then another. He bent his leg and draped his arm over his knee. Staring out over the open hills and valleys of the horse pasture, his expression darkened as though embarrassed by his checkered past.

"I got busted for shoplifting when I was fourteen," Kate said. "Twice."

Joe wasn't the only one who danced on the wrong side of the law for a time. One brow high, he turned his chin toward her, a slanted smile slashing his lips. "For thrills or to get back at Daddy?"

This time it was Kate who glanced away, embarrassed. She shrugged. "Both, I guess. My dad bought me from my mother for the low, low price of ten thousand dollars and a ticket to American citizenship. I was never anything more than a possession to him. My father's all about things he can buy. I could've had anything I wanted. The man's loaded."

"But you didn't want anything money could buy." Joe made it more a statement than a question.

The hairs at the nape of her neck bristled. She could feel him watching her, reading her. She wouldn't look at him.

She gave a half-laugh, bitter, but she tried to sound unaffected. "I guess I was proving I didn't need his money. The only times he really saw me were when he came down to the police station to bail me out. Sometimes I wonder if I got caught on purpose just so..."

She wouldn't finish the thought. She knew the answer. *Yes.* She would've done anything to get her father's attention. That was a long time ago.

Silence settled between them for several seconds, Kate nibbling on her sandwich, Joe inhaling his.

"He's your biological father?" Joe asked.

"Yeah. My mom was one of his maids. I have family in Mexico. Somewhere."

"That why you ran away? To hurt your dad?"

Kate shook her head, swallowing. "No. I don't give a shit about him. I wanted to find my mom. I searched for three years. The Thorndikes helped. They found out my dad had been paying people to feed me false information. I don't know why he didn't want me to find her. But he made damn sure I couldn't. I had to get away from him. So I did. Edward Mathers is out of my life."

Joe shifted uncomfortably beside her. Kate hazarded a glance. His sandwich was gone. He held the half-empty chip bag in his lap while the hand draped over his knee flicked the gold ring around his finger. He stared out over the fields again as though lost in thought.

"Okay, what's with the ring?"

Joe looked at Kate and then the ring. He tilted his wrist up, fingers splayed. "Police academy. Riley gave it to me the day I graduated."

"Means a lot to you?"

"Meant a lot to him. Tom Riley turned my life around. Got me off the streets. Gave me direction. Yeah. Means a lot."

Her heart pinched at the sincerity in his voice, the pain and love in his eyes. "He was more than a mentor to you," she guessed.

Joe stared at his hand, flicking the ring with his thumb. "My dad was a no-show. Mom was out of the picture before I turned twelve. And I was on the streets by fourteen. Don't know why Riley took me in, but he saved my life." His gaze shifted to hers, deadly serious. "I'd kill for him."

"I know what you mean."

"I figured." After a moment staring into her eyes, so deep she felt he'd seen her soul, Joe smiled.

The corners of his mouth flickered. The tightness around his eyes softened. "Never told anyone about Riley. Not really. Not how much I... Just never told anyone that before. Weird."

"He's your Mary Jane." Kate shoved the rest of her sandwich back into the small paper sack.

Joe cocked a brow, his smile brightening. "Say again."

"Soon as the bad guys find out how much Spiderman cares about Mary Jane they use her to get to him. Makes him vulnerable. Riley's your Mary Jane."

"No. I knew what you meant. I've just never heard a woman reference Spiderman before."

Kate gathered the paper remnants of Joe's lunch and added it to her bag. "Spiderman was always kind of my personal hero. My favorite."

"Mine too," Joe said. "'Cause he was always just a regular

guy."

Kate met his eyes. "Exactly."

They stared at each other, electricity bouncing between them like a summer storm. She swallowed hard and glanced away. "So...I guess you trust me." The meaning of it didn't sink in until she said it. He'd trusted her with something profoundly personal. Her and no one else.

"Guess I do." He reached out and brushed a flyaway strand from her eyes, tried to coax it back toward her braid. It didn't stay.

Her skin was so soft Joe couldn't help touching her cheek, running his fingers down to her chin. He held her between his thumb and forefinger, and coaxed her lips to his—a tender brush, his mouth on hers, warm and soft.

She smelled good, like wildflowers and vanilla. He breathed the scent of her deep into his lungs. When he leaned back he saw her eyelids flutter open. Green as jade, so beautiful her eyes made his chest hurt. Jeezus, she was lethal to him. She made him dizzy. Not good in his line of work.

His body warmed, blood surging to his cock in seconds. He dropped back to the tree trunk, tried to will his hard-on away. This thing between him and Kate was getting out of hand. Not that it should matter. Given enough time he'd screw it up anyway. He always did—somehow. The weird thing was, this time he actually gave a damn if he ruined things with Kate.

"Speaking of Spiderman." Kate moved to her hands and knees. She crawled closer, straddling his outstretched legs. "Y'know, some of those drawings used to get me really hot. Especially the way his tights hugged over his cock. I swear they gave him a hard-on when he was around the secretary, Betty. And you know the Black Cat's pussy had him strokin' off every night."

Joe's cock swelled, pressing tight against the zipper of his jeans, his heart rate quickening. "I think most guys had a thought or two about the Black Cat's pussy."

His line of sight gave Joe a clear view down Kate's pink sleeveless blouse hanging from her body and her plump breasts barely contained in her white lacy bra. He kept his hands loose in his lap, her erotic take on the comic deepening her voice and making his body tight.

Kate rubbed her hand up his leg, stopping to massage the tense muscle of his thigh. Her thumbnail brushed the jeans over his sex and then again, jolting sensation through his body.

"I remember staring at the bulge between his legs," she said, "thinkin' how hot it would be to pull down those tights and take his hard cock in my mouth. God, it'd be so hot to suck him off while he was still wearing the rest of the costume."

"Wonder Woman did it for me." Joe opened his legs as Kate's hand slid farther up his thigh. "She always had her legs spread when she flew around in her see-through airplane. Used to think about her flying overhead or tying me up with her lasso."

Kate palmed his cock through his jeans, stroking him so Joe arched against her hold on reflex. She squeezed then turned her hand and rubbed down between his legs, over his balls. He opened his legs wider to give her access, and she scraped her nails against the stiff fabric. His muscles pulled, sensation vibrating through his sex.

"Kate..."

"How about you be my Spiderman and later I'll be your Wonder Woman?" She didn't wait for an answer, her little hands moving to work his belt and unfasten his jeans.

Joe's fevered thoughts pushed concerns about ruining things with Kate from his brain. His cock was hot and swollen with need. He wanted her mouth on him. He wanted to drive his sex through those sweet red lips and feel her sucking him off. He'd worry about...whatever, later.

She tugged at the waistband of his jeans, and he marveled at how effortlessly worries faded when he was with Kate. It was easy being with her, natural. Then Kate's fingers touched the naked flesh of his cock and he couldn't think about anything else.

"Stand up." A wicked smile bloomed across her lips. "I've got an idea."

Kate rushed over to Wizard and untied the rope on her saddle and brought it back. "Give me your hand."

He did, and she looped the lassoed end around his right wrist then threw the rope over a tree limb a foot or so above his head. She pulled so his arm stretched up, and tied his left wrist to match.

The rope was thick and the knot loose. He could free himself easily, but that wasn't the point.

"Now I've got you, Spiderman." She crushed herself against him, rocked her hips to squeeze his cock along her belly. She flicked his lips with her tongue.

"This your lasso of truth?" he asked as she dropped to her knees.

"Better. That's a lasso of lust. Gives every man it captures a rock-solid boner." Kate jerked his jeans down past his knees. His cock wagged out in front of him, brushing her hair before she looked up at him.

He winked. "It works."

Kate licked her lips over her smile and caught his shaft in one hand, the other cupping his balls. Joe moaned, his hips rocking forward, his hands wrapping around to fist the rope.

She stroked him from root to head, kneading his balls, and licked a bead of pre-come from the very tip. His breath caught, his body shuddering, every muscle pulling at once. She opened her mouth on him, her lips hot and moist sliding down his shaft, her tongue molding around him, suckling.

Kate grabbed his hips with both hands pushing him back as his cock pulled from the hard suction of her mouth. Electric tingles hummed through the molecules of his body, all of it rushing down to his cock. She reached the tip and nipped with her teeth. And then she took him in again.

His hips found her rhythm without conscious thought. Like the surge of the tide, he rocked in and out of her mouth, the suction pushing and pulling him closer and closer to the brink.

Joe looked down at Kate, at his fat cock driving into her mouth, her red lips snug around him, her eyes closed, fingers digging into his hips. And he drove himself deeper, felt the soft back of her throat against the sensitive head of his cock.

Kate moaned and pulled his hips to do it again. The sight was mesmerizing, the sensation maddening. His heart thundered in his ears, pressure building so fast he could hardly breathe. His hips thrust into her, driving deep, careful not to push too hard. She took him, all of him, the suction so exquisite every muscle in his body seized.

His thighs trembled, his sack pulling snug. He was close, so close. Then she cupped his balls.

"Jeezus... Huuuu..." His cock popped from her mouth, sliding wet and hot along her cheek as he thrust. An instant later his knees buckled as Kate's mouth latched onto his balls, suckling as swift and sure as she had his sex. Her hand pumped his cock, frantic, as she drew on one testicle and then the other.

Fuck. A flood of heat washed through his body, his hips driving so fast he could scarcely stand. His body responded to Kate with an alarming force. He was free falling, control gone, tumbling in a swirling flood of sensation.

His flesh hummed over his body, his muscles tense, spring loaded, chest so tight he didn't breathe, release a coming promise he could nearly taste. She took him into her mouth again and the sultry warmth, the hungry draw was more than he could take.

"Kate, stop. No. I'm... Fuck. Kate." He couldn't talk he could hardly think. He plunged his cock into her pretty red lips again and again, too close to release to turn away. Joe yanked against the ropes, but he couldn't get free, he couldn't think. He couldn't think.

She held him, her fingers digging into his ass, driving his hips, controlling the pace, the depths and draws of his thrusts.

"I'm gonna come in your mouth." His jaw clenched. "Fuck! I wanna...come in your...mouth, Kate. I want... I'm..." Jeezus, he couldn't stop. He couldn't stop. And then it was too late to try.

Sweet pressure exploded through his body, liquid heat flooding from the top of his scalp down his chest and out his cock. Muscles flexed, turned to rubber, tension washing out of him in a rush, shooting out his sex, filling her mouth. And still Kate suckled him for more. She fondled his balls, teasing a fresh spasm of come through his shaft, until she'd emptied him completely.

When Kate pulled the sweet heat of her mouth from his cock, Joe shuddered from the loss. He staggered, struggled to catch his balance and his breath.

"Kate..." He swallowed, lethargy fogging through his mind and body. "That was amazing. Jeezus, I can barely stand."

Kate sat back on her heels, touching her lips with the tips of her fingers. Her smile looked a mix of pride and pleasure, her jewel-green eyes peering up at him through long black lashes.

"You're bound to go a little weak in the knees when Wonder Woman sucks you off," she said.

"Wonder Woman's got nothing on you, honey. No one does."

A half hour later one question kept repeating through Joe's head like the skip of an old LP. *What the fuck are you doing? What the* fuck *are you doing?*

He was falling for her, that's what. Joe knew the signs. Hell, they were hard to ignore. His chest squeezed every time he saw her, and her laugh literally made his heart skip. And that wildflower scent of hers had a way of going straight to his cock no matter what they were doing. Not good. He'd screw things up for sure now. And that thought, more than any other, made his hands shake. *Dammit.*

Joe hung his saddle and bridle on their hooks in the tack room and crossed the aisle to Kate's office. She didn't seem to notice him come in, her focus intent on the computer screen at her desk.

The blue screen cast a soft light on her face, giving her sultry features an angelic glow. Damn, why'd he have to go and fall for her? He liked having her around and now she'd wind up hating him. His love interests always did.

"I'm going to—"

"Ah!" She jumped at the sound of his voice, slamming against the captain's chest behind her, rattling pictures and trophies and horsefly spray.

Her hand went to her chest, eyes wide. "Geez, Joe. You scared me out of my skin."

"Something wrong?"

She relaxed, her shoulders dropping from their tense line as she shook her head and went back to the computer. "It's nothing. Just a weird feeling. I don't know. It's nothing."

Maybe her sixth sense was picking up his superhuman ability to royally screw up relationships. *What the fuck are you doing?* "Gonna grab a quick shower. You headed to the mess hall?"

Her attention stretched from the computer screen to him like a fly off flypaper, never quite breaking free. "Uh, yeah. Sure. In a minute."

"I'll wait." He was probably being overly cautious. He could see the mess hall from Kate's back office window. The big cinderblock building was down the small gravel drive and across the service road. Anyone standing in the doorway could see straight along the aisle of the stables.

Joe wasn't taking chances. He crossed his arms over his stomach and leaned a shoulder against the doorjamb.

Kate looked up at him. Smiled. "You don't have to do that."

Yes. He did. "I know. I want to."

Her smile brightened. She straightened, toying with a pen in her hands. "Honestly, Joe. Go take your shower. I'll meet you over there."

Joe shrugged. "Don't want to leave you by yourself."

Kate practically glowed, her smile sparking her eyes, pinching the high curves of her cheeks. She came around the desk and crossed the room to him, pressing her warm hands to his chest. Her wildflower scent swirled between them.

Joe's cock thickened. *Hell.*

"You're very gallant, you know that?" She pressed up against his chest on tiptoes and kissed him quick. But the chaste touch still sent his heart galloping.

"Right."

"Anyway, I'm not alone. There's a ton of people right across the way in the mess hall and I'm pretty sure I heard someone down at the other end of the stables cleaning a stall or something. Besides, this is my home. I'm never really alone. Trust me."

She was probably right. He needed a shower, or a frontal lobotomy. Something to dull the heatstroke effect of her in his head, on his body. He couldn't think straight.

"Five minutes." He held up as many fingers.

"Absolutely. I've got a few more things to add to this spreadsheet then I'll meet you over there."

He pinched her chin between his thumb and finger and kissed her. Lord, he was gonna screw this up. He should pull back now before that warm, sexy smile of hers turned to hate. Easier said than done. Joe pushed from the wall, chucked her chin and headed for his cottage.

The half-circle sun on the horizon warmed the breeze rustling through the trees around the stables, swirling across the gravel road and stirring the long grass in front of his cottage. Joe shoved his hands in the front pockets of his jeans, only half-aware of the loud crunch his sneakers made over the jagged white stones.

Maybe things could be different this time. Something was different, he just wasn't sure what. The only thing he knew for sure was that he didn't want her to end up like every other woman he'd had in his life—hurt and blaming him.

No. The odds were against this thing between them ending any differently. It wasn't worth the risk. He had to end it now before his natural wrecking-ball tendencies kicked in. Simple as that.

Hell, it wasn't like he was in love with her. *Yet.* The sex was fantastic, sure, but some things were just more important. Besides, once he got a handle on whatever was weirdly different with Kate, he could probably go back to enjoying the sex for what it was—outstanding.

Joe took the steps to his cottage two at a time. He grabbed the doorknob and twisted before the fluttering paper even registered in his brain. He blinked.

It was a photo.

A photo fluttering at eye level on his door.

A photo of Kate and him tacked to the door. There was notepaper caught underneath.

Joe stepped back. His brain cooled, focused, shuffled the information into coherent thought.

There was a photo of Kate and him tacked to the door, a notepaper fluttering underneath. He listened, glancing over his shoulder, scanning his surroundings, realizing he'd been walking around in a fog for days. Dammit, this thing with Kate had to stop.

He tried the door. It opened. His internal alarms didn't flash any warnings. He went in and made a quick check of the place, and stepped back out to snap the papers from the door. He pinched the photo and note between his fingers, laying everything inside on his chest of drawers.

The photo was of the two of them walking from the riding ring to the stable. Taken yesterday, judging by the clothes they were wearing. Someone had scratched out Joe's face. They'd made a hole.

Joe shifted his focus to the note. The handwriting so jagged and scribbled, he struggled to read it. After several tries he puzzled it out.

She's mine! You can't love her like I can! I won't let you!

Joe dropped everything and ran.

He smelled the faint haze of smoke the moment his foot hit the porch. Denial pushed it from his brain. He jumped the steps, racing for the mess hall, each footfall like a hammer strike in his head. His breaths whooshed in his ears, his heartbeat loud, echoing like he was in water. He was drowning, panicked, running blind.

His mind spun. She was there—she had to be. She was safe, eating dinner, just like she promised. Kate, the kids, they were all safe. Everything was fine. But the twist in his gut wouldn't let him believe it.

When he rounded the end of the stables and caught sight of the smoke billowing out through the wide entrance, he knew.

The stables were on fire.

And Kate was still inside.

Chapter Eight

"They're saying arson." Clayton twirled the melted curry brush between his hands. "Couple saddles are toast, most of the plastic brushes and stuff, and a few bridles. There's some damage to the inside wall and the roof, but other than that, the building's safe."

"Did you—" Like she'd inhaled fire, the back of Kate's throat was raw—made her cough. She swallowed, pulled the fireman's blanket tighter around her shoulders and tried again. "Vet?"

Clayton's blond brows creased while he deciphered her meaning. "Oh. Yeah. Vet's on his way. I think we got the horses out before they breathed in too much smoke. Not sure I can say the same about you."

Kate shook her head and centered herself better on the short tree stump she huddled on. "I'm fine."

"How'd it start?" Joe asked from behind her.

"He torched one of the saddles," Clayton said. "Fire spread to the ones hanging above it."

Joe cleared his throat, as though the smoke had affected him too. "Which saddle?"

"Yours."

"Joe's?" Kate tightened the knot of her arms across her belly, trying to hide her worsening tremble. "Why would anyone burn Joe's saddle? It's not even his."

Clayton shrugged. "Who knows?"

He didn't look her in the eye. Kate glanced over her shoulder at Joe. The soot shadowing his face made his scowl more intense than usual. He met her gaze but gave nothing away.

Kate turned back to Clayton. "You think it was...y'know, *him*?"

The possibility her secret crush had done this made her stomach roil. She hated even asking.

The worry in Clayton's eyes belied his words. "I don't know, honey. The fire chief says with the kind of kids we've got staying here, it's probably a prank gone outta control. Don't let it freak you out."

"It was him."

Kate and Clayton shifted focus to Joe.

"Left a calling card on my door." Joe stared off in the distance toward the stables as though he was talking to himself. Kate followed his gaze.

The throbbing red strobe from the fire trucks cast the night sky and surrounding building in a strange bloody haze. Smoke still thickened the air, stung Kate's nose and soured her stomach.

Maybe it wasn't the smoke. Maybe it was the fact that everything she ever cared about, everything she loved, had nearly burned to the ground, and her right along with it. If not for Joe.

Kate's stomach flopped, bile shooting up her throat. She held it back.

"You found another note? A photo? Which?" Clayton's tone was harsh, accusatory.

"Both."

"You didn't say anything."

"I was busy."

Kate stood to better see the exchange between them and

because she couldn't stop her knees from shaking. She looked at Joe still watching the firemen coming in and out of the stables, seemingly unconcerned with Clayton's mounting outrage.

Clayton huffed. "Lemme see them."

"Police have everything."

"Dammit, Garity. Who the fuck put you in charge?"

Joe's cold stare shifted to Clayton and Kate saw the quick blanch on her stepbrother's face.

Clayton's gaze flicked to Kate then back to Joe. He scrubbed his face with one hand, turning his back on the both of them.

"What's going on?" Kate asked.

"I'm spending the night at your place," Joe said.

Clayton spun around. "Like hell."

"Clayton." Kate stepped between them. Both men looked to have murder on their minds. She turned to Joe. "A girl likes to be asked, y'know."

Joe's steely gaze dropped to hers. "It's not a date."

She flinched at his chilly tone. "I see. You think I'm in danger?"

"Not takin' the chance."

"He burned *your* saddle not hers," Clayton said. "If anything, he's after you. Probably wants you out of the picture. And y'know what? I get that."

"That's why we're not staying at your place," Kate said to Joe.

Joe dipped his chin. "That's why."

Clayton moved up beside them, though neither Joe nor Kate looked his way. "She can stay in the main house."

"No. I want to sleep in my own bed." *With Joe.*

She wasn't cold, but for the life of her Kate could not stop her knees from shaking. Her heart pattered like a startled rabbit, and her hands trembled even when she balled them into fists.

Kate detested the fear that gripped her heart, but the only sanctuary she could imagine was in Joe's arms. It was such a romantic cliché. But since the moment he'd exploded through her office door, alerting her to the fire, saving her, saving everything, she didn't want to leave his side.

Joe calmed her. She could feel his presence like a protective force. He'd keep her safe. It was that simple. And that strange.

"You'll be safer in the main house," Clayton said. "It's got alarms and solid locks."

Joe swung his attention to Clayton. "It'll tip our hand. She moves out of her cottage, the stalker will know he's made an impact. Either he'll back off, regroup, and we'll never catch him, or it'll validate him. Prove he matters to her and he'll want more."

"So what, we're supposed to pretend nothing happened?" Clayton asked.

"Right. Me sleeping over won't seem out of the ordinary." Joe's dark eyes shifted back to Kate, the cool detachment melting away. "We've spent most of our time together from day one. Everyone's been led to believe something's going on between us. Overnight's a normal progression."

He made it sound like he'd set the whole thing up. Like their relationship, or whatever it was, had been part of some master plan from the start. Kate closed her eyes, forced the suspicion from her brain. The stalker, the fire, it was all making her paranoid. She couldn't deal with it now. She just wanted to feel safe.

Kate pulled the blanket off her shoulders and shoved it into Clayton's chest. "Whatever. Give this back to the firemen, will ya? I'm going home."

An odd kind of numbness wrapped around Kate as she

stood at Joe's front door waiting while he grabbed a fresh change of clothes. They hadn't spoken on the walk over from the mess hall, and left the silence undisturbed as they walked from his cottage to hers.

She sank into the fat cushioned chair by the TV the moment they got inside, and sat boneless as Joe pulled off her boots. She curled her stocking feet under her on the chair, resting her head against the soft back.

Joe draped an afghan over her shoulders, tucking the ends around her knees and under her toes, nice and snug. Kate didn't so much as blink. Her stomach churned and twisted. She felt hot but couldn't stop shaking. She was helpless, exposed, powerless to stop all this from happening again, or worse.

Her mind whirled. God, she couldn't live like this. How could anyone live like this? She didn't want to feel scared and vulnerable anymore. She had to get rid of this feeling. She had to do something.

"I'm gonna grab a shower," Joe said. "You okay?"

Kate looked to Joe.

Joe. Strong and capable. He never let anything get the better of him. Not even fire. He'd saved her. He'd put out the fire and saved the stables, the horses, everything. Nothing scared him. Nothing harmed him. God, she wanted that. She wanted to be fearless, invincible.

"You're lookin' kinda frayed at the edges there, dollface." Joe tilted his head to one side. "You hearin' me?"

Kate blinked, forced a smile, then nodded.

"Right." He brushed the tip of her nose with his finger and winked. "Yell if you need me."

The bathroom door clicked shut behind Joe. The sound of running water followed minutes later. And just like that Kate decided she wouldn't be scared and helpless anymore.

"Kate?" Joe knew it was her without pulling back the

shower curtain. He'd known she'd be coming before he'd closed the bathroom door.

She didn't answer. She didn't have to. He shifted back under the spray of water, rinsing the soap from his hair and face. He'd nearly finished when the curtain fluttered then peeled back at the other end of the tub.

"Hey, dollface." Jeezus, she made it hard for him to breathe.

Soot streaked her forehead, nose and chin, but when she stepped into the tub he noticed the shadow of grunge covered every part of her body that'd been exposed. He could see the line around her neck in the shape of a vee from her collar and the line at the round of each shoulder.

She smiled, but there was no spark behind it. Her hair hung loose past her shoulders. Her breasts and belly and legs pasty white compared to the black dust on her arms and face.

His gaze dropped, lingering on her breasts then lower to the tight curls over her sex. His body responded, his cock thickening, rising out from his balls, muscles tightening.

"Mind if I get in there?" Her voice was stronger than he'd expected judging by the haunted look in her eyes.

Joe stepped to the side and Kate made a point to rub her body against his as she passed. Her breasts and belly brushed soft against his skin, her hard nipples chafing an erotic line across his chest that his brain tracked on reflex.

She turned her back to the spray and inclined her head, lifting her arms to rake her fingers through her hair. Her breasts rose, shaping into two perfect teardrops, nipples rosy and puckered. Black-gray streaks raced down her chest, between her breasts, over her nearly flat belly and down her legs. The water pooled at her feet, turning ashen, then darker, before running clear.

Joe snagged the bottle of shampoo from the molded corner shelf and squeezed a dollop into his hand. The vanilla scent flavored the warm shower steam, filled his nose, connecting with every erotic thought in his head. His blood warmed, lust zinging through his veins despite his compassionate intent.

"Turn around," he said, and Kate opened her eyes.

A flash of little-girl-lost filled her wide green eyes before the woman settled in behind them. The corners of her lips trembled, sweeping up to the barest of smiles. She lowered her chin and turned. Her hair looked like a dark shiny curtain down her back, two inches past her shoulder blades.

Joe gathered the thick strands with one hand, the other coating the mass with the sweet-smelling shampoo. He worked the soap to a lather, massaging the small round of her head. Everything about her seemed miniature now, so delicate and vulnerable.

She could've been killed tonight. With all his training, all his hard-learned lessons, if he'd been a minute longer, thought a little slower, he would've been too late. Kate would've been gone forever and there was nothing he could've done to change it. *Dammit.*

Joe exhaled, closed his eyes for a minute. He pushed the swell of anger and triggering thoughts from his head. Kate's alive. That's what matters. For now.

He opened his eyes when he felt Kate reach for a smaller bottle. She squeezed a dab into her palm and washed her face while he continued lathering her hair. She leaned into the spray and rinsed, then reached to cover his hands with hers. He stopped his massage and Kate turned around, inclining her head into the stream again.

Joe stepped closer, his fully erect cock thumping against her belly. He took her wrists, pulling her hands from her hair.

"Let me." Gently, he pushed his fingers through her long hair. White foaming suds cascaded over the shiny curves of her body, catching around her nipples, dipping into her belly button, gathering around their feet.

Kate rested her hands on his hips. He could feel her fingers trembling. Anger stormed through him so fast his jaw locked.

When he caught the son of a bitch who'd done this, who'd shaken her, stolen her sense of safety... *It's not right.* Kate should never be frightened. He'd kill him. He'd—

Joe strangled the thought, reeled in his murderous anger, struggled for gentleness. He gathered her hair, squeegeeing the last remnants of soap with both hands, from the base of her head to the tips of her hair.

She edged closer so her breath warmed his chest, and her arms slipped around his waist. He kissed her forehead when she peered up at him, his cock pressed thick and needy between them.

Kate hugged him, resting her cheek on his chest, crushing the softness of her body against his. Joe wrapped his arms around her, held her while the warm water pattered his arms and over her back. He could've held her forever. He would've, but the snug hold of Kate's arms loosened and he let their bodies part as she wished.

"Ready to finish?" He reached for his sponge on the molded soap dish beside them and grabbed the bottle of liquid soap. Only half noticing the flowered picture decorating its label, he squeezed a mound of Kate's soap in the center.

The wildflower scent went straight to his cock as he lathered the sponge. Suds covered the back of his hand, halfway down his arm and he rubbed the soapy sponge around her neck, over her shoulders, down her arms. He lifted her hands and cleaned her fingers, her palms, then moved to the other.

Her naturally sun-kissed skin glistened, and Joe sponged soap over her chest, circling her left breast, then her right. His free hand followed the path, tracing the sensuous curve of her breast up to her nipple. Suds, piled in a small temple, braced on the tight puckered flesh, and Joe swiped his thumb over the hard nub, then gently pinched.

Kate's eyes fluttered closed. Her back arched, encouraging his fondling hand. Her chest rose and fell with her deepening breaths. His heart pounded, blood turning hot, swelling his cock to its limit. He pressed the soapy sponge down her belly, rubbing circles, before sliding around to her ass. He squeezed her nipple one last time then slipped his free hand around to hold both cheeks, holding her slick soapy body against his.

She wriggled, stroking his stone-hard cock with her body. Their flesh slid easy, pressure instead of friction, erotic and needy. Joe drew the sponge along the crease of her ass, soaping the inner sides of her cheeks. His other hand followed behind, pushing between the firm rounds, toying over the pucker of her anus.

Kate flinched at his touch, thrusting her hips forward, crushing the mound of her sex against the base of his cock. Joe caught his breath, every muscle in his body snapping tight. He rocked into her on reflex, cradling her against him with both hands on her rear.

Heat surged through his body, from his head down to his chest, tingling along his arms and legs. Kate's hands dropped to his ass and gripped, pulling their bodies flush. His thigh muscles shook, need pounding through his body and brain. She leaned back and wrapped her fingers around the thick shaft of his cock.

Instinct jerked Joe's hips back at her touch but Kate followed the move, quickly cupping his balls too. She arched into him, rubbing his cock along her soapy belly, lathering his shaft, so her hand slipped slick and easy along his sensitive flesh.

She stroked him from root to head, her fingers bumping over the smooth ridge at the top. Each stroke sent jolt after jolt of pleasure rippling through his body, humming along his skin, tugging the tightening knot in his groin.

His chest squeezed so hard he could barely breathe. His hips pumped his swollen cock into her snug little hands, faster, harder, pressure building. Joe dropped the sponge, grabbed her upper arms and spun her to the sidewall, pressed her back, his hips thrusting on instinct.

He took her mouth with his, tasting her, feeling her heat surround his tongue, enveloping him. She lost her grip on his cock, but his need continued the thrusts, stroking himself along her belly, the coarse hairs of her pussy brushing against his shaft. He moaned at his loss of control, at the sweet satisfaction of giving in to his primal urge, however briefly.

Her legs opened, though his height made his cock too high to find her sex. He slipped his soap-covered fingers through the wet folds between her legs, finding the heat of her inner body, hotter than the water warming the shower.

His fingers slipped from clit to anus, dipping in and out of her tight little pussy as they passed over, mixing her sultry cream with the wildflower soap. Her hips bucked, following the stroke of his fingers, her sex pulsing each time he teased her opening.

She grabbed his hand between her legs, matched him finger for finger, and drove the center two of both deep inside her. With their fingers doubly thick, filling her pussy, the muscles latched achingly tight around them. Kate pushed them deeper, and Joe stroked her inner walls, curling to find the spot that made her moan.

Her head pushed back against the wall, body arching, legs opening wider, as her muscles milked their fingers. Kate drew her hand out of her, riding only his. Joe cupped her mound, grinding his palm against her clit, watching her writhe for more. Her body tensed, her muscles squeezing around his finger, her hips rocking faster, suddenly frantic.

Kate's mouth opened, eyes closed, breaths coming in quick pants. "That's it. Joe. Yes. Don't stop."

Determination seized everything male inside him. With his fingers fucking her pussy, grinding her clit, he bent to take her breast into his mouth. Joe drew her in, flicked his tongue over the tight nub, nipped and suckled, feeling the instant her sex fluttered ecstatically around him.

"Ohgod... Yessss..." Liquid heat gushed through her sex, her orgasm pulsating her muscles.

The moment she stilled Joe pulled out of her. He turned her, faced her toward the end of the tub and braced her hands on the back wall. He pulled her hips back so her ass thrust toward him and spread her legs with his knee.

Joe stroked his cock, staring for a minute at the glistening sight of her, pink and open, plump and ready. He leaned forward and smoothed his hand down her back, over her ribs, curving his fingers around her waist, feeling that she was real, startling at how small and fragile she was. But she was alive.

He ran his hand over the firm round of her ass and traced a finger through her folds. A few more tight strokes on his cock and he guided himself to her sex. He plunged into her, his thoughts screaming in his head.

She could've been killed. Jeezus, he'd almost let her get killed. His hips thrust, driving his cock, pounding her sex. Kate drove back just as hard, harder. He couldn't get deep enough, close enough. He wanted to surround her, envelope her so nothing could ever threaten her again.

"Fuck." His voice was graveled, his emotions riding him rougher than he was riding her. Sensation swirled through his body, hot blood surging into his cock, swelling him, tightening her pussy's delirious squeeze.

His fingers gripped her hips, pulling her back as he pounded forward. The sound of their flesh smacking echoed loud off the tiled walls, but all Joe could hear was the thunder of his panicked heart in his ears.

She could've been killed. And there was nothing he could do to change it. He'd almost lost her. *Fuck. Fuck. Fuck!*

Her pussy hugged tight around him, sweet friction humming along his shaft, vibrating through his body. Nerves tingled, drawing sensation in a swirl to his center, his balls pulling tight, need building.

"Kate... God, Kate..." He threw his head back, his hips

bucking hard, pressure exploding in a hot rush down his cock.

He collapsed against her, spent—utterly. Kate leaned forward into the back wall to hold his weight, her shallow breaths matching his. Joe wrapped his arms around her waist, buried his face in the crook of her neck and held her. Lord, he'd never let harm come so close to her again.

Joe's stomach gurgled, empty, and suddenly he was awake. He narrowed his eyes toward the sun shining irritatingly bright through the cottage window. Kate nestled closer in her sleep. Spooned against him, her bare bottom wiggled against his morning hard-on, banishing all thoughts of food from his brain.

He hugged around her, burrowed his face through her long fall of hair to her neck. He kissed her, breathing in her scent. After a night of sex and sleep, the aroma was less wildflowers and more sweet natural Kate. His cock tingled, balls tightening. Damn, she smelled good.

Joe rolled to his back, his left arm trapped beneath her. He didn't try to free it. Didn't want to. He scrubbed a hand over his face, yawning, his cock tenting the sheets. The hard-on wasn't going anywhere, not with Kate lying naked beside him. *Hell, naked or not.*

He dropped his hand to his chest and closed his eyes, hoping for a few more minutes of sleep, wanting to stretch out the quiet contentment a while longer. Kate's bed was soft, and her sheets and pillows smelled like her. The sound of her sleeping breaths was better than warm milk.

The whole cottage was comfortable in a way he'd never been able to create for himself. There was nowhere else in the world he'd rather be. And then she woke up.

Kate stiffened, her eyes snapping open. She wasn't alone. *Joe.* God, she could smell him, distinctly male among her flowers and sweetness, naturally masculine, naturally Joe, all sexy and warm. She rolled toward him, slowly, his muscled arm under her neck.

He's asleep. Inky hair feathered the pillow around his face, his jaw and chin dark with stubble. Long lashes shadowed his cheeks, his mouth relaxed, perfect, kissable. The urge to touch her lips to the little scar at the corner nearly had her following through, but she stopped herself. He needed his sleep. He'd earned it...in more ways than one.

Kate took a moment to appreciate the delectable view. Muscled chest, bare except for the smallest brush of black hair around his nipples, faint lines running vertical across his abdomen then farther down where the sheet tented six or so inches high.

She lifted the edge of the sheet. Someone was having a good dream. Kate always said the morning hard-on is solid proof God's a woman. Men started their day ready to please. *As it should be.* Her hand itched to wrap around the darker flesh, to feel the velvet softness against her palm, to stroke the hard length of him. *Crap.* She wouldn't. He needed his friggin' sleep.

After a self-pitying sigh she laid the coverings softly back in place and rolled out of bed, careful not to jostle the mattress too much. She tiptoed around to the chest of drawers and picked out matching pink satin boy-cut panties and lacy bra.

She went to the closet, sliding the door as quietly as she could. The heavy wood rumbled over the tracks despite her best effort. It was quiet again soon enough and she pulled a butter-yellow riding blouse from the hanger. She slipped it on, buttoned it and grabbed cream-colored breeches.

She had other clothes, normal clothes, jeans, T-shirts, even a few dresses. But she lived and worked on a horse farm, on a horse. She mostly stuck to the clothes that worked.

"Goin' somewhere?"

Kate screamed, jumping nearly a foot off the floor. She panted, hand to her heart. "You scared the life out of me. I thought you were sleeping."

"You gonna answer the question?" He sounded grumpy.

She wiggled her knees, pulling her breeches up past her hips. She smiled. God, he looked good sex-rumpled in the morning. "You're not a morning person, are you?"

"Right."

She laughed, pulling the zipper and fastening the hook on her pants. "I was going to run out and grab us some breakfast from the mess hall."

His brows crinkled. "No home cooking?"

"Oh, no. I like you." *Silly man.* Her cooking was deadly.

Joe smiled and folded his arms behind his head, crossed his feet under the covers and did the one trick all males seemed overly proud of. He made his cock bob beneath the sheets.

He waggled his brows. "Come back to bed, dollface. Breakfast can wait."

Kate's gaze dropped to the tented sheets and she licked her lips reflexively. She raised a brow and offered what she hoped was a wicked grin. "Trust me. You'll be needing your strength."

She came around the bed and then leaned over him for a quick kiss. "I'll be right back."

Her hair brushed over his chest, and he snagged a fistful. "I like your hair down."

Their eyes met, so close she could see the tiny flecks of royal-blue and dark purple in his eyes that, from a distance, enriched the overall midnight color.

"I'll make a note." She straightened and he let the strands slip from his fingers.

Kate held her fat mass of hair in one hand and spit the rinse of toothpaste into the sink. *Pain in the ass.* But Joe liked her hair down and more and more she couldn't help liking Joe.

She rinsed her toothbrush and took another glance at her reflection in the mirror over the sink. She finger-combed her hair back from her face, gathered and twisted it at the base of her neck. She let go and the too-thick mass flowed loose across her back in seconds. *Darn it.*

"I like your hair down," she mocked in the mirror. Bet he wouldn't like it as much if the heavy mop were on his head. God, she was doing it again even though she'd warned herself against it.

She was sacrificing her own comfort to please a guy. And why? Because he was cute, sexy and lickable all the way down to his juicy center? *Okay, there was that.*

But he'd done more than just look good. Last night he'd sacrificed his own safety to save everything she held dear. That should be worth a day or two of her shoving hair from her face every five seconds.

That's it. She wasn't doing the giddy, lovesick girly-girl routine. She was being appreciative. And not because she was hoping there was more between them than hot animal monkey sex.

Heck, she'd hardly even thought about what spending the night, the whole night, in her bed meant to him. And no way was she overvaluing the countless things they had in common, or the easy way they joked and just plain talked with each other. He was probably like that with a ton of women.

But he did seem to go out of his way to be with her. Yeah, he was trying to nail the stalker, but private trail rides and road trips to the feed store, secret dips in the lake and quiet walks back to her cottage every night seemed above and beyond. And last night, when she was in his arms, there was something in the way he held her, a little too tight, a little too long. There was something. *Maybe.*

A loud knock at the front door broke Kate's dreamy train of thought. "Coming."

She jogged to the door and threw it open without even thinking of checking first who it was. "Clayton."

"Hey, Kate. Need to talk to Joe. He up?"

"No, he's—"

"What's up?" Joe's voice made Kate turn to see him standing in the bedroom doorway leaning his back against the doorjamb. His chest bare, he dipped his hands into the front pockets of his unbuttoned, barely zipped jeans, pushing them lower on the narrow muscles of his hips. He looked good. Too good. And she had the distinct impression he'd done it on purpose.

Kate shot her gaze back to Clayton. She could almost feel the rage rippling off his body. He was clenching his teeth so tight, the muscles along his jaw flexed. His ice-blue eyes shifted to her and she felt the chill all the way to her bones.

"I need to talk to your *boyfriend*. Can I come in?" There was something different about Clayton, something in his voice, in his eyes. He'd changed.

"Uh, yeah. Sure. Come in."

It wasn't until Clayton had passed her that she noticed the papers he held. He smacked his hand into Joe's chest, papers crumpled underneath. "Found these in Wizard's stall this morning. A new love note and photo. Figured you'd want to report it to Mathers."

"Mathers?" Kate said.

Joe took the papers, his face an impassive mask, his eyes fixed on Clayton.

Clayton stared back at him, though he was clearly answering Kate. "Edward Mathers. Joe's boss. Loverboy didn't tell you?"

"I...I don't understand. I thought Bill hired him." Kate's stomach rolled, nausea turning her skin clammy. "He's supposed to help figure out who's been sending the notes. He's a retired cop, a PI now. Right?"

"No. He's a bodyguard." Clayton turned to the side so he could see both of them. "Your father paid him to protect what was his. Make sure no one and nothing got near his property. You."

"Stop it, Clayton." *Shit.* She was going to be sick.

"I'd say he's done a pretty good job." Clayton crossed his arms over his belly and shrugged. "Though if ya ask me, I think he should've told you he was getting paid by the hour before he climbed into your bed."

"Get out." Kate swallowed hard to keep the bile down her throat.

Clayton rocked back on his heels, a smug grin playing across his mouth, his eyes narrowed on Joe.

"Clayton," Kate said. "Get. Out."

Her stepbrother's jaw dropped, his head snapping to Kate. "Me?"

She closed her eyes, struggled to keep from screaming, from crying, from throwing up. God, she'd been such a fool. "I want to talk to Joe. In private. Please, Clayton. Get out."

"You're kidding. Kate, this guy's lied to you from the get-go."

"Yes," she said, harsher than she'd intended. "And you knew about it. You lied to me too. The difference is you're like a brother to me. I thought I could trust you."

Clayton dropped his chin, stared at the floor and snorted. "Your brother. Yeah. Well, maybe that's the problem."

"Clayton."

He turned and headed for the door but stopped on the porch. After a deep breath he glanced back over his shoulder. "My head's been in a weird place for a long time where you're concerned. I know you're right. I know it. I just...need some time to get it straight. Y'know?"

"I know, Clayton."

He held her gaze for a moment, his bright blue eyes shimmering. "I'm sorry." Then he closed the door.

When she turned around, Joe had grabbed his T-shirt, gun holster and shoes, and was just coming back through the bedroom doorway.

His scowl creased his forehead. His sweet lips were tight and flat. He stopped short when he saw her waiting, the note and photo crumpled in his hand.

"You going to report to your boss?" The words choked her throat. Tears stinging her eyes.

"Right," he said, cold, unremorseful.

"Don't bother."

"Why's that?"

"'Cause you're fired."

Chapter Nine

Kate adjusted her seating on the rail next to Ginny. "No. Don't you see the difference?"

Ginny shook her head, watching the campers taking turns loping their horses around the ring. "I don't get what's changed. You were fine with it yesterday."

"Yesterday I thought he was a retired ex-cop, hired by the Thorndikes to help figure out who's been sending those notes and photos. Today I know he was hired by my self-important, money-can-fix-anything father to stick by my side however possible."

Including acting as though he had feelings for her and screwing her brains out when the need arose. Gawd, she'd been such an idiot.

"Ooohh, I get it." Ginny straightened as though understanding lifted a weight from her shoulders. "You think he was just *pretending* to like you."

Kate slouched. "Bingo."

"Ooo, that's harsh. So you really liked him, huh?"

Pride shook Kate's head. "No. I mean, well yeah. He's hot, right? And we had some fun, but he's just a guy."

Kate's belly flopped, tightening. The lie sank through her like cold iron, weighing her down. It didn't matter. She had to trust that if she kept saying it, kept forcing herself to believe it, eventually it'd be true.

"Exactly." Ginny flashed a mischievous smile, leaned close and spoke in a conspirator's whisper. "Least you got some great sex out of the deal. Right?"

"Right." There was that, although Kate had allowed herself to hope for so much more. The disappointment made it hard to breathe. She'd been such an *idiot*!

"When ya think about," Ginny said. "There's really no reason for you to stop. I mean, if it's just sex, great sex, then what difference does it make why he's here? He used his sex appeal to get close to you. Why not go right on using it?"

"I fired him."

"What? Why?" Ginny whined like a kid who'd dropped her ice cream.

"He lied. He lied to get into the camp, about who he was, why he was here and who he was working for. Who knows what else he's lied about? I can't risk him being around the kids."

"Oh." Ginny's slouch returned. "Yeah. I guess you're right."

"No. She's not."

Kate wrenched her chin over her shoulder to see Joe leaning against the stable next to the entrance. His arms crossed over his stomach and his left ankle lazy over his right, he looked like he'd been there for a while.

"Hi, Joe." Ginny smiled and Joe winked back.

"Hey, peanut."

Kate twisted around and jumped down from the railing. "What are you still doing here?"

"Working."

"I fired you."

"Doesn't count."

"Yeah, it does."

Joe pushed off from the stable wall, hooking his thumbs on the front pockets of his jeans. "Sorry, dollface. I work for your dad. Gonna have to take it up with him."

"I don't need a bodyguard."

Joe shrugged. "'Til I hear different..."

"That's stalking."

"Ironic, huh?"

"Ugh!" She couldn't argue with him when he looked like that—all smug and sexy, beard stubble shadowing his jaw, bedroom eyes dark, intense. The man was determined and it showed.

She bristled past him into the stables, feeling him follow a few lazy steps behind.

"For the record. I only lied about what I do for a living," he said when they'd reached the throughway at the middle of the stable.

Kate spun around, but Joe had plenty of time to stop. He didn't even have the decency to look surprised. "What about the camp application?"

"Your father took care of it." Joe shrugged. "Or one of his flunkies."

"You said the Thorndikes hired you to help investigate."

"No. I told you I was a retired cop. You assumed the rest."

Tension knotted across her shoulders, her hands balling into fists. "You followed me around everywhere making me think..." Dammit, she'd been such an idiot.

Kate exhaled, leaving the sentence unfinished and turned back toward her office. "Just go away, Joe. I don't need your protection. There are plenty of people around to look out for me."

"That's got nothing to do with it." He followed right behind her. "I'm not here to make sure you look both ways when you cross the street or that you eat all your vegetables. I'm here to guard you. To put myself between you and harm."

She stopped, glancing over her shoulder, her hand on the knob of her office door. "Why?"

Joe sighed, propping his hands on his hips. "It's the job."

"Nice." She didn't know what answer she was hoping for

but that wasn't it. Kate opened her office door and stepped in knowing full well slamming the door in his face wouldn't keep Joe out. So she didn't bother.

"First rule of bodyguarding: it's a job," Joe said. "Not a friendship, not a vacation, not a... Not a romantic rendezvous. It's a job. *You're* the job."

"What the hell does that mean?"

"*Christ.* It means I—" Joe stopped yelling. He took a breath, hands on his hips, and began again—calmer. "It means no emotions. Detachment. The principal's a thing, not a person. Do what needs to be done to keep it safe. Emotions make you hesitate. Dulls the edge. Makes you as screwed up as the stalker."

"Well, I'm not a thing, Joe." She dropped into her desk chair already exhausted by the conversation. "I'm emotional and messy and attached all over the place. And I like the people around me to be attached emotional messes too."

Okay, now she was just babbling. "People care about each other here. We're friends, family. I'd rather have someone who cares about me watching my back than a detached emotionless...machine."

"Right." He dropped his chin. Shook his head. Kate couldn't read him, and apparently that wasn't anything new.

Someone knocked on the open door.

"Kate?" Eddy said, mop-water bangs trapped behind his glasses. "I was... Oh. Didn't know *he* was in here again."

"It's okay, Eddy. Joe was just leaving."

"No. I'm not." Joe turned toward him, folding his arms over his muscled chest and planting his legs wide. He looked like a bouncer.

"You okay? You need help?" Eddy's bangs couldn't hide his deep scowl. If he had death-ray eyes, Joe would've been toast.

"No. I'm fine, Eddy. Thanks," she said. "What'd you need?"

The spindly young man stepped into the office, his big

brown eyes narrowed on Joe. Kate was surprised to notice they were the same height, though all of Eddy's muscles combined would only make up one of Joe's biceps. A fact Eddy didn't seem overly concerned with.

He closed the distance between him and Joe, shoulders back, jaw tight. He jabbed a finger at the bridge of his glasses. "Y'know, if the lady wants you to leave, you'll leave."

"That right?"

"That's right."

Joe cocked a brow. His dark eyes fixed on Eddy's. "You gonna make me?"

"If I have to."

"Hey." Sheesh, the testosterone levels in the room were enough for Kate to choke on. "This is my office. Nobody's making anyone do anything. Got it?"

Eddy blinked first, backing up without actually backing down. "Got it."

"Thank you, Eddy. What'd you want to ask me?"

He looked to Kate, his pitted cheeks flushing, eyes suddenly shifty, nervous. "I was gonna ask if you wanted to, uhm, I dunno, grab, y'know, lunch or something? Together, I mean. I thought we could maybe sit together. If ya want."

Flattered by his shy request, Kate's face warmed. It took a lot for him to ask. Eddy didn't make friends easily. People shied away because of his looks and oddball demeanor. But Kate knew the story behind the coke-bottle glasses, the reasons why he was offended and hurt so easily. Molestation, beatings, abandonment, those things will do that to a person.

Kate's heart ached for him. Eddy just needed a friend. "Sure. I'll meet you over there. Okay?"

Eddy's smile lifted his glasses. He nodded and threw Joe a triumphant sneer on his way out.

Joe's dark gaze tracked the young man's exit past the office windows and out the stable entrance toward the mess hall.

"Guy's not playin' with a full deck."

"Why? Because he wouldn't back down to you?"

Joe's gaze flicked to her, brows high. "Isn't that enough?"

Kate grunted her disgust. "Leave him alone. In fact, leave me alone. God, you think you're so cool. You think everyone's dying to be you, or with you. Whatever."

She dropped into her chair again, irritated that his confidence was justified.

"Right." Joe's glower stole over his face again. She could almost see him drawing into himself, closing off all emotion.

Ohmygod. I am a job to him.

Kate swallowed hard, trying to force her heart out of her throat and blinked at the ceiling. She wouldn't cry. Dammit, she was so not this person. Joe Garity was just a guy—another guy who wanted her, but not to keep.

She looked at him. "Listen, I'll call my father. Make sure he pays you. But I want you to go. Just...go. Now. Okay? I don't need or want a bodyguard. I've got people to watch my back. People who actually care about me."

"You talking about Clayton, Frank or Eddy?"

"What?"

"There another guy you've got turned ass backwards over you?" He snorted as though it was an inside joke, not at all happy. "Guess there is. At least two."

"What? No. I meant—"

"Forget it." Joe held up a hand, stopping her explanation. "Doesn't matter. They'll get you killed. People who care about you care about the wrong things."

"Rude."

"You're not listening." He slammed his hands on the desk, locked his arms. "They care if you're happy, sad, pissed, whatever. You don't want the guy protecting you worried about your mood. You just want him to keep you alive."

"And you can do that?" Her hands were shaking, her heart

skipping a mile a minute. "You can step between me and possible death because you don't *care* about my feelings?"

Joe straightened. He blinked as though he hadn't expected the question. He slipped his fingers in the front pockets of his jeans and met her eyes with his. "I care about keeping you alive."

"Same thing, right?" Kate's frown drew her brows tight, though for a moment he'd seen her chin trembling. Her eyes were moist and shiny, glittering in the sunlight.

Jeezus, don't let her cry. He knew the first tear would break him. "Doesn't matter."

"Yeah." She sighed, looked away. Her attention focused out the window, she blinked enough times he knew she fought against her tears.

What was he doing? He didn't want to hurt her. Hell, he was trying *not* to hurt her, trying to keep her safe, to keep her alive. He shouldn't have made love to her. He shouldn't have spent the night. And he sure as hell shouldn't have allowed his emotions to muck the works.

Her green eyes were still sparkling when she looked back at him. But her chin was firm and so, it seemed, was her resolve.

Kate pushed to her feet. "I won't have any part of my father in my life. He thought he could buy me when I was a kid and he's still treating me as a possession, assigning personnel to guard his property."

"Could just be protecting his daughter."

"If I was a daughter and not property, he would've talked to me. He would've told me he was worried, told me he was hiring someone to protect me. No. I'm a possession. A *thing*. But I don't have to explain that to you."

"Right." Joe clenched his jaw. Kept his damn mouth shut. She didn't get it, and he wasn't going to draw her a picture. If he'd been doing his job, if he'd kept to the rules, he wouldn't have been standing there. He wouldn't bother trying to help her understand.

What difference did it make that she was pissed at him? Who cared if her feelings were hurt, if she felt insecure about their intimacies? She was alive and he was going to make sure she stayed that way. That's why he was there, what he did for a living. Kate, the woman, shouldn't matter. Except she did. Jeezus, he was fucked.

"Fine. Then I want you to quit," she said.

"What? No."

She sucked a breath through her nose, her lips tight, hands fisted at her sides. "I want you to call Edward Mathers and tell him you're no longer working for him."

Joe pulled the folded note and photo from his back pocket. "You need to see this."

She wouldn't take them, so he tossed them on her desk and Kate looked at them for a second. It seemed curiosity won out.

She picked them up and unfolded the paper. He watched her eyes scan the words, watched them widen slightly then shift to the photo.

"What's this scribbled across your face?" Her voice was soft, shaky, though not an ounce of trepidation showed in her stance or in the frown creasing her brow.

"Betrayal."

Her attention focused back on the note. She read aloud, "*Fire purifies. Let it cleanse your heart. Our love can rise anew from the ashes. Don't be led astray again.*"

She looked to Joe. "I don't understand. He knew you lied to me?"

"No. Not likely."

"This was taken the day you followed me into the woods." She held the photo out to him. "Our clothes and hair are wet. He says not to be led astray again. He knows you betrayed my trust."

Joe's muscles tensed. A knot tightened at the back of his

neck. "It's not about that."

"Of course it is. He cares about me. He doesn't want to see me hurt."

"He doesn't want you fucking other men."

Kate blanched, drew the photo back to her. "What?"

Joe sighed, rolled his head trying to loosen the knot. "You betrayed him. With me. It's a warning. Don't do it again—or else."

"He burned *your* saddle."

"Burned me out of your life," Joe said. "Purified with fire."

"But..."

"He's turned a corner. Upped the stakes." Joe took the note and photo from her hands so she'd stop staring wide-eyed and paled at them. Her gaze tracked him folding the papers, slipping them into his back pocket.

"He wasn't like that before," she said. "The notes. They were sweet and then you came."

"He was courting you. Must've thought it was working. When you and I started, he knew it wasn't."

"But I didn't do anything to make him think—"

"You exist. That's all he needed. He's in love with you, Kate. He's dangerous. To you, to everyone around you—including the kids."

Kate's eyes flicked to him, the pupils so big the emerald green was only a thin trimming. "No. It doesn't make sense. If he loves me, he wouldn't hurt me. He wouldn't hurt the people I care about."

"Not the way he loves. He's obsessed. You're his drug. You're a constant itch he can't scratch. And trust me, dollface. Sooner or later he'll either find a way to scratch or eliminate the itch."

"Me."

Joe dipped his chin. "That's right. And if the kids are around when he does... Nothing else matters to him, nothing else exists. Just you and him."

"We have to call the police." She reached for the phone.

"I did. Gave them the last message and photo."

"And?"

"Forget it. They dusted for prints. Came back clean. They can't tie the guy to the fire beyond speculation. There's no overt threat made in any of the notes, so their hands are tied."

Kate hugged herself, eyes dazed, unfocused. "What do I do?"

"Lemme do my job."

She looked at him. Her eyes suddenly steeled. "No."

"Kate."

"I can't. No." She shook her head. "You don't understand. I can't let Edward Mathers back into my life. Not even for this. You don't know what it was like."

She looked away, gave him her profile, but he could see the rush of emotions shuddering across her face. He wanted to touch her, to hold her. He didn't dare. Dammit he'd never been afraid of anyone in his life, but he was afraid of her, afraid of her rejection.

Kate began talking, her voice soft, distant, as though her mind was in a far-off place or time. "My whole life, not once, not one kiss, one hug, nothing. He bought me everything I could possibly want. Gave me a beautiful room. It was my place, like a photo on a shelf. It's where I was put, kept. If it weren't for my nanny, I would've never left the house. I was home schooled.

"Thirteen when he finally allowed me to attend private school. Thirteen when I realized in the backseat of his limo there were people in the world who wanted to touch me, to love me. I was sixteen when my father realized it."

She brushed her fingers over her cheek, under her eye. They came away wet. She sniffled and Joe's gut twisted.

Kate raised her chin and cleared her throat. "I was sixteen years old when Edward Mathers finally found a use for the daughter he'd bought and paid for. Sixteen when he told me to go *talk* with one of his male associates. Said his friend was lonely and he'd like having a pretty girl to *sit* with."

She laughed, bitter. "I was so naive. I wanted to please him, even after all those years."

Joe's hands were balled into fists in his pockets, his jaw clenched so tight his teeth ached. "Did he..."

She shook her head. "I left that night. Walked away from the only man who's ever wanted to keep me. I won't be owned. I won't allow that man back into my life."

"You can't handle this alone," Joe said. "Without training, experience, someone's gonna get hurt."

"I know." She turned. "That's why I want you to quit. Tell my father you're not working for him anymore."

"Kate."

"Tell him you're working for me."

Chapter Ten

"I'm not one of the queer-eye guys," Joe said, his back to the open changing-room door.

"It's a simple question. Blue or green? Doesn't take a degree in fashion or an orientation switch."

Joe did not want to look. Kate was doing it deliberately. He turned anyway. "Green."

"That's it? Green. That's all you have to say?"

He'd been asked his opinion on everything from which pair of six-inch fuck-me heels best accentuated her legs to which shade of blowjob-red lipstick looked better with her skin tone. *Seriously? All of them.*

This time though, he knew it was coming. The pert nipples on faceless mannequins wearing lingerie in the showcase windows were clue enough. He'd prepared himself—he thought.

Joe's nails dug into his palms, arms tight across his chest. His hard-on squeezed beneath his jeans so thick he was about to bust a seam. He clenched his jaw, his gaze dropping despite his best effort to the silky negligee smoothing around her body.

Definitely green. The shiny fabric bared her arms in a halter style and plunged between her breasts, snug over nipples hard as pencil erasers, leaving the supple inner curve of each breast teasingly exposed. A band of dark lace edged the neckline and defined the waistband high beneath her chest.

The effect was an eye-catching frame for a well-endowed body like Kate's. The bottom swung loose and airy to the top of her legs. A heavy sigh would flash panties or pussy. Intrigue and suspense enough for any man.

Plus, he noticed suddenly, the color kind of matched her eyes. "Green. That's all."

Kate's thin brows bunched, her lips pursing to a sexy pout he wasn't sure she knew was sexy. Her arms dropped from the stretched pose on the doorframe. Defeated, she sank down from her tiptoes.

Oh yeah, it was deliberate.

"Would it kill you to tell me why?" she asked.

He sighed. "It's the one you're wearing."

"So if I'd come out in blue?"

"Then blue." He checked his watch, trying to remember how to breathe. "Almost done? Going on two hours now."

Kate's frown deepened. Resigned she glanced away for a second and then dropped her gaze to the bulge at his crotch. *Busted.* Her brows shot to her hairline, an ecstatic smile blooming across her lips.

She met his eyes, her glee lighting her face, glowing over her skin and making the tightness in his chest worse. "All done. But I'm going to need help with the fasteners on this thing. You mind?"

Not waiting for his answer she turned and stepped closer to the mirrored wall inside the changing cubical. She swept her hair up with both hands, exposing the delicate run of fabric-covered buttons and loops behind her neck.

Joe didn't move. It'd take a moment for him to reel in the urge to strip her bare and run his hands over her naked body. He concentrated on inhaling, then exhaling. *Inhale. Exhale.*

"Joe." Her gaze met his in the mirror. "Little help?"

Hell, he couldn't win this game. What man could? Fair or not, when it came to restraint and seduction, the deck was decidedly stacked against men.

He wasn't sure how the ridiculous challenge between them

had even started. It'd been a full day since she'd hired him and exactly a half day longer since they'd last had sex. She was pissed about him working for her father, and Joe figured he'd give her time to get over it. But now it felt like weeks had passed.

Apparently the window of opportunity had slipped by without his notice. Though, as far as he could tell she never really lost that chilly edge to her tone. But he wondered if the reason behind her cold shoulder had changed.

He'd waited too long. She resented it and now seemed to be daring him to try. Hell if he'd make a move knowing he'd be slapped down for his effort. Unfortunately for Joe, or not, his libido was quickly overriding his stubborn will. He stepped into the changing cubical, his hands big and clumsy over the tiny buttons.

The smell of vanilla and wildflowers swirled around him like an erotic eddy. He closed his eyes, letting the scent seep through to his center. His muscles pulled, blood rushing hot through his veins. His cock jerked when his fingers brushed her skin, soft and warm. God, she always smelled great.

He edged closer, the skirt of her negligee, brushing feather light against his jeans. The air between their bodies thickened, energized. A deep breath from each and they'd touch. Joe's hands shook. He gritted his teeth against the tremor.

"Green looks..." He cleared his throat and tried again, his voice soft, sincere. "Matches your eyes."

The silky hairs at the back of her neck moved with his words. He swung his gaze up to the mirror, saw her lips sweep to a smile.

"Thank you."

He worked the last button, holding the ends of the fabric, stroking his thumb over the petal-soft skin at the nape of her neck. He watched her eyelids lower, desire warming the clover-green color.

"Need me for anything else?"

Baby-fine hair tickled his knuckles, his hands drifting apart, her top going slack. His skin tingled with her nearness, her weight shifting back so her bare shoulders brushed his chest. Joe held his breath, closed his eyes, riding the flood of heat zinging through his veins.

"No." Her voice was a whisper, too soft to make him believe the statement.

He pressed his palms to her skin, holding either side of her neck, smoothing out toward the rounds of her shoulder, the ends of her negligee pinched between his fingers. His breathing shallowed, the satiny fabric gripping earnestly to the sharp points of her breasts, all but her pebbled nipples exposed to him.

Joe tightened his grip around her upper arms, shifted her back to his body, pressing the marble-hard line of his cock against her bottom. She let him. And his breath gushed from his lungs at the feel of her. Kate's arms drifted to her sides, her hair falling thick and heavy between them and over his shoulder, fragrant like a warm breeze over a summer field.

He leaned down wanting to touch her skin with his lips, needing to taste her and Kate inclined her head to the side. The high silver ring on her ear caught his eye. He kissed the tender flesh it pierced and flicked his gaze back to hers.

Her eyes were hooded and dreamy, their gazes locked in the mirror as he lowered his mouth to her neck. He could feel the heat of her flesh on his lips before they touched, her sweet heady scent enveloping him, making his mind sluggish.

"Excuse me. Hey. Excuse me, sir."

Joe snapped straight, shot a glance over his shoulder at the salesgirl.

"You can't be in there. Only one person to a dressing room, *sir.*" She sneered.

And just like that the cold front moved back in.

"Joe, be a doll and get me a fresh soda," Kate said from the center seat at the overcrowded counselors table.

Joe didn't move from the wall he leaned against five feet away.

"Oh, wait." Kate glanced at her fellow diners. "Anyone else need a refill?"

Ginny waved. "Me."

Eddy scooted his chair closer beside Kate. "If he's fetchin' I'll take one."

"Me too," another counselor said.

"Diet for me," said another.

Kate swung her attention back to Joe. "You get that?"

"Abso-fuckin'-lutely." Joe didn't budge.

He wasn't her damn assistant, although that didn't stop Kate from ordering him around like one. Carting him off to the mall pushed his tolerance level to the max, though where she went he would follow. But Joe was nobody's flunky. And he sure-as-shit didn't *fetch*.

Behind his thick glasses Eddy's eyes narrowed on him. He swiped his stringy bangs to the side and tipped his chin toward Joe. "Why's he always hanging around?"

Kate turned to look at Joe, though she likely knew who Eddy meant. "He's a…"

Joe and Kate had agreed it was best to keep his true profession secret from the male staff so as not to tip off the stalker. They'd maintain the cover he'd established, affair and all, though nothing official was ever stated, in hopes of driving the creep out of the shadows. Kate was safe. He'd make damn sure of it.

But Joe knew the summer-affair scenario was lacking authenticity lately. A fact he'd have to rectify—for professional reasons, of course.

"He's just hanging out like the rest of us." A smile flickered at the corners of her mouth. She turned back to Eddy. "Besides, he's kind of old to stay with the other campers. Don't you think?"

"Yeah, but he doesn't actually talk to any of us. It's creepy."

Joe pushed from the wall and closed the distance to Kate.

"He's shy. He talks to me," she said. "Sometimes."

Eddy's spine stiffened. "Still think it's weird. He your boyfriend?"

"Ah...we're, ah—"

"Yes. I am," Joe said from behind Kate.

She jumped. His name whooshed through her lips on a breath. "Joe."

He leaned over, bracing his hands on the table, caging Kate between his arms. Her scent wafted up to play havoc with his libido, but Joe ignored his body's quick response.

"Ready, dollface?" He bent at the elbows and pressed a kiss to the crown of her head. Jeezus she smelled good and her hair felt like spun silk against his lips.

"Ready?" she asked.

The table had gone eerily silent. Joe flicked his gaze. Just as he thought, all eyes were on them.

"Ready to..." He bent lower, his upper body surrounding her. He rested his lips to her ear. No one would hear clearly enough but Kate. "We're lovers. Remember? Hot 'n' heavy. Time we acted like it."

He kissed the tiny nub of flesh at the entrance to her ear— because people were watching and because he needed to kiss her.

Her breath shuddered. Her voice came weak and airy. "Ready to go to the breeders? Uhm, yeah. Sure. Let's go."

She shoved her chair back and Joe huffed, doubling over. White, blinding light streaked through his brain. The searing pain of a hot poker stabbed through his groin and his balls shot up into his body lodging somewhere in the vicinity of his gut. Then it really started to hurt.

Kate glanced at Joe's groin as they walked down the stable aisle at the breeders. He was still limping a little. Lord, she hoped she hadn't broken anything.

He caught her looking, must've read her worried expression and shot her a frown laced with male embarrassment.

She mouthed the word, "Sorry."

He shook his head, brow tight, and turned his attention to the man between them leading the way. Albert Finnegan, head breeder at Maple Run Farm.

Joe glanced around then back to Albert. "Horses need all this to, ah…"

"Copulate?" Albert said with a slender brow cocked high over the frame of his glasses.

"Right."

"No. Don't be stupid." Albert walked on, passing the run of stalls on either side. He had a peculiar feminine sway to his hips that said as much about him as the sass in his tone and the flaring swing of his arm.

"Horses, like any creature on earth, are quite capable of propagation naturally, without aid," Albert said. "This facility simply ensures their safety and provides efficiency nature has not."

"That right?" Joe looked quizzical and irritated at the same time, staring at Albert's back.

"Indeed." Albert wore the white lab coat Kate had come to expect, though she was never sure why. She suspected it made him feel official. There was a lab in the building, with a cryogenic freezer, microscopes, big syringes and other scientific-type equipment, but as far as she'd ever seen, Albert was more of an overseer than a lab technician.

"Your mare is up here." He flipped his wrist in the direction. "We're ready to bring in the stud."

"Just in time for the show," Joe said with a smile and wink in her direction.

Albert spun, small blue eyes narrowed behind his glasses. His slender face flushed all the way up through the sparse hairs neatly pressed to his head. His cheeks sank in below impossibly high bones and the spot of hair beneath his tightly pursed lips emphasized the sharp point of his chin.

"We are not seventh graders here, Mr. Garity. This is a serious, delicate procedure. Not a way for you to..." His gaze made a quick sweep of Joe's body, ending with a raised brow and appreciative smile. "Get your jollies. I trust you'll keep your brutish male urges in check?"

Joe slipped his hands into the front pockets of his jeans. "Right."

Albert twirled back around and led on. Joe flashed Kate a questioning wide-eyed look. She shrugged. What could she say? The guy was flaming.

They stopped near the end of the stables where three mares were tied, asses out, in narrow stalls. Two padded chains below the mares' rumps stretched across each narrow opening a foot apart.

Memories sent a flush of heat to Kate's face. She knew what was coming. She'd seen it countless times before, but she hadn't considered how she'd feel about watching the "procedure" with Joe.

"You two over there." Albert pointed to a spot past the mares, closer to the end of the stable.

One of the farmhands, a young man Kate recognized but had never met, led a horse down the aisle toward them. The large bay stallion perked its ears as he neared, his nostrils flaring, his flaccid cock swinging long and pink to his knees.

He brought the stallion's muzzle close to the wet sex of the first mare, her tail swishing, feet shifting, stomping the ground uneasily. The stallion snorted and nuzzled the mare. She squealed as though she'd been bitten, ears pinned then thrust her rear leg back hard and quick. The big stud flinched, but the chain stopped the mare's kick, sparing him certain injury.

"Tease," Joe said.

Albert glanced over his shoulder. "That's nothing. Equine copulation is a passionately violent act. So driven are they by their lusts, kicking and biting, deep gashes from hooves during mounting, even risk of death won't dissuade them." He looked back to the horses. "Marvelous creatures."

The scene was repeated twice more with the other mares, the large stallion growing more excited with each taunting whiff. In the end, his fat pink organ curved long and solid beneath his belly. His powerful hoofs pounded the ground before his mares, his need calling him to mount them despite the small space and the chains that separated them.

Kate stared at the impressive organ wagging thick and stiff beneath the stud's belly. The animal's arousal fairly sizzled in the air, electricity tingling over her skin. Her body warmed. She watched as the stallion thrashed his thick neck, dancing closer to his females. Light gleamed over his tight muscled hindquarters, his powerful body driven by his need to plunge himself deep inside them.

"He's ready." Albert looked to Kate. "Take your friend in first before we bring the stallion to see Jessie."

Joe leaned close, his arm slipping around Kate's waist. "Jessie?"

"Short for Jezebel. The farm's whore. She's in here. C'mon." Kate nodded toward the wide-open doorway at the very end of the stables to their right.

She took a spot against the inside wall and Joe edged in, his arm going around her waist, again tucking her close. She closed her eyes for a moment, relishing the warmth of his body, the firm strength of his muscles against her.

"What the hell is that?"

Kate opened her eyes, belly fluttering, as she glanced at his expression, seeing his mind puzzling out what they were about to witness. She followed his stare.

The room was twenty foot by twenty foot square, with a dirt

floor and corrugated sheet metal for the ceiling and walls. On one end the wall held a door and a long window into the lab. A small group of people stood huddled in quiet conversation near the lab door. Several wore elbow-length plastic gloves. One had added a clear face mask.

"That's Jessie," Kate said shifting her attention to the large contraption at the center of the room. "Basically a big wooden sawhorse covered by thick foam pads and built at a slant to make, ah, *mounting*, easy and pain free."

"A horse sex doll."

"Pretty much." Kate shrugged. "She's easy and safe. A stud's wet dream."

Joe looked askance at her, his smile crooked, a flash of heat in his dark eyes. "Right."

Though she'd never admit it, she enjoyed a secret thrill watching the breeding processes. Seeing the stallion's fevered excitement, his primal undeniable need, the voyeuristic charge of watching another creature in a sexual act made her body pulse, her blood run hot.

Just thinking about what was coming creamed her sex. If she didn't know better, she'd think Joe was affected the same way.

The handler led the stallion into the room. Albert followed taking a spot against the wall on the other side of the door. He folded his arms across his chest, his right hand moving to his mouth, his eyes focused on the stiffly aroused horse.

The stallion pranced toward the stationary mare, repetition putting a knowing excitement in his step. One of the gloved technicians smeared the real mare's creamy scent along the foam padding, further coaxing the stallion.

His neck stretched, nostrils flaring, cock hard and thick, the stud sniffed twice then reared up to straddle the imitation horse.

Joe's hand fisted the waistband of her breeches at her side, tugging her closer. Kate glanced at him, but his eyes were fixed on the masturbating stallion.

Before the stud found his position the masked technician swooped in, a long, flexible rubber tube in his hands. He fitted it over the stallion's wide stiff cock and stroked his length, both hands gripping the tube.

The powerful animal thrust his hindquarters, ramming his long erection into his imaginary mare. His muscles rippled beneath his shiny fur, driving hard and frantic. The sawhorse shook from his strength. The technician under him stroked a counter rhythm squeezing his hands, his face grimacing, his arms taut.

Muscles deep inside Kate tightened, her sex tingled and slicked. Joe's hand opened on her hip, his fingers hot, kneading the side of her pelvis. Kate looked at him, his jaw clenched, eyes narrow, riveted on the scene before them. She glanced down, intrigued to see the faint line of his cock in his jeans.

She felt him look at her and she met his gaze. He didn't smile. His eyes were so filled with desire her breath caught. His hand squeezed her hip. He pressed her body against him. He wanted her then, undeniably, unmistakably, finally, and every bit as much as she wanted him.

"For all the good it did me," Kate grumbled hours later, falling backward onto her bed. She lay sprawled over her comforter, horny as hell and without a cock in sight. Joe's cock might as well be a hundred miles away as good as it was to her on the other side of her bedroom wall.

They should've come straight back to the cottage after the breeding farm. They should've found a room, a stall, a dark corner, somewhere where they could've taken care of the frustrating ache between her thighs. They hadn't, and the moment was lost.

Not that she could really blame Joe for not making a move. She'd been throwing out so many mixed signals even Kate wasn't sure what she wanted.

After everything she'd told Joe about her father, how could he have even considered continuing to work for him? It made her heart hurt. But worse than questioning his ethics, she questioned Joe's motivations, his reasons for being with her.

The night of the fire she'd been so sure he felt something more for her than lust. But now? She'd once worried his constant, focused attention was a requirement of his job. Now she knew for a fact it was.

Kate wiggled up to her pillow, raised her legs and pulled the comforter out from under her. She snuggled underneath and squirmed out of her panties.

"This bites," she said under her breath and pushed her hands down through the wet curls of her sex. After a few seconds Kate knew masturbating would be as satisfying as an ice cube at an all-you-can-eat buffet. She didn't want her finger inside her or her happy-bunny vibrator. She wanted Joe—or at least her body did. Her heart was still on the fence.

She threw back the covers, kicking her feet free and stood. "If Daddy dearest can pay Joe to follow me around and have sex with me...so can I."

Kate yanked her nightshirt over her head and tossed it in the corner. She grabbed her fluffy terrycloth robe from the end of the bed and went to the dresser mirror. She slumped when she saw her reflection. The thick comfy robe made her look like a belted pillow. To make things worse, she had bullet head from her riding helmet.

"Crap." Nothing she could do about it. The robe was the only one she had. Warmth over sex appeal had been the order of the day when she'd bought it. She finger-combed the thick waves of her hair, refusing to examine her reflection below the neck.

Better. She went to the door and took a few deep nerve-calming breaths. Was she really going to do this? Did she need sex this badly?

"Abso-fuckin'-lutely," she whispered and creaked open the door.

The living room was cast in dusky shadows. Joe slouched on the couch across from the bedroom door. His face was in profile to her, his head lolled back, his arms in his lap. Kate stepped out on tiptoes. She stopped, narrowing her eyes. Something in his lap was moving. She stared, waiting for her vision to adjust.

Joe made a soft groan, shifted his hips and Kate noticed the rhythmical pump of his hand.

She swallowed hard, her belly fluttering. She knew she should look away, at least let him know she was there, but she couldn't. She couldn't move. The sight of his big hand stroking up and down the stiff shaft of his cock, his left hand cupping his balls, made her muscles tight, her thighs wet.

Joe rocked his hips once and then again. His jaw clenched. His eyes shut tight. The soft sound of friction, skin against skin, finally reached Kate's ears.

He made another soft sound. "Kate."

Her name on his lips while he pleasured himself sent a fresh wash of heat through her pussy. Joe's hand gripped his shaft hard enough to raise the veins in his forearms. His rhythm quickened, turned rough. Dark veins roped up the side of his neck. His hips rose, leg muscles tensing, and Joe pumped himself faster, harder.

Gawd, she'd come just watching him. Kate edged forward, hoping he'd somehow feel her presence. He didn't, obviously too lost in the build of sensation.

Kate moved closer, stopping at the arm of the couch. She could see clearly now, the front of his briefs pushed down under his balls, his cock standing straight and stiff, the shiny head poking up and down through the rim of his fist.

She licked her lips, her mouth cotton-ball dry. "Want help with that?"

Joe jumped, reaching lightning fast for the throw cushion,

covering himself. "Fuck, Kate. Warn a guy."

She caught her bottom lip between her teeth. "Sorry. I didn't mean to embarrass you."

Joe looked up at her, his wavy hair curtaining around his face. His brows drew tight above sexy dark eyes. "You didn't. Just startled me. How long have you been there?"

Kate fingered the edge of her robe, her body hot, excited. "Long enough."

"Just watching me?"

She nodded.

Joe reached up and took her hand, pulling her to stand in front of him. He shoved the coffee table back with his foot then untied her robe.

"Say it, Kate."

"What?" She swallowed, her thighs trembling.

He parted her robe, pushing it off her shoulders, exposing her naked body to him. "Tell me why you were watching me jack off. What you want."

"I want..." She allowed him to lower her hands, so the robe slipped to the floor. "I want...I want the same deal you gave my father. You work for me, like you did him."

His eyes flicked to hers, his brow etched with confusion. "That's right. What deal, sweetheart? Tell me."

"You fucked me in order to stay close. To guard me. Now you work for me and..."

"You want me to fuck you because I work for you? Because you're paying me? That's what you think?"

Her heart skipped, a ripple of insecurity shuddered through her belly. "I don't know... I just want...I just need you inside me. I don't care why you're there."

A sob choked at the back of her throat. She fought hard to swallow it down. *Dammit,* she did care. But her body ached to be filled, to be satisfied. Her need far outweighed the silly wishes of her heart.

"Kate, I—"

She grabbed his face with both hands, stopped him before he said something that would make it impossible for her to continue. Like apologizing that she'd guessed his reasons exactly.

"Just do as you're told. Don't talk."

Joe's brows shot to his hairline, then fell with his sexy smile. "Yes, ma'am. What would you like?"

"Kiss me."

He shifted forward to stand, but Kate held his shoulders. "No. Not on the mouth."

Joe leaned back, lowered his gaze to her pussy. His smile widened. "Yes, ma'am."

He slid his hands up her thighs, his palms rough, still warm from masturbating. "Spread your legs."

She did and he grabbed the pillow off his lap, threw it then leaned forward, clamping both his hands on her ass. He buried his face against her, his tongue darting out, toying over her clit, firm and moist. Kate's chest squeezed. She held her breath, her body melting in his hands. Her hips rocked forward on reflex, her muscles tight, desperate for more.

His tongue pushed lower, driving through the sensitive folds, stroking back up to her nub. He suckled her, drinking her in, sweet suction, pulling sensation from every nerve ending in her body. Her hands raked through his hair, fisted, held him to her.

Joe didn't resist, his vigor increasing with hers. His hand slipped around, cupped her ass between her legs, tracing down between her cheeks to her sex. He plunged his thick, stiff finger inside her. Her muscles squeezed around him as he added another, pushed deeper, drawing hard on her clit.

Sweet, undeniable sensation swamped over her, billowing out from her core. His fingers pumped her sex, like air into a balloon, building the tingling pressure. She was so wet, his strokes and suckling triggering a flood of cream through her pussy. He pulled his fingers out and replaced them with his thumb, his wet fingers cupping around to her anus.

Kate gasped with the feel of his fingers teasing the tight entrance, her body going slick at his touch. His thumb shoved deep into her sex, made her knees weak and her breath catch.

He held her hip steady, suckling her clit, pumping her sex, pushing past the slicked opening of her ass. Her mind spun, her heart thundering in her ears. She bucked her hips, riding his hands, his mouth, forcing his face to her pussy.

"I'm coming... Joe. Yes. Yes." Everything inside her gathered to a tight, tight ball. She inhaled. Held it. Then suddenly all she held broke free, throbbing through her ass, gushing hot and wet to her pussy, pulsating in the nub of her clit.

She writhed against him, riding the storm of pleasure raging wild through her body. Second by second the razor-sharp sensation ebbed, fading to a warm sated comfort.

Kate opened her hands on Joe's hair and he kissed along her belly until his dark eyes peered up at her, his chin resting just above her coarse curls. Ridiculously adorable, he made her heart ache for what she couldn't have.

"You satisfied or do I have to put in some overtime, *boss*?"

His words sliced through her like a stab of ice. Was he joking? Did he resent what she'd asked him to do? A moment ago she'd have said no. But now? She couldn't tell. Her mind was spinning, her orgasm too fresh, her emotions too raw. It didn't matter. Dear lord, she'd just paid a man for sex.

Kate sucked a quick shoring breath, stepped back and picked up her robe. "Actually, I'm good, thanks. Feel free to go back to what you were doing."

She turned on her heel and strolled back to her room, dragging her heart behind her.

Chapter Eleven

"You didn't deserve that."

"Damn straight." Kate refused to look at Clayton. Staring out the inside office window at nothing. She didn't want his sad, pretty blue eyes spoiling her righteous indignation.

"Part of me really thought he'd told you already."

"And a part of you knew he hadn't."

Clayton didn't confirm or deny. "Sorry."

"Forget it."

She'd actually gotten over Clayton's accidentally-on-purpose slip about Joe working for her father shortly after he'd walked away. He wasn't the one she was angry with—just the easier target. Paying Joe to perform sex acts was all her doing.

"So it's over between you two?"

Kate looked over her shoulder to see Clayton still sitting at the desk. He leaned with his forearms in front of him, his hands bending and twisting a paperclip beyond recognition.

"I don't know. Yeah. I guess." Her stomach twisted. "Not sure there was ever anything real between us to begin with."

"'Cause he lied to you."

"That'll do it." She shuffled over to the chair on the other side of the desk and dropped.

"If he hadn't?" Clayton swung his eyes to her, peering beneath his favorite cowboy hat with the rim curled tight toward the center on either side. "How serious was it, Kate? Did you really... Did you fall for him?"

"Doesn't matter. Like you said, he was paid to be here. That changes everything."

"That's not an answer."

Kate sat forward. "Why are you asking?"

His face flushed and he looked away. "I just need to know."

A cold shudder tickled down her spine. Her belly rippled. Joe's insistence about Clayton and the things Clayton had said that day made her dread his possible reasons.

She smiled, trying to lighten the tension. "It's kind of weird discussing my love life with my brother."

"Knock it off, Kate. I'm not your brother. We aren't kids anymore."

"Clayton..."

"Stop." His gaze collided with hers, held it. "I can't do this, Kate. It's tearing me up."

"What is? Clayton, you've seen me with other men before. What's with you?"

He shook his head. "It's different this time. I can see it in your eyes. The way you look at him. Even when he's not around it's there."

Kate sat back. "I don't know what you're talking about. He's just a guy." Her throat constricted on the words. Her eyes stung. She pushed the reaction from her mind.

"Then say it's over. Not because he hurt you, but because it didn't mean anything to *you*."

"What difference does it make?" Kate said.

"Can you say it?"

"Why?"

"Because I need to know I haven't lost you."

Shit. "What?"

Clayton pushed to his feet, strode around the desk and scooped Kate up from the chair. Her hands bracing on his chest were all that kept her from being pulled completely into his arms.

He held her waist, his other hand tenderly brushing flyaway strands from her eyes. He ran his fingers down the side of her face then cupped her jaw. A rush of tingles washed over her body.

"I'm not asking you to marry me or professing undying love. I just... Just consider me." Clayton's short, towhead blond hair, bright eyes and rock-hard farm-boy body were enough to cream the panties of most women he met. His features were chiseled and had sparked the interest of two modeling agencies in the past. He'd turned them both down when they told him he'd likely be asked to pose naked at some point. He wasn't that kind of guy.

Kate wasn't oblivious to his looks, but Clayton had always kept a distance. "I've never thought of you that way."

"So, start."

"Why now? Why the sudden full-court press?"

He dropped his hand to her waist, his thumbs stroking her sides. "I still remember the day I saw your skinny butt get off that bus in Pittsburgh. Did you know it was my idea for Dad to give you a job? To bring you here rather than a shelter. He thought I was being altruistic. I was eighteen and horny."

"That was fourteen years ago. You've never even made a pass."

"Didn't want to scare you off. You were such a little thing."

"I was sixteen."

"You were a baby. Your father had messed with your head. You were alone, vulnerable. You needed taken care of, protected. You needed time."

"I don't anymore?" she asked.

"Time's running out. I'm going to lose you. I always figured you and I would come together eventually, when the time was right. But when I saw Joe, saw the way you looked at him, I thought I'd waited too long. Have I?"

Kate swallowed, staring into those shining blue eyes. Her heart hammered a mile a minute. Her throat went dry. She slid her hands to his biceps, allowed him to nudge her closer.

Clayton was more than any woman could ask for—never mind his looks. He was kind, intelligent and honorable. He'd never hurt her, never lie or mislead her. There'd be no surprises. The only time he'd kept anything from her was when he'd learned the truth about Joe and even then he'd kept quiet to protect her.

He knew her better than anyone. He'd seen the good and the bad, and still welcomed her into a family she'd desperately needed. He was safe. Unlike Joe, Clayton had wanted her, *to keep*, from the start. Now more than ever that was a comfort she couldn't ignore.

Kate smiled, still trying to lighten his somber mood. "Clayton, we've never even kissed."

"I can fix that." His fingers crawled around her waist, gathering her closer to his body. His lids lowered, his gaze dropping to her lips. He leaned to her mouth and Kate's belly rolled. A moment before they touched she changed her mind. But then it was too late. They were kissing.

His mouth was warm and moist. He tasted like bread or white rice, not unappealing but not especially memorable. His lips were strong, driving the kiss, his tongue sweeping into her mouth predictably. Muscles bunched under her hands, his arms tightening around her, not feverously but expectedly. His body was hard against her, his chest muscled and warm, his stomach and groin a comfortable, if flat, press to hers.

Clayton broke the kiss abruptly. His head cocking back for a better view without loosening his hold on her. "You're not trying."

"Yes I am."

"Give me a chance, Kate."

Kate exhaled. She slid her arms around his neck and

kissed him again.

White rice and comfort, no sparks, no body-melting heat. It was nice, like chicken soup and crocheted blankets—safe. Then his hand slid to her ass and squeezed. Kate gasped against his mouth and Clayton nipped her tongue, then suckled. Just like that heat stirred low in her body, her nipples tingling. She shifted her hips on reflex and Clayton's body roused to life.

They were man and woman, the parts would fit, but Kate's heart wasn't where it needed to be and she suspected neither was Clayton's. She broke the kiss, separated the press of their bodies. "I'm sorry. It's not working, Clayton. It can't."

"It can. Maybe not fireworks and shooting stars but that'll come in time."

"I don't think so. I don't want to lose you either, but I can't pretend to feel something I don't. You deserve better. We both do."

Clayton dropped his forehead to hers, his hat nudging back. "Maybe it'd be different if we had been raised together from birth. Maybe we'd know where we fit with each other. Something would feel right. Nothing does now. I don't know."

"I'm not Amy, Clay. Even if we were raised together from infancy, you wouldn't feel for me the same way you did for her."

"I know that." He straightened. His tone was sharp. She'd expected as much. The subject of Clayton's sister was a complicated, tender topic. Kate let it go.

"How about we stop trying to label it and just be? I'll be in your life and you stay in mine. And in forty years if neither of us is married...we'll buy a cat together."

A smile flickered at the corners of his lips. He snorted. "A cat?"

"Yeah. Old ladies love cats and old men love pussy."

"I get it." They laughed, forcing the weighty tension between them to dissipate. "Was the kiss really that bad?"

She wrinkled her nose in a mock grimace. "You tell me."

Clayton shrugged and opened his mouth to answer.

"Looked cozy enough to me."

Kate and Clayton parted, turning to see Joe leaning a shoulder against the doorjamb, his arms crossed over the Superman emblem on his snug gray T-shirt.

"How long have you been standing there?" Kate asked.

"Long enough." His dark eyes slid to Clayton. "Nice ass?"

Clayton folded his arms, unrepentant. "As a matter of fact."

Joe gave a half nod, scowl securely in place. "Right."

Gawd, he looked good, effortlessly sexy. He hadn't shaved today and Kate's hand itched to scratch her nails over the bristle of stubble. His hair was a casual muss, black shiny waves over his brow and down to his collar. Kate's heart skipped. Liquid warmed her sex, memories of those soft lips nuzzling her pussy making it hard to breathe.

"What are you doing in here, Joe?" she asked.

"My job."

Clayton dropped his arms. "You think she needs protection from me?"

"I go where she goes."

"I'm fine," she said. "Besides as you can see, Clayton's here. You don't have to stay so close."

He looked at her, his eyes like black ice. "Right. Know if I'll be puttin' in overtime again tonight, boss lady?"

Kate's face flamed hot, her ears burning. She couldn't look at him. "No. Absolutely not."

"Understood." He pushed straight, the deep creases across his brow softening. "Be out here if you need me."

"Fine." She watched him walk several stalls down to lean against the opposite wall where he could still keep an eye on the door.

"You have fallen for him."

Kate blinked and looked at Clayton. "Wha? No. Why do you say that?"

"Christ, Kate, your whole face lights up when you look at him." Clayton shuffled back a step as though dazed. "Your entire being changes. I can see it. Anyone could."

"Clayton..." Heat washed over her cheeks and up through her ears. She looked back to Joe.

A group of counselors huddled together talking and laughing a few feet from Joe. Craft hour for the campers meant free time for most of the staff. They ignored Joe for the most part, but it was Ginny who finally walked over and leaned against the stall wall next to him. Her breast pressed against his biceps. Joe had his hands in his front pockets. He dropped his gaze, stared at her chest for several seconds, then raised his eyes to Ginny.

Kate couldn't hear what he said, but Ginny's bright smile faltered. She straightened. Nodded. Then returned to the group. Joe's dark eyes swung to Kate, his expression tight, unreadable.

Clayton watched through the office windows. "Him too. He's just as hung up on you. If you both weren't so bullheaded..." He looked back to Kate. "What happened?"

She shrugged, trying for nonchalance. "Nothing. I hired him. That's all."

A flash of light caught the corner of her eye. Kate looked across the aisle to the tack room. The door was open, the room dark. "Did you see that?"

"No. What'd you mean you hired him? How? For what?"

"I asked him to quit working for my father and work for me instead. He's still my bodyguard except now, I'm paying him."

Clayton's white-blond brows shot high. "Oh. Wow. That's..."

"Awkward."

"Yeah."

Another flash from the direction of the tack room and Kate turned in time to see a blur of movement at the darkened doorway.

"Now *that* I saw," Clayton said.

Kate glanced down the aisle to Joe. He was already striding toward the tack room. Clayton was through the office door in front of Kate, a half stride behind Joe. Just before they reached the tack-room door, someone sprinted out.

Joe and Clayton gave chase, but Joe was closer. His long reach snagged the back of the runner's shirt collar a few feet outside the stable entrance. Joe yanked him around to face Kate.

"Frank," she said.

Joe fisted his collar high so Frank's shirt hiked up, pulling at the pits of his arms. He'd lost his ratty cowboy hat in the sprint. His prison-short hair, round features and pronounced underbite made him seem acutely devious.

Frank squirmed. "Le'go. Le'go. You're gonna rip my dang shirt."

"Camera." Joe held out his hand.

"Screw you. I ain't got no camera. Lemme go."

Joe yanked his shirt higher.

"Hey, hey. Okay, wait a sec." Frank pulled a silver camera about the size of a wallet from his back pocket and slapped it into Joe's hand. "Don't break it. It's new."

Joe glanced at it, front and back, then handed the camera to Clayton.

Clayton made short work of figuring how to operate it. "He's got pictures of the damage to the tack room and of you, me..." He flicked his attention to Frank, his eyes turning to ice. "And Kate."

Something in Joe's face changed, turned cold, emotionless, deadly. Kate shuddered at the stark, lightning-fast transformation. Without warning Joe whirled the dangling Frank around and shoved him hard against the side of the barn.

Frank hit with a loud thud against the wood. "Uhff."

Joe had a hold of him again before he could recover,

flipping him around, pinning him with an iron hand to his chest. "Explain."

"Get off me." Frank tried to push away from the wall, but he couldn't budge Joe's leveraged hold.

"Explain the pictures. Why?" Joe asked.

"It's a free country, asshole," Frank said. "I can take all the pictures I want and I ain't gotta tell you dick."

Clayton planted himself next to Joe, feet wide, thick muscled arms knotted over his chest. He gave a nod toward the dark purplish bruise shading across Frank's nose and under both eyes. "That your handy work?"

"Yeah," Joe said, brows tight.

"Feel good?"

"Hell yeah."

"Figured." Clayton spoke to Frank. "This is private property. You're trespassing."

"Nu-uh. I'm here on business."

"What business?" Joe asked.

Frank dug into his back pocket again and pulled out a neatly folded paper. "Delivered ten rounds of hay. See?"

Joe ignored the paper he waved, his eyes cold on Frank.

Clayton snagged the thin rustling sheet. "Sales receipt. He's telling the truth."

"This is the guy." Joe pushed harder against his sternum. "Call the cops."

Frank grimaced. "Hey. You can't. I didn't do nuthin'."

"You're a stalker," Clayton said.

"Fuck you. Am not."

Joe jabbed harder. "Then why the pictures?"

"Ouch. Knock it off. Some guy paid me. Okay?"

Kate stepped forward. "Who would pay you to take photos of me?"

Frank's brown eyes swung to Kate. "Not just you, pony girl.

Everything. The farm, the fire damage, everything. Said he'd pay extra for pics of you and your boyfriend. 'Cept I couldn't tell which of these numnuts has been buryin' his cock in ya, so I got some of both."

Ice tingled down her spine. Her stalker was hiring the job out to people? It was beyond bizarre.

"Who is he?" Joe said.

"He don't want people to know."

In a blur of movement Joe shifted, pressing his forearm across Frank's throat. "Who?"

Frank made a choking sound, his voice going raw. "I dunno, I dunno. I got an email addy. That's it."

Clayton leaned in. "He contacted you through email?"

"Yeah." Frank's eyes stretched to the limit, his mouth wide, lips curled back from his teeth. "Get off. Get off, I can't breathe."

"What's the address?" Clayton said.

Kate moved closer. "Joe, he can't breathe."

Joe's face remained an implacable mask, his eyes inhumanly cold, riveted on Frank as the man's face reddened. Veins began to bulge.

"Don't know. Didn't...didn't memorize." Frank choked.

"I want the address." Joe pressed harder.

"I'll get it. I'll get it."

"Joe." Kate said, but Joe showed no signs he'd heard her. "Joe, you're choking him. He can't breathe."

Clayton flicked his gaze to Kate then back to Joe as though waking from a dream. He straightened but did nothing to stop him.

"Dammit, Joe. He told you he'd get it." Kate squeezed Joe's biceps. The marble tense muscle didn't give. "Frank can't give you the address if you suffocate him. What's wrong with you?"

Sanity flashed through Joe's dark eyes. The rigid lock of his arm eased. He stepped back and Frank fell to his knees gagging and coughing.

Joe blinked. His gaze swung to Kate, shock fading to calm indifference. He raked a hand through his hair and headed back into the stable. "He'll live...if he gets the email address."

Jeezus, he could've killed the little jerk. *If Kate hadn't...* Joe didn't want to think about it. He was so tied up in knots he *couldn't* think.

Was Frank the stalker? Was he lying about being hired through an email? Joe didn't know. But he should. There was a time he'd known if a guy was guilty or not just by watching his eyes, listening to him talk. Not anymore. *Shit.* Joe didn't know a damn thing.

"Hey. I want my camera back," Frank yelled from behind him.

"Delete the pictures," Joe said without stopping. "Give'im the camera."

He'd already committed assault, no reason to add theft to the possible charges. Frank didn't strike him as the type to go whining to the police though. And Joe's gut told him his story made sense. At least it was provable. Couldn't say as much for him being Kate's stalker. Trying to press harassment charges could tip their hand to the real stalker.

Unless Joe's gut was as screwed up as his brain and Frank was the stalker. In which case he was letting the guy who'd nearly killed Kate get away. Who knew?

Fuck. Kate had him twisted ass backwards. He shouldn't have agreed to work for her after they'd already crossed the line between principal and guard. There was a difference between client and principal. He worked for the client, guarded the principal, unless the two were one and the same. Then he didn't fuck either—ever.

He'd never crossed the line before, never, and now he knew why. She believed their working relationship superseded their personal exchanges. Believed he'd slept with her because of the job rather than despite it. And then she'd acted on that belief. Yeah, that kind of pissed him off. Sex with him was a fuckin' business transaction to her.

Joe stopped short, hands propped on his hips and shook his head. What the hell was he thinking? Their working relationship *should* supersede their personal exchanges. And business was the only thing that should pass between them. Any other way and he risked a foggy brain, slow reactions, poor judgment and possibly Kate's life.

"I need a signature here."

Joe's gaze shot to the office and the delivery guy standing with an outstretched clipboard. Joe closed the distance between them in three long strides, pushing past him into the office.

"Hey. Can ya sign?" the man asked, nudging the bill of his blue company ball cap with his pen. He followed Joe into the office.

Joe took the clipboard and motioned to the basket of rainbow carnations, balloons and long-stemmed roses in a windowed white box. "Who're these for?"

"Dunno. It's on the order slip there. Mathers. Kathleen or something."

"Katharine," Joe corrected, scribbling his name. He handed the clipboard over then stopped and pulled it back. "Don't see roses on this receipt."

"Didn't deliver roses."

"Roses?" Kate stepped through the office door.

Joe gave the delivery guy a ten and a nod, sending him on his way. "Don't touch."

Kate jerked her hands back from the box. "Why?"

Joe didn't answer. He rushed back out the door into the stable aisle. Someone had left the roses—gone in and set them on the desk while he was interrogating Frank.

"What's with you?" Clayton strolled toward him from outside. "Looks like you've seen a ghost."

Joe considered the beefy farm boy for a second. Could he have slipped in when Joe and Kate were busy with Frank? Joe shook the question from his head the instant it formed. Wasn't possible. They'd caught Frank together. But someone had gotten by him.

"Stay with Kate." Joe jogged past him out of the stables.

Off to the left, several yards away, Frank was standing by the open door to his pick-up talking with two male counselors. Joe's mind shuffled possibilities. Frank was in the tack room when Kate and Clayton were in the office. He and Clayton had been lured out by the flashes from Frank's camera and then further by his conspicuous attempted escape. He couldn't have left the roses. Unless...

Joe eyed the interaction between the three young men. They were friends. Made sense. Kate said all the counselors were college students and Frank used to be one of them. Stands to reason he'd still have friends on staff. Could he have convinced one of them to leave the box of roses while he drew everyone out of the office?

He made a mental note of their faces. Joe spent most of his time with Kate. There was a lot of staff he didn't know. The counselors talking to Frank were two of them.

Mental picture formed, he scanned the area between the stables, the service road and the mess hall beyond. There was no one else around. He turned, jogging back down the stable aisle, throwing a glance through the office windows as he passed. Clayton was with Kate. *Good.*

Clayton had a wealth of friends on the farm and a loyal staff. Would any of them hesitate to do him a favor and leave the box for him when no one was looking? Was a man like Clayton capable of the cowardly antics the stalker displayed? He certainly had long-held feelings for Kate as motivation. Joe filed the slim possibility in his mind and kept moving, kept searching for suspects.

The group of Ginny, Ashley and two male counselors from

earlier were still conversing in the center of the aisle watching the goings-on with quiet interest. They moved to the side when they saw Joe coming.

Joe evaluated the group as he passed, noting faces, shifting facts and previous observations in his mind. Could one of the two males be Kate's stalker? Possibly. But Joe's impression told him both were far too interested in bedding Ginny or Ashley to have a secret obsession with Kate. Unless that's what they wanted Joe to think.

He reached the center throughway, stopped and looked in both directions. The main house was off to the left. He could see the trees by his and Kate's cottages. The parking lot in front of the stables held a few cars but no people.

To the right was the entrance to the indoor arena several yards out. He caught a glimpse of a horse and rider inside, working. Beside the arena he could see the cars parked in front of the bunkhouse, but again, no people. *The damn place is deserted.*

Joe moved on, jogging down the aisle, looking back and forth into stalls as he passed. He reached the end of the stables where the riding rings and paddock areas were. *No one.*

He spun and doubled back, this time taking the turn toward the indoor arena. The late-afternoon sun was still bright enough to cast the insides in shadow. Joe couldn't make out details until he stepped through the wide entrance.

Eddy. He rode a large black horse around and around at an easy lope. When they came to Joe, he pulled to a stop. "Problem?"

"How long you been here?" Joe asked.

Eddy shrugged. "'Bout half hour, forty-five minutes. I'm warming up Wizard for Kate."

"She know you're on her horse?"

Eddy sneered. "Yes. Of course. You think I'd ride her without Kate's permission? I don't take things that aren't *mine.*"

Joe's gaze dropped to Wizard's neck and the gleam of sweat

over her furred chest and more at the edges of the saddle pad. He figured it likely took time to work up a sweat on a horse. He didn't know much about horses. Could Eddy have left the box and still had time to give the horse such a workout? Anything was possible.

"You mind?" Eddy swiped long bangs to the side with two bandaged fingers. "Wizard doesn't like people standing at the edges inside the arena."

Joe gave a nod. "Right."

Everyone he suspected of being the stalker was within distance at the time the roses were left, but it wouldn't have been easy for any of them. Joe headed back to the office and stepped through the door just as Kate read the card from the basket.

"Happy birthday. Affectionately, your father, Edward Mathers." Kate flicked her gaze to Joe. "What? He thought I might be confused who 'father' was?"

"Think he's just out of practice." Joe moved up beside her and stared at the boxed flowers.

"Maybe." She folded the card back into the envelope. "Guess I can overlook the signature and the fact he sent them two days early, since he also sent roses. Even got the color right."

Joe opened the long white box. The white roses filled the container from end to end, green tissue paper wrinkled and messy underneath. He checked the ends, then carefully sorted through the bunch.

"These aren't from your father," he said.

Clayton stiffened across the desk from Joe. "They came with the other flowers and balloons."

Joe looked at him. "No. They didn't. These have been cut straight at the ends. Florists cut them at an angle. The tissue paper looks used and there are only ten roses."

Clayton stuck his hands in the front pockets of his jeans. "You can buy roses in any number."

"Yeah, but if Edward was trying to win the affection of his daughter, why send only ten roses? And these aren't long stemmed, they're bush roses. Someone's stripped the branches to leave one rose on each."

"You know a-scary-lot about roses." Despite her tease, he could hear the uncertainty wavering in Kate's voice.

"Sent my share of apologies. Start to recognize quality." They stared at each other for a moment. Was she wondering if she'd be receiving his apology bouquet soon, too? Maybe she should. He'd certainly screwed things up between them. *Par for the course.*

Joe broke the connection first and looked back to the box. He dug under the tissue paper, along the sides and both ends.

"So who sent them?" she asked.

He pulled out the small folded paper from under the very center. "Not sent. Left, dollface."

He read the note then handed it to Kate.

"*To my future bride?*"

"They're from him."

She swallowed hard enough he could see her throat work. "The stalker. But we were just in here. He was that close?"

"He won't get closer." Joe reached for her, held her arms, caught her widening gaze. "I won't let him."

"How do we stop him?"

"You're moving into the main house," Joe said. "Now."

Chapter Twelve

"You are quite the professional, Joe," Kate said a few strides in front of him. "All that stuff about the flowers and finding the note. Now, being big enough to bow out and put the target under lock and key."

"Not bowing out, dollface. Hunkering in."

She glanced over her shoulder at him, her riding boots crunching against the white gravel drive. "You seriously think I still need you five feet away inside the main house? The place is like the Louvre after dark."

"It's my job."

Her brow creased, lips tightening to a near flat line. "Yeah. Your job."

"That's right."

When she reached the patchy grass just beyond the gravel in front of the cottages she spun around. "You're pretty dedicated to your *job*. Aren't you, Joe?"

Joe stopped beside her, slipped his hands into the front pockets of his jeans. "Right."

The air was warm, the sun low on the horizon, but Kate clutched her bare arms as though she were freezing. "Always on duty, right? Ready to follow me anywhere."

"Where you go..."

"Even into my bed...if the job calls for it."

The muscles along his shoulders tensed. "Something like

that."

"You follow me because it's your job. Because you're paid."

"That's how it works."

"And how you feel about me, how I feel about you, none of that matters." Her voice wavered, her chin trembling for moment before she steeled her expression.

His jaw clenched, anger flaming hot and fast through his veins. "That's what you... You really believe that?"

She gave a solid nod, but her hardened expression flickered.

"Jeezus, Kate." He wiped his palm down his face and over his chin. "Don't you get it? It's not my job to worry about how we *feel*. Feelings muck things up quick. We crossed a line we shouldn't have. There's no going back. It's done. But now I have to do what I can to get my head straight. To keep it straight. To keep you alive. The rest... No. I can't let it matter. Not now."

She flinched as though he'd slapped her. "I see." She turned on her heel and continued her trek toward her cottage.

Joe was two steps back when his gaze scanned ahead and noticed the door to Kate's cottage was unlatched. He lunged for her before she took the first porch step.

"Wait here," he said in her ear. Her back to his chest, his hand tight around her upper arm, her scent surrounded him, vanilla and wildflowers. He ignored it and left her where he'd stopped her to check out the cottage.

Joe tried hard not to make a sound on the steps. His hand itched to pull his gun from his ankle holster. He didn't. With kids nearby he couldn't risk making a mistake.

He peeked around the very edge of the front window and saw the mess inside, then rolled back, body flat to the wall. He looked to the door, nudged it wider with the tips of his fingers. Listened. Nothing.

One last motion to Kate to stay put. She nodded. *Smart.* Then he turned and went in low. He scanned the living room.

Empty. Peeked into the bedroom. Empty. Joe crossed the distance from the front door to the hallway quick then found the wall with his back. He crouched again—bad guys hardly ever aim down—and peeked around the corner.

The kitchen was clear. The bathroom door was open, the room empty. There was no one in the cottage—anymore. But there had been. Joe stood and took in the devastation. Someone had made like a tornado in Kate's home. Pictures were torn off walls and shattered on the floor. Lamps and end tables were overturned. Magazines she'd had on the coffee table were shredded and thrown everywhere, and the couch and chair cushions were gutted.

The bedroom was more of the same, mattress overturned, feather pillows decimated. Drawers were emptied and broken, clothes everywhere, some ripped beyond repair. Joe turned and walked back to the front door.

"Kate."

She hurried up the steps with no more encouragement. "Oh, shit."

Joe watched her face pale. His chest pinched. He wanted to hold her, to gather her into his arms and shield her from the loss and fear that stretched the dark pupils of her eyes. He couldn't. Wasn't his job. He'd never guarded anyone he truly cared about before. He only knew how to keep the principal safe one way. No emotions and a clear head. In his mind, it was Kate's best hope and he'd give it to her. Damn the cost.

"Pack a bag."

"I don't understand." Kate tossed her blue Nike duffle bag on the bed in her room at the main house. "Why would he say he wants to marry me and then destroy my home?"

"Love and madness," Joe said. "Same thing."

She smiled, but it didn't light her eyes. "Yeah, right."

Joe set her laptop case next to the small roll-top desk in the corner then readjusted his own bag on his shoulder and switched his gun case to the other hand. He turned to see her watching him, green eyes haunted, needy.

He hooked his thumb on the shoulder strap and sighed. "He loves you, Kate. He wants you so bad it hurts. No one wants to want like that. He starts to resent the person who's causing it. So he lashes out. Doesn't mean the wanting goes away, though."

"You make love sound horrible."

Joe shrugged. "It is what it is."

"Wow. Who squashed you?"

His gaze shot to hers. "Come again?"

"Some girl must've given you a pretty good smackdown to leave a mark like that."

He shook his head, a smile tickling at the corner of his mouth. "No."

Joe wasn't the one forever getting hurt in his relationships.

"C'mon I told you my humiliating ride down love's terrifying highway. Your turn. Besides," she said catching his gaze, her voice softening, "I could use the distraction."

Her eyes were greener than he'd ever seen them, the pupils glistening. She was scared and hating it. But that wasn't his problem. Not his job.

She leaned a hip against the tall queen bed, old lace decorating the canopy overhead. The maroon flowered comforter looked thick and heavy, pillows piled three deep along the headboard. His mind flashed on an image of her sprawled naked on that bed, her dark cinnamon hair curling around pillows, the thick comforter a tangled roll at the end of the bed. His body warmed, chest tightening. How easy would it be to undo the distance they'd put between them? How great would it feel to tumble back into her bed?

Didn't matter. For her sake, they couldn't go back. "Got nothin' to tell."

"You've never been in love?"

Joe took less than a second to consider the question. "No."

"Never?"

"Not once." He dropped his army-green canvas duffle on the floor next to the wingback chair behind him. He turned and set the silver gun case beside the duffle. He'd take them to his room next door when Kate was settled.

"What about your mother?"

Joe straightened. "What?"

"Your mom. How were things with you and her?"

Joe ignored the twisting feel in his gut and shrugged. "Fine. Why?"

"Well, if you've never been in love then the only significant, influential woman in your life was your mom."

"She wasn't."

"Wasn't what? Significant or influential?"

"Both."

"Right," Kate drawled. "So tell me about her."

"No."

"Joe..." she said, pleading with her greener-than-green eyes. *Damn.* Those eyes would get them both killed one of these days.

He folded his arms. "What'd you want to know?"

"Everything. Anything. When's the last time you saw her?"

"Twenty-seven years ago."

Kate snorted. "And..."

"She waved from the back window of a cop car. Arrested for drunk and disorderly. We were shopping for school clothes."

"How old were you?"

"Eleven. Anything else?" His gut twisted tighter and he couldn't keep his jaw from clenching when he closed his mouth. Rip off his fingernails one by one and he'd enjoy it more.

Kate didn't seem to notice or was too lost in the imagery to break free. "Eleven. You never saw her again?"

"No."

"What happened? Where was your father? They just leave you there?"

"Never met him. She was too drunk to tell the cops I was with her. When the store closed the manager found me and called social services."

"That's when you went into foster care."

"Right."

"Wow, I hadn't put it together."

"Uh-huh." The knot in his stomach wasn't Kate's fault, but he wanted the conversation over. He grabbed his bags. "Gonna put my gear next door."

"So you didn't really have a mother. No one to help you relate to women."

Joe stopped, the weight of the duffle and gun case sagging his shoulders more then they should. His head lolled back, staring at the ceiling while he found the tolerance to continue.

He looked at her. "I had a mother. She was a drunk. She was a woman who blamed every man she slept with for her fucked-up life until there weren't any men left. Then she started blaming me."

"What'd you do?"

He shrugged. "Nothin'. I was kid."

His gut pinched so hard bile shot up the back of his throat. He fought it down without letting on. The years he'd spent trying to please his mother burned through his mind. He couldn't make her happy. He'd never make anyone happy, least of all her. So he stopped trying.

"Joe…"

He shook his head. "Forget it. I survived."

"Yeah. But at what cost?" Kate made another little feminine snort. "And I thought I had issues."

Joe faced her. "I don't have issues. I relate to women just fine."

"Oh, obviously."

"Trust me, dollface. I get no complaints."

Kate blushed all the way up to her ears. She looked away, recovering, then looked back. "There's more to it than being good in bed."

He flashed a crooked smile he was only half feeling. "But I am good in bed. Aren't I?"

Their eyes met. She smiled. "Yeah."

Joe's smile widened. "Never had problems pleasing a woman in that department."

"But what happens when you get out of bed? You said you've never been in love, but love, for a lot of people, is the reason for sex."

Joe tried to follow her logic. It wasn't easy. "Satisfied is satisfied. In bed or out."

"No. There's a huge difference between physical and emotional satisfaction. You know that, right?"

"You fall in love every time you have sex?" He didn't know what answer he was hoping for, but his gut wobbled.

"No. But that's taken practice. It's not the same for me." Kate toyed with a cream-colored tassel on the comforter. "I'm not that kind of person."

"Neither am I." He readjusted his grip on his bags. "Sex is sex. The women I've been with were satisfied. Afterwards...yeah maybe I screw that part up sometimes. But not because I don't care. *Not* because of my mother. Some women are just impossible to please. What's the point?"

"But that's not—"

"Enough." He didn't mean to bark, but the tension pinching between his shoulders and roiling through his gut was starting to make his skin crawl.

The *tick-tock, tick-tock* of her wall clock announced the passing seconds.

Joe exhaled, like letting steam off a boiling pot. His voice was calm when he spoke. "I'll be next door. Don't go anywhere without me. Understood?"

Kate nodded, her eyes a little wider than they should be, a little greener.

Not his job. Joe turned and left her room.

The mile-long trail ride along the winding Youghiogheny River was an end-of-camp treat. After nearly four weeks the campers were normally confident enough in their riding skills to make the trip without difficulty. The kids who'd attended camp before charged the anticipation for the new kids with vivid descriptions and fun stories along the way.

"You goin' down the bum slide?" Tony asked, wedging his horse next to Sunshine. There was plenty of room for two horses on the path but Joe and Sunshine both looked out of sorts.

"Hey, kid, pick an end," Joe said. "Front or back. The horse doesn't like you squeezin' in beside her like that."

Kate smiled and swung her gaze forward again. Almost two weeks of riding lessons and Joe still looked as though he was holding on for dear life.

"Yeah, okay, but are ya?" Kate knew without looking Tony had stayed right were he was.

"Uh...I don't know, kid. What's a bum slide?"

"It. Is. Awesome!" Tony squealed.

Kate glanced back to make sure the other kids and horses following in line behind them weren't spooked by Tony's exuberance. Single-line trail rides tested a child's restraint and patience. These kids more than most. Kate tried to be lenient.

"See, the river gets really slow and wide where we can go swimming. It's not deep. Except in spots."

"That right?" Joe said.

"Yeah." Like he'd open a floodgate Tony spoke in a gush. "There's one place that's real high and you can jump off 'cause the water's deep, but you gotta jump straight down or you get squished by the rocks, then there's this other part where the water runs down over rocks into the wider part and the rocks are all smooth and the water runs real fast and it's like a trench and you can sit and slide all the way down into the wider part, that's the bum slide. Get it? Ya sit on your bum and slide—bum slide." Tony took a breath.

"Got it."

"Single file, Tony." Kate met Joe's gaze for a half second before she turned back around. Her belly tingled.

Their talk the night before shed light on the inner workings of Joe's all-male mind. Still, Kate couldn't help thinking, no matter what Joe said, he knew what it was like to be in love. Even if he didn't, he had to feel the chemistry between them. It couldn't all be in her mind. It was more than sex, more than the job. No one pretends that well.

Fine. He had issues. Who didn't? But it was as though Joe was doing everything in his power to keep the yawning distance between them. The more he pushed away, the more Kate was willing to risk to bring him back. Sure she could get him into her bed, but she wanted more than his body this time. She wanted him there on her terms, because he had feelings for her, not because she paid him. All or nothing.

She couldn't be the free milk, the open candy dish. Not with Joe. Not anymore. It'd been years since she risked her heart to win someone's love. This time it just might kill her.

"Switch out bridles for halters and leads, campers, then tie your horses," Kate said when they reached the swimming hole. She dug out Wizard's halter from the saddlebag. "No one leaves their horse until a counselor checks your knot."

The tie rail ran over a long wooden trough, overflowing with hay to keep the horses busy. Agnes, Hickory Farm's head chef, had brought lunch to the picnic tables around the bum slide in her modern-day chuck wagon—a restored concession truck. The sun was out, the skies were clear and the air was hot. The day was gearing up to be a much-needed fun-filled escape.

Joe tied Sunshine next to Wizard. He and Kate stood back to back. Ginny was on Wizard's opposite side and the other counselors were spaced between the campers on both sides of the tie rail. The only person who'd opted out of the trail ride was Clayton.

Kate didn't push him when he'd looked her in the eye and said, "I can't."

She knew there'd been a wealth of meaning in those two words, and a day spent river wading wouldn't change anything. They'd find their place with each other though. She could see it in his eyes. Clayton wouldn't walk out of her life—ever.

"Bum slide," Joe said over his shoulder. "How painful are we talking?"

Kate turned. "I've seen jean butts worn straight through in one afternoon."

Joe winced and shook his head. "You going down?"

"I already did about four weeks ago with the first group of campers to come through."

"Ah. You're swimmin' though, right?"

"Is that a professional inquiry?"

Joe met her gaze, his face coloring. He smiled. "Right."

Her cheeks went hot and she looked away to hide her ear-to-ear grin.

By the time she finished checking knots on lead ropes, Kate was the only one left at the tie rail. Children squealed over the rush of water, and a line had formed for people waiting to jump off a precipice into the deepest section of the swimming spot. Ten feet to the right or left could be a deadly leap. Counselors assured above and below the children were safe. They called it the high dive, though no one actually dove. Cannonballs, however, were aplenty.

Kate had just stepped out of her shorts and was undoing the buttons of her blouse when a male voice startled her from behind.

"Change your mind?"

Kate spun, hands clutching the edges of her blouse to her chest. Never mind she had a bathing suit on underneath. "Wha? No. I was changing."

Joe's gaze traveled over her body, making her skin tingle and her heart pound too fast. When their eyes met again, he smiled and Kate felt it all the way to her toes.

"Need help?"

"No," Kate said hotly and finished unbuttoning. It felt too much like a striptease the way he watched her, but she motored on, refusing to meet his eyes until she'd folded the blouse into her saddlebag. "I'm good."

Joe's left brow shot to his hairline. "Right."

Kate laughed, nervous, and for the first time really looked at Joe. He was wearing a bathing suit. Not cutoffs or old shorts but an actual man's bathing suit.

The blue suit was snug, square cut, and hugged around his muscled thighs and narrow hips. With lighter stripes around his waist that came to a V in front, the elastic material shaped like a second skin over the firm muscles of his ass and clung to the tennis ball round of his cock.

"You mind?" Joe said. "There're kids around. Bad enough I'm listing baseball stats in my head already. Cut me some slack."

Kate snapped her gaze to his, but from the corner of her vision she could see the swell at his groin continued.

"Racing suit looks good on you," he said.

She looked at herself. "Thanks. Need a different body type for bikinis."

Skimpy two pieces made her look like Arnold Schwarzenegger on estrogen, too many muscles, too much flesh, not enough material. The racing suits fit better, felt better and stayed on a hell of a lot better. Until now nothing else had mattered.

"Green's your color." His gaze fixed on hers.

"You noticed?" She hugged herself. "Didn't think that was part of your job."

"It's not." Joe held out a hand to her, his eyes dark, his face relaxed, confident, sexy.

Kate blinked at his hand. Her belly fluttered. Maybe Joe was more open to exploring the feelings between them than she'd thought.

She couldn't stop the smile blooming across her lips. "You sure?"

"Absolutely."

She took his hand.

"Gotta keep up the cover, right?"

Connecting romantically with her bodyguard would be a whole lot easier if it weren't for his annoying, and potentially life-saving, obsessive work ethic.

"Oh. Cover. Right."

Romance or survival. Decisions, decisions.

Chapter Thirteen

"Ready?" He breathed into her ear. His stubble-rough cheek brushed against her skin, his sweet musk scent enveloping her.

Kate closed her eyes, nodded, clutching the thick knotted rope to her body. "Ready."

Joe kissed her lobe and sent a ripple of tingles over her flesh. "One. Two. Three."

He pushed and Kate swung out over the river, her feet perched on a fat knot at the end of the rope. She held as tightly as she could, but her hands were slipping. She ignored her stinging palms and held on until she reached the apex of her swing. Then she let go.

Freefalling twenty-some feet, Kate squealed, arms flailing. Seconds later cool water exploded around her, flooding out the light, and she was in the river. When she came up, the kids and counselors were still hooting and clapping. Who doesn't love a good rope swing?

"Good one, Kate," someone said.

"That was awesome, Miss Kate," said another.

She'd no sooner brushed the hair and water from her face than a tsunami-sized wave swamped over her. Kate blinked, spitting river water from her mouth, clearing her vision in time to see Joe come back up, the ripples from his cannonball landing still sloshing around her. He flicked his head to sling his hair from his eyes and followed her toward the shore where they could touch bottom.

"Thanks for the warning," she said.

His arms snaked around her waist, pulled their bodies together. "Warning. What fun is that?"

"Drinking a gallon of river water is not fun."

He kissed her, pressed his mouth to hers warm and hard, then stopped just as abruptly. She gasped, her body suddenly humming with need, her mind working fast to catch up.

"Not my fault you were hangin' out in the kill zone."

Her lips tingled. She ignored it. "I came up for air. I wasn't hanging out."

"Right." He shifted her in his arms, coaxed her to wrap her legs around him beneath the murky water. They could've been naked from the waist down and no one would know. Her sex spread open against the tight muscles of his belly. Kate hugged her arms around his neck, loving the secret intimacy of the position.

"Get a room," Rick, a counselor, yelled from the hillside. Kate looked his way. A line had formed behind him for the rope swing, and all eyes seemed to be on her and Joe.

"Yeah. You lovebirds go make goo-goo eyes at each other somewhere else," one of them said.

Joe nuzzled her ear, made her muscles flex low in her body. "Everyone's buying the cover."

Kate's belly sank. He was pretending. Of course. She knew he was. He'd been laying it on thick all day. But there was only so much teasing her body could take. She wanted his heart to lead him back to her bed, but after a day half-naked, acting as though they couldn't keep their hands off each other...she couldn't.

She wriggled against him, pressing the heat of her sex along the hard muscles of his stomach. "Shall we give them an encore?"

Her wriggling inched her lower until she felt the unmistakable swell of his cock nudging her bottom. His body couldn't lie. This was no act no matter what he said.

Kate's heart skipped and she tried her best to sound impassive despite the surge of adrenaline zinging through her blood. "Thought you were pretending."

"I am."

She laughed, her breasts tingling, nipples pulling tight. "Yeah. Then I think your cock's hoping to win an Academy Award."

Joe glanced over his shoulder, then the other. He leaned his face close to hers, looked directly into her eyes. "This *is* an act, dollface. Understand?"

Kate swallowed hard, her pride lodging in the back of her throat. "Could've fooled me. 'Cause that's not *my* hard-on poking me in the ass."

"Reflex."

Kate dropped her legs from around his waist, pushed off from his chest to put distance between her and his hard, ready body. "Reflex, huh?"

"Right." He reached for her, snagged her elbow and tugged her back into his arms, his dark eyes focused on her lips. "Like the reflex that had your pussy creaming against my stomach just now." His gaze flicked to hers, brows tight. "Reflex. That's it. I don't fuck my clients."

"You already did." She tried to squirm free but his arm was steel around her waist, pressing her firmly against him. His body heat warmed her, contrasting the cool water, making his embrace a haven she didn't want to leave. But pride wouldn't let her stop trying.

"Things changed," he said.

"Because you're working for me instead of my father?"

"Yes. No. Not only that. It's complicated."

"What's complicated? You didn't have a problem the night we got back from the breeders." Her face went hot with the memory.

"That's what you want?" His dark eyes turned hard, cold. "Like it was that night?"

No. That night was sex, pure and simple. No emotion. No connection. Kate wanted so much more. Raw sex wouldn't be enough, not by half. But having Joe back in her bed was at least a place to start. There was more between them than sex, she was sure of it. She just needed a chance to bring them close again. Kate wasn't experienced enough in this sort of thing. She didn't know any other way.

"Is that my only option?" she asked.

His fingers pressed into her sides. She could see his jaw muscles flex. He stared at her for several seconds, his breaths heavy, his brow deeply furrowed.

Something flickered behind his eyes finally and he looked away. When he turned back she could tell he'd found a measure of calm. He set her away from him.

"Damn it, Kate. It can't happen. This is the only way I know how." He swam to the shore.

Kate was still trying to figure out what the hell she was missing in Joe's answer that would have it make sense when the group arrived back at the stables.

This is the only way he knew how to do what? And what'd it have to do with sex? She hadn't asked him to explain. There wasn't another moment when they were alone. She'd been left to try and puzzle it out on her own.

It was giving her a headache. She couldn't think about it anymore. Between trying to decipher Joe's cryptic explanations and enduring all of his pretend advances, her brain was fried and her body was screaming for relief. Hell, even Eddy was starting to look doable. If they didn't catch her stalker soon she'd be dead anyway. *Can a person die of sexual frustration?*

Kate pushed it from her mind, losing herself in the simple pleasure of brushing Wizard. She filled the hay box and water bucket, then gave the big mare's strong neck a few loving strokes. The fresh, sweet smell of hay mixed with the more pungent aromas of the stables swirled around her in the stall and Kate breathed it in. Like a secret elixir her tensions eased. Nothing soothed her like the smell of horses.

She emerged from the stall renewed. "Tony, you're going to be late for dinner. What took you so long to water Coco?"

He looked over his lopsided shoulder at her, a water bucket dangling at the end of his arm, his other arm high in the air as counter balance. "This is Sylvester's. Already did Coco."

"Why isn't Nisha watering her own horse?"

Tony's tan face pinked with his explosive grin. "Told her I'd take care of it. Girls like it when you do stuff for'em."

Dating advice from a ten year old. She should call Joe over to take notes. Speaking of the devil, where was he? Kate shot a glance back toward the office. She could see him through the windows, his white T-shirt hugging nicely over his muscled back.

"Can I go? This is heavy." Tony shifted the bucket to his other hand. Water sloshed out, soaking his jeans from the knee down. He didn't seem to care.

"Sure, sweetie. But from now on, Nisha takes care of her own horse. If she can't take care of Sylvester, she can't ride him."

Tony nodded quickly as he turned and waddled on down the aisle. Kate headed in the opposite direction. She heard Clayton's voice before she saw around the corner into the office.

"She doesn't need to see them."

"Wrong," Joe said.

"See what?"

Both men threw her somber expressions. Kate looked at the photos in Joe's hands. Bile churned her stomach.

"Not again." Her voice was barely a whisper.

"They're just photos," Clayton said. "Taken with a high-powered lens. Proves we're doing good. He wasn't able to get close."

"Proves he's desperate," Joe said. "Probably pissed."

"He's sending something every day now?" She caught Joe's gaze. "Is that because of us?"

His scowl faltered, a hint of tenderness flickering through his eyes. "Not likely. He needs things between you to start coming together. Probably sent these to prove he's able to reach you no matter what we do."

She held out her hand for the pictures. "Lemme see."

"No, Kate," Clayton said. "You don't need to see."

"She does." But when Joe tried to give her the pictures, Clayton snatched them away.

"You trying to scare her?"

"Yes." Joe's attention stayed fixed on Kate. "She needs to know this is serious. Not a time for distractions."

"Let me see, Clayton." Kate held her hand out to him, waiting.

Clayton sighed, resigned, and gave her the photos. "We won't let him near you."

Kate swallowed her heart out of her throat, scanning the pictures. "Clearly, he doesn't have to be near."

There were five in all. She was naked in every one, wet in the shower. The pictures were shaking.

No. Kate's hands were shaking. She looked to Joe. "How?"

"Window was open. He must've been in a tree behind the main house."

"He climbed a tree? That sounds so..."

"Desperate."

"Yes," Kate said.

Joe shoved his hands in the front pockets of his jeans. "He's got a timeline. Time's running out."

She held a hand to her stomach wishing it to calm.

"When?"

"Your birthday."

"Tomorrow?"

"Right."

She couldn't think. Her head was going to explode. She shuffled to the desk and tossed the pictures onto the blotter, then dropped into the chair. Joe and Clayton tracked her progress, Clayton worried and hovering, Joe stoic and determined.

Kate ignored them both, propping her elbows on the desk, holding her head in her hands. "How do you know about a timeline?"

She hadn't said his name, but Joe answered. "He sent a letter to your father. Told him he was asking you to marry him on your birthday."

Her gaze shot to his. "And you knew this when?"

Joe didn't even have the decency to look ashamed. He folded his arms over his chest and stiffened his jaw. "It's why he hired me."

"You didn't say a word."

"Better you didn't know."

"Why?"

"It'd skew your perspective. Make you feel you're only in danger on that day. You're not safe 'til we catch him."

Was it true? Maybe. Hell, she didn't know. Kate stared at the pictures fanned on the desk between her elbows. He'd caught her at her most vulnerable. Naked in the shower. How long had he stayed in that tree watching her?

"Where'd he leave these?" she asked without raising her head.

"There," Clayton said. "On the desk. In the envelope."

Kate's gaze shifted to the left. She read her name printed in block letters, a red heart pierced with an arrow drawn over the final three letters of her last name.

She looked back to the photos. They showed her from her chest up, grainy, but unmistakably her. She stood with her head tilted back into the stream of water, hands raking through her hair, breasts bare for all to see.

Kate looked up at Clayton. "You found them?"

"Um, yeah." Clayton's fair, towheaded complexion reddened.

"Shit." Tears stung her eyes. She blinked them back, looked away. Gawd, she hated him. Hated the person who'd taken these photos, hated Clayton for seeing them, hated Joe.

Her stalker stole her privacy, stole *her*. He'd exposed her, stripped her bare in front of him, in front of everyone, and there was nothing to be done about it. He'd seen. They'd all seen.

She swung her gaze to Joe, his scowl so deep the wrinkles over his brows shrank his forehead. She'd had sex with Joe. He'd touched her naked body, but this was different. She was a thing in these pictures, no rights, no privacy. It didn't matter how strong she was, how nice, how innocent. She wasn't a person. Her stalker had taken everything that was her.

"Bastard." Her voice was soft and weak, emotions clogging her throat. She stared at the photos, her body going numb. She couldn't feel the chair beneath her, the desk under her elbows. She couldn't hear over the pound of her heart, and the tears pooling in her eyes began to blur her vision.

"Enough." Joe grabbed the photos from the other side of the desk, straightened them into a stack and shoved them into the envelope.

"Hey." She stood, her gaze tracking the photos. "What're you going to do with them?"

"Are you pissed?" Joe folded the envelope so it was no bigger than the pictures.

"Yes."

"Good." He shoved them into his back pocket. "Then they've served their purpose. Stare at them any longer and they do more damage than good."

"Joe, answer the damn question." Kate didn't give a shit why he'd shown them to her. She wasn't about to let them leave her sight.

"Into a file with the other—"

"No. Shred them."

"They're evidence," Clayton said.

"Shred them." She could hear her voice going higher, shriller. She couldn't help it.

Clayton moved next to the desk. "Kate, no one will ever see them."

She snapped to him, venom in her voice. "*You* saw them. So did Joe. This ass shouldn't have been able to take the photos in the first place, but there they are. No one could stop it from happening. If they exist, so does the risk. I want them gone."

Kate looked to Joe. His deep scowl had smoothed to a shadowed frown, and the look in his eyes seemed resolute. His mouth held an easy part between his lips, the small scar in the corner the only flaw. His broad muscled shoulders relaxed.

"No one will see them unless they're needed as evidence."

"No."

"Kate. You can destroy them personally once we're sure. Trust me." Joe had an air of quiet confidence that somehow helped slow the tremor shaking through her body.

She exhaled, tried not to puke and dropped into her desk chair. "Fine."

"We'll get'im, dollface," Joe said.

"Promise?"

"Promise."

"Stay." Kate's voice was soft and fragile. So unlike the woman he knew her to be. Damn the son of a bitch who was doing this to her.

"I'll be right next door."

"I want you here. I need…" Her voice wavered as though she'd cry. She glanced away for a moment tucking strands of flyaway hair behind her ear.

Her brows knitted tight, she laced her fingers in her lap and met his gaze. No tears. "Please."

Joe's heart pinched. "I can't."

"You won't."

She was right. He should've left already. Hell, he should've never come in. He should've seen her to her room, waited in the hall for her to turn the lock and then gone to his room next door. Instead he stood on the wrong side of her closed bedroom door leaning his shoulder against it, hand on the knob.

"It's not how I work," he said.

"You've never slept in the same room as someone you're guarding."

Joe slipped his hands in his pockets, tried not to notice the way her night-top clung to her breasts, the way the darker flesh of her nipples shone through the thin fabric. The way her mint green panties peeked between her legs as she sat cross-legged on the bed. And the way her room already smelled like vanilla and wildflowers.

He tried. It wasn't working. "If I stay we wouldn't be sleeping."

"And that's why you won't stay?"

Joe rubbed the knot tightening at the back of his neck, ignoring the growing discomfort lower on his body. "I'm here to protect you, not fuck you."

"Then don't fuck me. Make love to me."

"Kate." His gut twisted. He knew where this was going and it made his palms sweat. His heart was like a freight train in his ears. He couldn't stop what was coming and he wasn't sure he wanted to.

"There's something between us, Joe. I know you've felt it. And I know it scares you. But I don't know why."

"Doesn't matter."

"Dammit, Joe, just admit it. I know you care about me. Just say it."

Jeezus. He pushed from the door, angry and scared and horny and everything else. "I care. Alright? Yes."

She flinched at his sharp tone but didn't miss a beat. "So what's the problem?"

Joe stepped closer. He barely realized he'd moved. "Listen, I'm good at my job, Kate. Damn good. But I'm a disaster at relationships."

"Welcome to the club."

He moved closer. "No. Don't you see? I've never guarded someone who meant something to me. I don't know how. I can't think straight. And I won't risk your life because of my lousy hang-ups. I'd rather lose you as my lover than lose your life. I won't risk it."

A smile, barely there but so sexy it made his gut tighten, blossomed across her lips. She pushed to her knees. "I will."

Kate had his T-shirt fisted in her hand before Joe realized he'd moved all the way across the room to the bed. She yanked him to her, crushed her mouth to his, her tongue teasing along his lips, sweeping into his mouth.

His body responded with mind-numbing speed, heat scorching through his veins, shaking the muscles of his thighs. He couldn't fight her. He couldn't fight his need for her. He didn't want to. Joe scooped his arms around her waist and pressed her body to his.

She was lean and strong but so soft her body molded perfectly to his. He could feel the stiff points of her nipples against his chest, the warm give of her belly pressing along his sex. Sensation sizzled and tingled over his skin, coiled in the constricting sac of his balls. She tasted honey sweet on his lips, her wildflower scent warming through his mind and body.

They broke apart for several heated breaths, panting as she jerked his T-shirt up his chest, her hands greedy over his muscles, pushing and yanking the fabric up his arms and over his head. Joe got his second hand free while Kate worked his belt and jeans.

He framed her face with his hands, held her still for a deep, soul-quenching kiss. But when her hand fondled over his naked penis, his breath caught. He pulled back to see her fist tight around his stone-hard cock, his jeans shoved down to his knees.

"Make love to me." She leaned in, kissing and nibbling his neck even as she pumped his shaft.

His hips rocked with each stroke, he couldn't help it. "Kate. I don't want to screw this up. Don't want to lose you. I can't."

She stopped, leaned back to look him in the eye. "You won't," she said, her tone sure. "This is right. I feel it."

Kate scooted back off her knees, braced her arms behind her, legs open so he could see how her cream had moistened her panties. "Do you feel it, Joe?"

Everything inside him snapped tight. His heart skipped. A warm shudder tickled down his spine. She was so beautiful, her dark hair blanketing over her shoulder, a thick wave resting above her breast. Her eyes were that brilliant green again, like the morning sun through stained glass. Only now lust weighted her lids adding a sultry gleam that made his hands clench and his chest squeeze.

She was braless, sexy in the nearly see-through white tank top, her body radiating sexual need. He could feel it, see it, and it made everything male inside him go weak and hard at once.

Joe toed off his shoes and ripped his socks off with his jeans and underwear. The Velcro ankle holster came off in one quick yank and he mounted the bed then her without registering the movement. She fell back, his body covering her from chest to groin. He wanted to feel all of her, her soft curves, tight puckers and warm wetness.

He kissed her, exploring her mouth with his, tracing kisses along her cheek, nibbling her ear. He took her wrists in one hand, dragging them up above her head, perfecting the teardrop curve of her breasts. Her nipples jutted toward him, tenting the sheer fabric so he couldn't resist shifting lower to suckle her.

Kate wriggled with the tender draw on her flesh, her hands fiddling with something. "Oh, shit."

Joe looked and only then noticed he held her wrists beneath the tall stack of pillows. Something firm yet soft, rubber, brushed his knuckles. "What is that?"

"Nothing. Leave it."

Joe pulled it out. He got to his knees, Kate's legs on either side of him. "A vibrator?"

Her ears were blood red, her hands covering her face. She shook her head, her voice muffled against her palms. "Shoot me now. Just shoot me now."

"Relax. I'm a man. We love toys." The dildo was less than half his size and it dawned on him he may have hurt her the other times they'd been together. She hadn't said anything, but he made a mental note to take greater care. He flicked the button on the battery pack and the vibrator hummed to life.

Kate's hands came off her face, eyes wide. "What're you going to do?"

He made his smile wicked and bobbed his brows. "Playing. Now, take off your panties."

Her breath shuddered but after a moment's hesitation, Kate obeyed. She tossed her little green underwear to the floor and started to squirm out of her top.

"No. Leave that." He liked the way the sheer material lay like gossamer over her full breasts and molded wet to her nipples where he'd tasted her. The darker flesh wrinkled tighter as he watched, her nipples like dark juicy raisins.

His gaze dropped to the glistening folds of her pussy, her curls wet with cream. He dipped his finger into the heat of her body, smoothing easy through the soft flesh.

"Oh, Joe..." Kate arched into his touch, her legs spreading

wide as he sank his finger deep inside her. He stroked her from the inside, feeling her muscles hug around him. His cock twitched in envy, need a tightening knot in his balls.

He leaned in, drawn by her feminine scent and her sweet soothing heat. With the very tip of his tongue, he tasted her clit. She flinched but then rocked into his face, so his mouth covered her. He drew the sensitive swollen nub into his mouth, a gentle scrape of teeth as his fingers drove in and out of her pussy.

Her orgasm thundered over her without warning, swelling her walls around his fingers, drenching her sex in a gush of release. Her hips bucked, pressing her clit hard against his mouth and he took all she willingly gave. When she'd stilled he replaced his mouth with her toy and Kate's body roared back to life like a furnace freshly stoked.

"Show me where you like it," he said after a few seconds, sensing he hadn't quite hit the mark.

Her eyes nearly closed, her face radiantly flushed, hair wild around her head, she reached down and guided the toy with his hand. She found the mark instantly, her back arching as the vibrations hummed through her sex. Her hand shifted to the toy, took control.

"Jeezus, Kate that's so fucking hot. Yeah. Keep playing with yourself."

His hands free, Joe stroked himself as he edged closer, the other hand catching under her knee, lifting. The slick entrance to her body flexed before him. He drove into her hard and fast, his eyes locked on the pink bunny-eared vibrator working her clit.

The dildo vibrated her pussy around him, the hum of it tingling up his shaft, pulsating through his balls. "Fuck..."

The threat of release swamped him fast and it was all Joe could do to resist teetering over the edge. His chest tightened. He held his breath as her muscles milked his cock, hungry for every thick inch of him. He buried himself inside her, going harder, deeper with every thrust.

Both hands held her under her knees. The sound of their bodies slapping together echoed through the room, sending jolts of sensation ricocheting through his body. Sweet friction sizzled along his flesh, a swelling pressure building up from his gut, driving his hips, squeezing through his chest. He clenched his jaw, fought the primal urge to ride the wave of pleasure over the edge.

He looked at the connection of their bodies. The sight of his cock slipping in and out of Kate, her fingers spreading the lips of her pussy while her other hand guided the dildo made his cock thicker, tighter inside her. He wouldn't last much longer. He didn't have to.

"There. Yes. Don't. Don't stop." Kate's head pressed back into the pillows, her body pounded by his, the bed frame knocking a frantic rhythm against the wall.

She turned and muffled her raw howl with the pillows, heat flooding her sex, muscles throbbing wildly along his cock. Joe couldn't resist a second longer, needing to thrust harder, faster, like he needed air. The sweet pressure her body had built in him rose fast, squeezing through every muscle, tightening through his chest until he couldn't breathe. Sensation exploded inside him, charging through his veins, roaring from every corner of his body and out his cock.

Spent, Joe collapsed forward, catching himself before his full weight rested on top of her. Her vibrator hummed between them and Joe found the power button on the battery back to switch it off. He nuzzled under her thick fall of hair, pushing the pillow out of his way to plant kisses on her neck. Her sweat salted his lips and he licked her, making her squirm.

She twisted under him, turned her face to his. Her smile warmed something deep inside him and he had to kiss her quick or go mad from the urge.

Kate blinked, caught her breath. "I've done a lot—sexually speaking. But I've never done that. Never played with myself in front of anyone."

"You're a fuckin' pro."

She blushed. "You're no slouch yourself."

"Bah. Just warming up." He kissed her again because he couldn't be this close to her lips and not taste them.

"You'll stay?" She asked when he released her mouth.

"I lost that argument the second you snagged my T-shirt, dollface." And he had a feeling that's not all he'd lost.

Weird. He didn't care.

Chapter Fourteen

Kate snuggled into the spoon of his body and mumbled something about God being a woman. Joe didn't agree. He smiled to himself, rocked his hips forward, pressing his morning hard-on against the soft give of her ass. Only a male mind could make an ass that fine.

He rooted through her thick swag of hair to her neck and kissed. She tasted like sex and heat, a salty sweetness that stirred his blood and pulled a nice tug through his muscles.

"Morning." She encouraged his kisses with a tilt of her head. "So, five hours' sleep and you're ready to go again?"

"Been trying to hold still the last two," he said against her neck. "Figured you needed your rest."

She laughed, a small feminine snort that made him smile, and caressed the arm he held around her waist. "Thanks for the restraint, stud."

"Welcome."

"Although." She squirmed around to face him. "That does explain my dream. I was a witch and my broomstick was being *very* naughty."

"Broomstick?" Joe rolled to his back scooping Kate along for the ride. She straightened, pressing her hands to his chest, her knees on either side of his waist. The soft lips of her sex spread open on his belly, her sultry heat sinking through him to the bone.

"Oh. I mean, well, of course it was a very long, thick, meaty broomstick."

"Thank you."

She rolled her eyes and laughed. "Men."

Joe squeezed his hands on her hips, his thumbs fitting along the crease of her legs. He lifted her, scooting her back so the head of his cock teased against the hot entrance to her body. "You lodging a complaint?"

She wriggled, trying to settle herself lower on him. Her green eyes flicked to his. "Absolutely not."

"Good to hear." He lowered her, painfully slow, feeling her muscles grip hungrily around him, drawing his body deeper and deeper into hers. Every muscle in his body coiled, awareness centering on the connection of their bodies, the heat spreading fast. His breath caught.

A loud bang startled them both. Joe jackknifed in bed, instinctively pulling her into the protection of his arms. It seemed endless seconds ticked by before his sex-fogged brain could puzzle out the sound.

"What was that?" she asked, breathless, her cheek to his chest.

"The door." He stared as though it might make the noise again. "Someone slammed it."

"Someone was watching us?"

He looked at her. "I can find out. You okay?"

"Yeah. Definitely. Go." She pulled the sheets to her chest and slipped off his semi-hard cock. The room air cooled his sex and returned him to a manageable state before he'd finished pulling on his jeans.

Joe stopped at the door and glanced back at her. Worry wrinkled her brows, caught her bottom lip between her teeth. Her dark cinnamon hair tangled over her bare shoulders, the queen-sized bed dwarfing her, making her seem all the more precious and fragile.

He'd never allowed himself to care for his principal before.

But in that moment Joe's drive to protect her was more a part of him, more a primal need than any professional ethic could ever elicit. He would die for her. And that truth made his chest hurt.

"Lock this. Stay put," he said then left.

It was early. The wide carpeted hallway was empty. Though in a house this size, empty halls were likely the norm. Joe glanced to his right. Kate's room was the last on this end. A high windowed wall was only twenty feet away.

He turned and jogged on his toes toward the staircase at the center of the house, pausing for a quick listen at doors as he went. His gut told him whoever it was hadn't risked hiding in an occupied room, but he needed to be thorough.

Two doors down from Kate's room, another two from the center of the house, the alarms suddenly blared. Seconds later voices yelled from the lower floor and Joe ran full-out to the stairs. Taking them three at a time he reached the bottom of the wide staircase in seconds and the front door four strides later.

"What's going on?" Joe said over the trumpeting siren to the elderly man stabbing a control panel with his floppy gloved finger. He had a thick cap of butterscotch hair that touched the collar of his dirty blue overalls—pruning shears poking through a hole in his back pocket.

"Someone triggered the alarm. Can't get the number punched in." The man's long face stretched, exaggerating the words as he yelled. His withered skin was like an old piece of crumpled vellum smoothed in the shape of a face. Lines that had nothing to do with worry or laughter, creased every which way over sun-ravaged skin that sagged beneath his eyes and chin like a basset hound.

"What's the number?"

The man eyed Joe warily. Joe held his out hands to his sides, harmless. The man shrugged and stepped out of the way. "Two, fifty-eight, thirty-six, one, twenty-four."

Silence.

"Who are you?" Joe asked him.

"Ralf Patroni, gardener. Who're you?"

"You set off the alarm?"

"'Course not." Ralf's tight brow added to his wrinkles. "Who are you?"

Joe turned and headed for the entrance to the kitchen under the fat oak staircase, answering as he walked. "Joe Garity. Chief bottle washer."

He broke into a jog before he crossed the threshold, then stopped short on the other side. The room was large, twenty by thirty easily, with high ceilings and a long island running parallel to the sidewall, cabinets above and below a long countertop.

There was a worn round wood table to the right where a barrel-shaped woman in a black maid's dress and white frilled apron sat reading a newspaper. Another woman, older, thinner, wearing gray instead of black and a no-frills apron, stood at the sink on the far wall. She glanced over her shoulder at him just as the maid raised her eyes.

"You ladies set off the alarm?"

The maid at the table shook her head, her attention dropping back to the paper. "Ask Ralf."

"No. Wasn't him."

The woman at the sink turned, wiping her hands on her apron. "You sure? He forgets to come in and out through the backdoor. Mr. Thorndike doesn't turn the alarm off 'til after breakfast."

"The backdoor's not armed?"

Both women, now affording him their full worried attention, shook their heads.

"Where?"

They pointed behind him toward a narrow hallway in the far left corner of the kitchen. He followed the passage to the small rear entry room noting the slated closet door and the archway at the back of the little room. The exit led to the front foyer beyond. He checked the back door, yellow steel. It wasn't locked.

The hallway continued past the backdoor into a large empty dining room. He checked then backtracked and took the archway from the rear entry room and passed into the main foyer. The grand front door loomed before him, to the left the staircase and beneath it the entrance to the kitchen.

"Garity." Joe glanced up the stairs at Clayton. "You pissin' with the alarm system?"

"No."

Clayton stopped. "Ralf?"

"Not Ralf."

"*Shit*," Clayton whispered, lips tightening to a flat line.

"Right."

The big towheaded blond jogged the rest of the way down the stairs and met Joe next to the control panel at the front door. "Where's Kate?"

"Here."

Both men turned toward the balcony railing before the stairs. Joe's chest squeezed. "Can't be. Kate's waiting behind a locked bedroom door."

"Get over it." Kate tugged the silky tie of her robe and trotted down the steps. The luxurious material split over her naked thighs as she moved, fluttering around her calves like smooth green liquid.

"Was it Ralf?" she asked when she'd reached them.

"No," Joe said.

Clayton's jaw hung slack, his eyes full of male hunger, staring at her. Joe gathered Kate close, tucked her under his arm. Strictly territorial male, and it worked. Clayton's mouth snapped shut, his white-blond brows slamming low over angry blue eyes.

"You two rush right out of bed? Couldn't stop to dress or

215

button your jeans?"

"Right," Joe said.

"It's not even six-thirty," Kate said. "Clayton..." Their eyes met and Joe saw something pass between them.

"Yeah. Sorry." The man shook his head and turned to the control panel.

"It looks like the front door's the one that tripped the alarm." Clayton's voice wavered for a moment, but Joe had to hand it to the guy, he pulled himself together quick.

"So who?" Joe asked. "Another staffer?"

"The house staff has keys to the backdoor," Kate said. "Ralf's the only one who's ever forgotten."

Joe hitched a thumb toward the kitchen. "Talked to the maid and cook. They thought it was Ralf too. Poor geezer."

"That's everyone." Clayton propped his hands on his hips. "If it wasn't them, then someone's here who shouldn't be."

Joe gave him a nod. "You check upstairs, I'll take this floor."

"Yeah." Clayton jogged toward the stairs.

"What about me?"

Joe snagged her hand and pulled her along behind him through the archway to the back entry room.

"Stay." He positioned her next to the wall while he opened the backdoor and examined the lock.

"What're you doing?"

"No sign of forced entry." Joe closed the door, shifting the puzzle pieces in his head.

"Why's that light on?" Kate was at the slated closet door before Joe could stop her. He scooped an arm around her waist and put her behind him just as the door swung open.

"Eddy?" she said over his shoulder.

Wedged between the vacuum cleaner and mop bucket, the gangly young man gnawed his thumbnail, knees to his chest, back against the wall. His brows were high beneath his long bangs, eyes wide, glasses perched at the end of his nose.

All the fear and worry and rage that had built up over the past two weeks crashed through Joe's mind and landed on Eddy like a big red bull's eye. He reached in, fisting the collar of Eddy's Star Wars T-shirt in both hands, pulled him out and set him on the wooden bench across the room.

It felt like he'd done it in one swift move. Blinking, Joe wasn't sure he'd let Eddy's feet touch the floor. *Must've.* Somewhere in the back of his head he heard Kate scream his name, but it took her elbow to his gut before the madman haze dissipated from his brain.

He staggered back as Kate wedged between him and the horrified Eddy. She clutched the edges of her robe together between her breasts and leaned over resting a hand on Eddy's shoulder. "What were you doing in there?"

"I was... I...I was waiting." His too-wide eyes darted back and forth between them.

"In the closet?" Joe asked, suspicious.

Eddy ignored him and spoke to Kate. "I mean, well, I started up to see if you were awake. And then I, um, I saw I had mud on my shoes. Figured I'd wait in the mudroom."

Joe pointed to the floor. "This is the mudroom. That's the cleaning closet."

Eddy's brows pinched, eyes going narrow on Joe, attitude winning out over fear. "Had to get somethin' to clean up the dirt clumps. Didn't I?"

Joe had a mind to adjust his attitude and shifted forward, but Kate shouldered him back. "Wait. Why were you waiting? Why'd you come?"

He shrugged, the snide glint in his eyes vanishing. "You have a morning class. Thought we could work on my psych project beforehand. Then maybe, I dunno, have breakfast together or something."

"You tell anyone you were here?" Joe asked. "How'd you get in?"

Kate didn't let Eddy answer. "We already did the camper evaluations."

His pocked cheeks reddened. He glanced away. "I know. I just thought... It was fun talking about the kids and the farm and stuff. Like colleagues, y'know? Like we were...close."

Joe's mind seemed to be clicking on a two-second delay. Eddy's responses were trickling through in spits and gurgles. He put a hand on Kate's arm and nudged her to the side. "You were going to her room?"

Kate glanced at Joe then back to Eddy before he answered. "How'd you know where my room was?"

Eddy ignored Joe. "Clayton showed me last summer. He pointed out your old bedroom window. Figured that's where you'd be since you moved back in."

"You didn't just *start* up the stairs. You made it to her room." Joe was sure enough he'd made it a statement. Instinct prickled at the back of Joe's neck, puzzle pieces shifting again.

Kate paled, straightened, clutching her robe tighter. "That was you? You were at my bedroom? You were...watching us."

"No." Eddy's whole body lurched like he'd stand, but Joe was quicker with an easy shove to keep him in place. "No. I wasn't watching. As soon as I saw... I mean, I closed the door right away."

"You freaked," Joe said. "Took off running."

Eddy's gaze slid to Joe, brows snapping tight beneath his bangs. "Did not. I left. That's all."

Joe folded his arms, shifted his weight to his heels. "Tried to run out the front door?"

Eddy brought his stubby thumbnail to his mouth, dropped his gaze. "Just wasn't thinking."

"And when the alarm went off you panicked and hid in the cleaning closet," Kate said.

"I was gonna leave, but *he* came down so fast." Eddy flicked his narrowed eyes to Joe. "What are *you* doing here so early?"

"What'd it look like?"

"Joe," Kate said, ears flushing blood red. "Eddy, this is the Thorndikes' home. It's not appropriate for you to go wandering around. From now on, wait for me at the stable office. Understand?"

"Fine." He stood, then jabbed a thumb toward Joe. "What about him? If I go, he goes."

Joe dropped his hands to his hips and opened his mouth for a blunt retort. But Clayton beat him to it when he emerged from the hallway to the kitchen.

"Garity's gotta grab a few things he forgot in his room. Like his shirt and shoes. They'll both be down later, buddy. Happy birthday, Kate honey. I'll take care of this." Clayton winked at her and steered Eddy by the shoulders toward the archway to the front foyer.

"Happy birthday, Kate," Eddy said over his shoulder then glared at Joe. "Don't understand why it's okay for him to wander around the Thorndike house and not me."

"She's his girlfriend."

"So?"

"Maybe we should have a talk about what girlfriend and boyfriend means at their age?" Clayton said before distance muffled the rest of the conversation.

Kate's belly fluttered. *Girlfriend.* Was she? It was too foreign a concept to consider. She glanced at Joe who was still glaring at Eddy as the front door closed behind him.

"He's just a kid," Kate said.

"Wrong."

"Well, he's like a kid." She walked around Joe, through the hallway to the kitchen, trying to keep the strange word from her mind. She passed by the long center island to the far end of the kitchen and into a short hall. There was a pantry to the left and a narrow twisting staircase on the right.

She started up the stairs. "Eddy's had a hard life. Abuse, abandonment, you name it. But he's innocent. It's like he's stuck in a perpetual childhood and I'm kind of his...big sister."

"No. You're not."

Kate led the way down the long hall, past the center staircase and on to her room. "Yeah. Okay, you're right. But he is very naïve. I doubt he even understood what he saw when he opened my door. Besides, he needs friends."

Joe closed the door behind them then leaned against it, reaching a hand up to massage the tense muscles at the back of his neck. "I'm not buying it. Somethin's off about that guy. Doesn't feel right."

She riffled through her suitcase on top of the dresser, grabbing a bra, underwear, her charcoal gray riding breeches and coral button blouse. There were a sprinkling of clothes she'd left behind in the dresser and closet, but the silk robe she had on was likely the only thing she'd wear that she hadn't brought with her.

Kate rolled her eyes at Joe as she headed for the bathroom, trying to seem casually unaffected when she was nothing of the sort. "You said the same thing about Clayton."

"Right."

She cringed but swallowed the expression before she turned to face him. "Okay. Maybe you were right about Clayton. But even if Eddy is a few bales short of a full barn, I think I can handle him. I mean, he weighs, what, sixty pounds?"

"More like one-sixty. About sixty pounds more than you." Joe pushed from the door and strolled toward her, dropping his hands to hook his thumbs on the back pockets of his jeans.

Awareness hummed over Kate's body, a primal, acutely feminine sense responding to the approaching male. Her gaze skittered over his body, the round muscles of his arms and chest, the angled lines at his hips, the open vee of his jeans and the spray of dark hair hinting to his sex. Her heart skipped then set a faster pace, muscles tensing low in her body. Her palms went hot and moist like the lips between her thighs, and her breasts tingled against the cool silk of her robe.

Good lord, she was in deep, deeper than she'd been in years. She cared too much, what he thought, how he felt. *Girlfriend.* She wished she didn't want it so much. But he'd said he cared. That was big, right? It was something. Worth a little faith, especially with someone who made her feel comfortable and exhilarated at the same time—strange.

Joe was the *one*, if ever there was a *one* for a woman like Kate. She took the gamble, allowed herself to believe in the possibility of love, to believe in Joe. He had a huge chunk of her heart snug in the back pocket of those damn jeans. Maybe he had her whole heart and she just couldn't admit it yet.

Shoot, this is gonna hurt if I'm wrong.

"I didn't forget." He closed the distance.

"Forget?"

He reached for the collar of her robe, running his hands along the fold down between her breasts, knuckles brushing the puckered edge of her nipples. Tingles rushed over her skin like a million tiny caterpillar feet. Her breath trembled.

"About your birthday. Just didn't get you anything."

"Oh." She wasn't expecting a gift. But geez, saying it kind of felt like he'd kicked her dog.

"I'm no good at that sort of thing. Couldn't think of the right thing to give you, so I didn't get anything."

"That's okay. It's fine. Really. I'm gonna take a shower. You'll be here when I'm done?" She edged backward into the bathroom hoping the no-gift conversation was over.

He hadn't let go of her robe and when she moved his fists tightened. He yanked the collar and she stumbled into him. In one seamless move Joe caught her mouth in a kiss and stroked his knuckles up over the sensitive press of her nipples. She gasped at the sudden touch and he broke the kiss.

"I swear I didn't forget," he whispered, his forehead resting on hers.

She caught her breath and smiled. "I believe you."

Kate could tell it was important to him that she understood. He cared what she thought. That *was* big. Kate leaned back and kissed his forehead. He let her go, turning without meeting her eyes. She closed the door.

When she'd finished, forty-five minutes later, Joe sat on the edge of her unmade bed twisting his academy ring around his finger. His dark eyes swung up to her when she opened the door, then dropped back to the ring. He started talking as though they'd been in the middle of a conversation.

"You're right. I don't know how to relate to women, not really. The example I had, it wasn't the best. My mom, she was used to getting what she wanted. Didn't like settling. Said she was a daddy's girl and she'd never had to." He laughed at that.

"Never met her dad. Guess once she got knocked up, Daddy wasn't so proud of his little girl anymore." Joe shrugged, twisting his academy ring. "The guys she dated never measured up. Didn't make enough money, didn't spend enough money, couldn't read her mind, whatever. It was nuts. Some of them really loved her, really tried. She dumped them anyway. I mean, what's the point, right?"

Kate leaned against the bed beside him, wanting to touch him, not sure she should. Despite his casual tone she could see the tension along his shoulders, the tightness in his arms. He wasn't enjoying rehashing his past. So why was he doing it?

"Anyway, the drinking just made it worse. She used to say I was the only man in the world worth a damn. I was fuckin' six. By the time I was ten, I'd failed her too."

His dark eyes swung up to Kate's, glistening. He forced a smile so at odds with his true feelings his lips trembled trying to hold it. "Pretty pathetic when a kid can't even make his mother happy."

"I'm sure she didn't mean it."

"She meant it." He looked back to his ring, twisting.

"Thought Tom Riley helped me get past all that, the anger, the lashing out. Never realized how truly screwed up I am."

Kate stroked his hair, she had to touch him, brushing it back from his eyes. "You're not screwed up, Joe. You're one of the most clearheaded, insightful men I've ever met. Your mother was selfish and inconsiderate. Her father obviously spoiled her."

"So?" He looked at her. "Your father spoiled you. Least he tried. Gave you everything. Her father stopped loving her when she got pregnant. Your father wasn't much better, loving you when it suited him."

Kate hadn't come out of her childhood unscathed. But for the first time in her life she felt she'd begun to heal the wounds—thanks to Joe. She wasn't sure she would've come as far without him. "Your mom was wrong to make you feel responsible for her happiness. It wasn't fair. But I'm sure her problems had more to do with her than you."

"No, her problem was she didn't know what she wanted. Even when she had it, she didn't know. Or she was too much of a chicken shit to admit it." His gaze slid up to hers. "I'm not my mother's son."

Kate's heart pinched. "What'd you mean?"

His gaze dropped to his hands and Kate's followed. He twisted his academy ring one last time then tugged it off his finger. "This was the first thing I ever did that was worth a damn. The only thing I gave a shit about."

Joe took her hand, fumbled for her ring finger and slipped his beloved ring over it. "Happy birthday, Kate."

She held out her hand, staring. She couldn't breathe, couldn't swallow her heart out of her throat. The ring was too big. She didn't care. Her brain was spinning, her chest tight, her knees trembling. This couldn't mean what she thought it meant.

Kate smiled, easy, playful, despite the tears stinging her eyes. "What, we going steady now?"

Joe held her gaze. "Something like that. As long as you

have that ring, Kate, you have me."

"And if I never want to take it off?" she asked, butterflies rioting in her belly.

"Then I'm a lucky man." He stood in one liquid smooth move, framed her face with his hands and kissed her.

Kate gasped at the suddenness of it, lost her breath and kissed him back anyway. Her hands went to his hips, squeezed his warm flesh, felt his fat ring separating her fingers. And it was good, very good.

When their lips parted, his expression turned serious, brows low over the darkest blue eyes she'd ever seen. "Promise me one thing. If I screw this up, you won't cut out on me."

"Oh, honey. You screw this up and I will kick your ass." She pushed up on her tips toes and kissed him quick. "That's a promise."

Chapter Fifteen

"Surprise!" The indoor arena echoed the roar of a hundred happy partygoers.

Kate's hand jerked and squeezed his, even though she knew it was coming. Joe laughed. He let her go the instant he felt her grip open. Rug rats swarmed around her, hugging her hips and waist, nudging Joe out of the way.

"Happy birthday, Miss Kate," Tony said, his pointy birthday hat perched at the crown of his head.

Delmar, Nisha and Carmen sang together, "Happy birthday."

"You look older today," Garon said.

Savion elbowed him without uncrossing his arms. "She is old, stupid."

He and Garon were part of the too-cool few who didn't rush Kate. They fringed the edges of the group, jaded in all their ten to twelve years of hard life. Pointy party hats pressed into their mussed hair and creased around each of their solemn faces, hinting to the little girls and boys buried deep inside.

All the camp had turned out, including kids Joe had only seen in passing over the past two weeks. Nearly fifty children and almost as many adults counting counselors and farm staff.

Joe scanned the faces, allowed himself to be nudged four feet from Kate but no farther. Conversation and laughter echoed off the metal walls and ceiling. Somewhere in the large open building music blasted. Four lines of colored paper streamers hung in twelve-foot swags along the walls, and an enormous balloon arch stretched over a raised platform where the cake and refreshment tables sat.

"Put a lot of work into this," Clayton said from behind him.

Joe glanced over his shoulder. "Right."

Clayton stepped beside him. "Nothing but friends and family. People who love her. You can dial back the eight-hundred-pound-gorilla look. No one's gonna hurt her here."

He looked at Clayton again, raised a brow. "That a fact?"

"Yeah. You think you're the only one who wants to protect her?"

"Just the only one who knows how."

"Christ, you're an arrogant ass."

"I know." Joe stepped forward, hoping to end the conversation. There were too many people here, too many faces he didn't know. He should be paying attention to Kate, to the people getting too close to her, not measuring dicks with Clayton.

Joe scanned the arena, noticed all the horses were tied at the far end, including Sunshine. He did a double take. Were they wearing party hats? Big, horse-size party hats and their hooves were painted colors to match the riot of helium balloons tied to the walls and hitching rail. They didn't seem to mind.

His attention shifted back to the people strolling in and out through the huge opened doors on either side of the arena. Other partygoers squeezed in around Kate, hugging and touching and shifting her a yard farther away without notice.

Joe pushed at the little shoulders closest to him. He wanted to shrink the distance, but then didn't. They were kids. What'd he think they'd do, gnaw her ankles? *Shit.* Maybe he *was* being an eight-hundred-pound gorilla. His feelings for Kate were clouding his judgment, throwing up red flags out of fear instead of tactic and logic.

The whole scenario set off Joe's internal alarms, but for the first time in his career he wasn't sure he could trust them. And that really pissed him off.

"Yeah. Probably best. For now."

Joe startled at the sound of Clayton's voice. He'd nearly forgotten he was there. "What?"

"You being all hovering and suspicious." Clayton rocked back on his heels beside him. "'Course once this is all over, it's gonna drive her crazy."

Joe slid his gaze sideways to Clayton. "You think?"

Clayton wrinkled his chin and nodded, arms folded across his chest. "Oh, yeah. Kate's not the type to be tied down. Never able to stomach a guy for long, especially the clingy ones. Usually bolts. Just sayin'."

"Thanks. I'll keep it in mind." Joe's gut twisted. Would he ever be able to dial back his protective impulses when it came to Kate? The thought of losing her made his chest tight. Whether she walked away or was taken, he couldn't stop one without risking the other. Jeezus, he couldn't think about it. How did a person survive caring about someone this much?

"Hey, that's Joe's ring."

Joe turned, Clayton stepped around him, both focused on Tony. The curly-topped boy stood with his nose inches from Kate's paper cup and the hand on which she wore Joe's academy ring. Her gaze flicked to Joe as Tony called in a second opinion.

Savion took Kate's wrist and turned it, nearly toppled her drink before she managed to switch it to the other hand. Several more campers, Delmar, Nisha, Carmen, gathered so close Kate's arm was lost behind bowed heads.

"Yep. That's his ring alright," Savion announced.

All eyes turned to Kate and hers held Joe's. A smile flittered across her lips, cheeks flushed, ears redder still. Her brows creased up to a point, a mix of tempered happiness washing her face.

"This mean you're his girlfriend?" Tony asked.

Kate's mouth fluttered opened and shut. She shrugged still looking to Joe. "I'm...I mean, we're..."

"Yeah. That's what it means," Joe said trying hard to hold his scowl and failing miserably. *Man*, he wasn't prepared for how much he'd like saying it out loud.

Kate's smile spread full bloom to match his, lighting her eyes, turning them that unreal green that made it hard for him to breathe.

Ginny crowded close beside her, reaching for her ringed hand. "Was it a birthday gift?"

Kate nodded, turning to follow her appendage while most of the female staff and a few of the males ogled Joe's ring.

"Says police academy." Eddy swung his bug eyes behind his glasses to Joe. "You a cop?"

"Used to be." Joe slipped his hands into the front pockets of his jeans to the knuckles, shifting gears from pleased new boyfriend to undercover bodyguard in a heartbeat.

"What's that mean?"

"I'm retired. Injured in the line," Joe said.

Eddy shoved his glasses up the bridge of his nose and eyed Joe from head to foot. "Don't look injured."

"That right?"

"He was hurt very badly," Kate said. "Almost died. Joe's a very brave, strong-willed man."

She sounded proud and damn if he didn't like it.

"More like old and lucky." Eddy glanced back at the ring. "Probably turn your finger green."

No one seemed to pay Eddy any mind as he turned and left. Ashley slipped into his spot beside Ginny like water, leaving no sign he'd ever been there.

Ginny threw Joe a wink. "I'd take it if he'd offered it to me."

"Yeah. Ya got any little brothers at home?" Ashley said.

"Sorry ladies, Joe's one of a kind," Kate said.

"Thank the lord for small favors," Clayton grumbled. "We gonna get this show on the road or not? Time to cut the cake. Garity's not the only one who got you a gift."

The crowd moved like a school of fish, all of them swarming around Kate. En masse they swept up onto the platform stage, squeezing in around the cake table as they sang and watched her blow out the candles. Joe hadn't even made it up the small steps. He could've forced his way to her side, should've, but didn't.

She was safe. He was close enough. These people weren't a threat to her. He said the words in his head, but the impulse to throw his body over hers like a shield and whisk her away from the pushy crowd nearly choked him.

Thumbs hooked on his pockets, Joe fisted his hands, dug his nails into his palms and moved around to the front of the platform. At least here he had a clear line of sight, albeit a level below and ten feet away with the thin metal railing edging the stage between them.

If things went south he'd never make it to her in time. *Unacceptable.* Joe shifted his weight back toward the steps then stopped when he caught Clayton watching him from the stage. How the hell had he made it to the cake table?

Dammit. If either of them should be standing on that stage next to her while she passed out cake and opened gifts it was Joe. After everything they'd been through, all the hang-ups and misunderstandings they'd overcome, they'd earned their chance together. He'd be damned if he'd let Clayton bogart even a second of his time with her.

"He's loved her for a long time."

Joe turned to see Bill Thorndike, Clayton's father, standing in his path to the steps. "Yeah? It's my turn."

The man was tall, like Clayton, with the same bright blue eyes and thick muscled body. Even in his late sixties Bill was a hardcore cowboy in his pale blue and white checkered shirt and worn faded jeans. His hair was shorter than Clayton's, showing pink scalp beneath soft white stubble that matched his Magnum P.I. mustache and bushy white brows.

"Not like that," Bill said. "Oh he might argue at first, but he knows what his feelings are really about. Can't help himself. Just hard for him to admit."

"What's that?"

"Amy." Bill's gaze drifted to his son. "My daughter. Nine years old when she died. Leukemia. Clay took it hard. We all did. But he was her protector and when she passed..."

"Right." Joe looked from Clayton to Kate. Clayton felt he'd failed his sister. Yeah. Joe could wrap his brain around that feeling.

"Clay was fourteen. He couldn't accept there was nothing he could've done to save her. Four years later, Kate gave him another chance."

Bill snorted at his memories. "Lord, she was a sight. Thin as a string bean, with them wide green eyes. All alone in the middle of a big-city bus station. Was fate we were there that day. Been to that station maybe ten times my whole life."

"That right?" Joe narrowed his eyes on Clayton, shifted the information in his head. He saw it. The way Clayton looked at Kate. Love, for sure, but beneath it—something else. It wasn't jealousy he'd read in his tone and manners—it was bridled fear.

"If it hadn't been for Amy, things might've been different between them," Bill said. "But what they needed from each other was deeper than anything physical."

Joe turned back to Bill, caught the stone-cold look in his eyes. "My boy's not a threat to you, Garity. But you take that little filly away from us and you'll kill'im sure as shootin' him. They're family. We all are. I'd be obliged if you kept that in mind down the road."

"I can do that."

"Hey, Joe. Ya gonna play?" Tony yelled from the center of the arena. He sat atop Coco's bare back, the bay mare's party hat protruding from the side of her head.

Joe looked back to Kate and Clayton and the seven or eight friends who were left surrounding her. "What're you playin'?"

"Dollar bareback first, before the horses get sweaty and the fake dollars stick to them."

"Go. She'll be fine," Bill said, obviously following Joe's gaze. "My boy won't let her so much as stub her toe. Besides, she'll probably be out there in a minute anyway. Where you go, she follows."

Joe glanced over his shoulder at Bill. "Yeah?"

Bill closed his eyes to nod, then smiled. "Yeah."

A quick breath of a laugh huffed out of Joe before he could stop it and he returned Bill's nod with a smiling one of his own. After one last glance to Kate, he turned and started toward Sunshine, the last horse left tied at the far end of the arena. "I'll play, kid. But I'm takin' that hat off. Looks like she's tryin' too hard."

Damn, he was happy.

"You know these games drive him crazy?" Kate leaned her shoulder against Ginny's, squinting against the bright afternoon sun as they watched the activities in the outdoor ring.

"I know. He throws a fit every time he drops the egg." Ginny lowered her voice to do her best Joe impression. "Not everything's meant to be done on horseback, people."

The two women laughed but stopped when the ring rail they sat on wobbled. Kate looked to see Eddy leaning his forearms against it beside her.

"He just doesn't get it." Eddy brushed Kate's knee with his knuckles. His eyes, big and round behind his glasses, swung up to hers. "Not a horse lover like us."

Kate's body stiffened despite herself. She didn't want to hurt Eddy's feelings. He was fragile that way. But something about him today, about the way he looked at her, spoke to her, touched her, made her flesh squirm.

She caught herself in the reflex action and forced her muscles to relax. "Actually, I think he's doing amazingly well. Two weeks ago he would've never sat bareback on a horse playing egg toss."

Eddy sneered at Joe. "More like egg drop. He sucks."

Ginny leaned forward, peering around Kate. "Least he looks good doing it."

"Looks like an idiot to me."

"Hey, Eddy, you've got something right there..." Ginny pointed to the corner of her mouth with her middle finger. "Oh, wait. That's jealousy. Never mind."

"Go bleach your mustache."

"Shut up, ya bug-eyed freak."

"Stuck up—"

"Enough." Kate threw up her hands, palms out like walls on either side of her. "Geez, you two are worse than the kids."

Eddy pursed his lips so tight the skin turned white around the edges. He swung his gaze back to the riders at the center of the ring, his angry breaths hissing through his nose. Ginny giggled.

Kate closed her mind to it. She wouldn't waste a second of her birthday on Eddy and Ginny's daily feud. Both were convinced the other was stuck in old high school stereotypes, the geek and the cheerleader. Kate couldn't care less. Not today. Not on her best birthday ever.

"Throw it underhand, kid. I'll catch it," Joe said.

Nisha swung her head back and forth, her stiff black braids brushing her shoulders. "Nu-uh. You're gonna miss, then start talkin' all crazy 'bout glue factories and dog food. Your face will turn red and that icky vein 'long side your neck'll swell up n'start thumpin'."

The little girl's detailed description had Joe rolling his head on his neck, relieving the growing tension knots no doubt. Kate didn't worry for a second.

"Throw. The egg." Joe was a storm cloud of passion and a mountain of control. Definitely no Mr. Rogers, but he had a heart as big as the moon and the hidden soul of a child.

Nisha tossed the egg. Joe caught it. Everyone exhaled.

A warm shudder tickled across Kate's shoulders. He was hers. He'd told everyone. And she was his. Gawd, could this day get any better? She'd remember it forever.

Kate's cheeks ached from her wide grin and she couldn't stop her thumb flicking the big academy ring around and around her finger. It was really there. Life was good.

"Kate?"

She dropped her gaze to Eddy, still feeling lost in a dreamy fog. "Huh?"

"I, ah, wanna give you your birthday gift."

"Oh, Eddy, you didn't have to—"

"Yes, I did."

His abruptness snapped her mouth shut. "Oh. Well. Okay."

He looked around. Besides Ginny next to her and the twelve campers, including Joe, playing egg toss in the ring, the grounds were alive with people. Clayton and Bill stood at the far end of the ring, closer to the main house side, deep in conversation.

Counselors and campers gathered in small groups talking and more mulled around in and out of the indoor arena and barns.

Eddy tossed his head to gesture toward the stables behind them. "C'mon. I can't give it to you out here."

The hair at the back of Kate's neck bristled. "Why not?"

"It's personal."

"No one's paying any attention," Kate said. "Here's fine."

Eddy glowered at Ginny beside her then looked back to Kate, barely tempering his noxious expression. "You afraid to be alone with me or something?"

Goose bumps washed over her body, icy fingers scraped

down her spine. She didn't want to hurt his feelings but something wasn't right. "Of course not. I just... I told Joe I'd watch him play egg toss."

Eddy looked to the center of the ring, shoved his finger into the bridge of his glasses. "'Cause he's your boyfriend."

"That's right."

Eddy's eyes narrowed to slits. His jaw clenched so tight she could see the muscles working beneath his scarred cheeks. He snorted without an ounce of humor. "He won't even notice you're gone."

"I'm sure he will. Besides, it would be rude not to tell him."

His gaze flicked to hers, a calculating sharpness glinting in their depths the likes of which she'd never seen in Eddy before. He tipped his chin toward Ginny. "She can tell him."

"I don't—"

He took her hand and Kate's stomach lurched, stopping her protest. "C'mon, Kate. It'll only take a minute. I left it in your office."

"You're a pain in the ass, Eddy." Ginny sighed and looked to Kate. "Don't worry. If Joe asks I'll tell him your charity case needed some private hand holding."

"See?" Eddy said. The vacant smile he gave Kate made her skin tingle like ice crystals forming, but she wasn't sure why. She knew Eddy, trusted him, but something wasn't right. He tugged her hand.

She swiveled her legs to the other side of the railing and climbed down. She glanced at Joe, tossing the egg back to Nisha, then to Clayton talking to Bill. She turned and noticed the familiar faces talking and laughing at the opening to the indoor arena as Eddy led her to the stables. No one stopped them. No one raised an eye. She was the only one who felt it.

Inside the stables the long aisle seemed dark despite the run of fluorescent lights down the center of the ceiling. It was such a bright sunny day, warm and happy, but Kate's blood ran cold.

"You okay?" Eddy said. "You look pale."

He asked with the same innocent sweetness he always did and Kate questioned her gut reaction. This stalker business combined with the riot of emotions Joe sent running rampant through her head had her whirling on the razor edge of sanity and paranoid madness.

She laughed at herself and shook off the frost of apprehension still chilling over her nerves.

"I'm fine. There's just been some, *stuff*, going on." Kate stepped into her office, Eddy close behind.

He closed the door. "The stalker?"

She turned to face him, her desk beside her. "How'd you know about that?"

Bill and Clayton had informed the farm's regular staff about her secret admirer, but the counselors were left purposely uninformed since most were new and potential suspects. But naturally, Kate figured, people talked.

Eddy shrugged, fingering his backpack he'd left on the guest chair in front of her desk. "Didn't know much for sure 'til after the fire. Heard the firemen and Joe talking to the cops. Why are you calling him a stalker?"

"Well..."

Eddy's magnified eyes swung up to hers, expectant. Kate's nerves shuddered like ants marching cold little feet all over her body.

She swallowed. "It's kind of complicated."

"No it's not. He's been nothing but nice to you, hasn't he?"

"Nice?"

"Yeah." Some of Eddy's sweet innocence melted away with his rising agitation. "He sent you roses, didn't he?"

"Yes, but—"

"And he writes you poems. He's taken beautiful photographs of you. Like works of art."

"Art?" she said. "Eddy, they weren't works of art. They

were—"

"Yes, they were. All the greats painted nudes. Michelangelo, Da Vinci, Van Gogh, Rembrandt, their stuff is art. Just 'cause these were photos instead of paintings—"

"Eddy." Kate's fingers gripped the edge of the desk. "How did you know I was naked in some of the photos?"

Eddy's mouth snapped shut. He stiffened. "I...I changed my mind. I don't want to give you your present here. Let's go somewhere else. Somewhere special, more private."

"No, Eddy. Answer my question."

"It has to be right," he said as though he hadn't heard her. "It has to perfect. C'mon."

He grabbed his backpack and swung it over one shoulder, then turned for the door. When she didn't follow he looked back to her.

Kate's stomach clogged her throat. She couldn't swallow, could hardly breath. Her chest was tight and her palms were cold and clammy. Gawd, how could she have been so stupid?

"I'm not going anywhere," she said.

Eddy sighed and walked back to the desk. He set his backpack next to her hand white-knuckling the edge. His attention dropped to the finger on which Joe had placed his ring.

"That thing's fuckin' ugly." His voice was so cold and heartless she barely recognized it as Eddy's. "Who gives a woman a man's ring? Doesn't even have a diamond. Everybody knows women love diamonds."

"What do you want?" She fought to keep her voice from shaking.

It didn't seem like he'd heard. "If he really loved you, really knew you, he'd have gotten you a ring that fit. One with a diamond."

"Joe will be looking for me. I have to get back out to the ring."

"No he won't." Eddy locked gazes with her, radiating confidence. "Ginny's gonna tell him you're with me. The bitch thinks I'm a sniveling, four-eyed dweeb. She won't let Joe worry."

Kate's heart hammered in her ears. "Should he worry?"

He shrugged, smiling devilishly. "Depends. He thinks you're his. Are you?"

She didn't want to answer that. Wasn't sure it'd be wise. "Eddy, are you the one who's been leaving those letters and photos for me?"

His smile broadened, his attention dropping to his backpack as though hearing only what he wanted, responding as he chose. He unzipped the largest section. "Okay, okay. I'll give you *half* your present now, but you'll have to wait 'til we get to our special place for the rest."

Eddy pulled out an eight-by-ten frame, stared at it for a second, smiling, then handed it to Kate. When she reached for it, she noticed her hands were shaking. She couldn't make them stop. She grabbed the picture.

"Wrote the poem myself," he said.

Kate stared at the image of her standing on the shore of the river near the bum slide and waterfall. Joe was far off to her right, watching her. At least she assumed he was watching her. It was hard to tell after Eddy had scratched a hole through the photo where his face should've been.

All the faces were scratched out, the children sliding through the fast current, the counselors wading in the swimming hole below. Even the smaller faces of people on the opposite shore had been picked away leaving an ugly jagged hole at the top of their necks.

"Well? What'd you think?"

Bile shot up the back of her throat. Kate's body lurched. Her hand flew to her lips. She caught the edge of throw-up in her mouth and swallowed. "Oh, God."

"Read it," Eddy said, oblivious to her sickened response.

Kate's gaze dropped to the lined paper pressed behind glass under the photo. *"My love for you will never die, lest for another your heart does cry. From this world into the next, my soul is yours until we rest. Should the world turn you 'round, and your heart become unbound. 'Til our dying breaths I'll fight, to steal you back and make things right."*

Kate looked to Eddy. His proud grin pinched his shiny cheeks, his long mop-water bangs twitching behind his glasses with his blinks. "Pretty good, huh? And I mean every word. We're gonna be so great together."

"Eddy, I—"

"No. Wait." He held out a hand to stop her. "I know. I'm getting ahead of myself. I want everything to be perfect. It *has* to be perfect."

He grabbed the strap of his backpack and tipped his head toward the door. "C'mon. Let's get out of here before that idiot cop comes and interrupts us."

Kate dropped the framed photo on the desk, shaking her head, though she didn't connect the motions with conscious thought. "No. I can't leave with you. I won't."

Everything she'd ever heard about kidnappings and murders started with the victim allowing the attacker to lead her away. She would not make that mistake. If he was going to hurt her, he'd have to do it here where someone would find her quickly or happen by to help her. No. She wasn't going anywhere.

"Aw, Kate. C'mon," Eddy whined. "It's gonna be really great. Promise. I have a gift for you. But I can't give it to you unless we're at our special place." His voice was straining, growing louder. "Everything has to be perfect. Just like I planned it. You have to come, Kate. You have to."

"No."

Eddy's exhale huffed out of him. His shoulders slouched. "Fine. I didn't want to do this, but sometimes tough love's the only way. All the songs say it. Love hurts. Right?"

He reached into his backpack and pulled out a gun. "And I do love you, Kate."

The weapon was silver, thick metal and utterly indistinguishable from any she'd seen on hundreds of TV shows. The only thing Kate knew about guns was they could kill people. That's all she'd ever wanted to know.

She sucked a breath, shored her courage and prayed to God he was bluffing. "If you're going to kill me, you'll have to do it here. I'm not leaving with you."

"Wha? No. This isn't for you...yet." He looked at the gun in his hand. He wasn't pointing it at anything, but she felt the threat just the same. "You have no idea how much I get you, Kate. How well I understand you. I knew I couldn't wave a gun and force you to come with me."

"Then what're you going to do?" Her voice cracked at the end. Kate cleared her throat though she doubted it did any good.

Eddy shook his head staring at the gun. "It *has* to be perfect. It has to be at our special place. I'm sorry, Kate, I know how much you care about these kids. So do I. We have so much in common. But if you won't come with me... It *has* to be at our special place."

He looked at her, eyes big as quarters behind his glasses. He shrugged, then turned and went to open the door. When he stuck his head out Kate couldn't tell what or who he saw down the aisle.

"Hey, Lucy," he said. "Lucy. Lucy. Hey, c'mere. I wanna show you something."

Kate shot to his side, grabbed his arm trying to pull him back into the office. "Eddy, no. You wouldn't. You're not going to hurt a child."

Eddy glanced over his shoulder at her. He was tall and thin, but Joe had been right, she was no match for him. He hadn't budged and his expression was stone-cold evil. "Not me. You. You're the one who's making me, Kate."

"Hey, Eddy. What'd ya got?" The little raven-haired girl was suddenly there outside Kate's office door.

She and Eddy flinched, but Eddy recovered quick. Swinging his gun hand behind him, he pushed the door wide. "It's really cool. C'mon. It's in here."

Kate's flesh squirmed over her bones at the lecherous sound of his voice. "Lucy, no. Go away—"

"Don't move, Lucy." Eddy looked to Kate even as he reached out and snagged the shoulder of Lucy's Tweety Bird T-shirt. "Miss Kate didn't mean it. She needs you to help her make a decision."

He dragged Lucy over the threshold. The little girl stumbled, eyes wide, as though instinct warned of a danger she couldn't possibly comprehend. Her uncertainty played against her, kept her silent and compliant when she should've been anything but.

Eddy held her in front of him, his gun hand behind his back, his free hand stroking her long shiny black hair. "Lucy, I want you to ask Miss Kate if she'll let you see the surprise I've got behind my back."

Cold sweat tickled down Kate's spine and between her breasts, chin trembling with an emotion she would not allow. Kate clenched her fists, jaw tight, anger warring with fear as she dropped her gaze to Lucy.

"Miss Kate?" she asked, timid. "Can I see the surprise?"

Kate swallowed but her voice still came as a whisper. "No."

Eddy leaned down and spoke next to Lucy's ear. "Ask her why not."

Lucy's big brown eyes locked with Kate's. "Why not?"

Eddy stood and Kate's gaze followed. *Bastard.* "Because. Eddy and I are leaving. Now go."

Her small body shifted, but Eddy stopped her. "Thank you, Lucy. You were very helpful. Why don't you go score another piece of cake?"

Lucy's sugar lust won out over trepidation. Her smile bloomed from ear to ear. "Really? Cool."

She raced from the office and with her Kate's best hope of getting a message to Joe. Eddy closed the door and shoved the gun down the front of his pants. He went to the desk and grabbed the strap of his backpack, slinging it over his shoulder.

"Time to go," he said.

Kate held her head high and took a cleansing breath. She marched past him to the desk and slipped Joe's ring from her finger, then set it on the picture Eddy had given her with a tiny click when it touched the glass.

Eddy watched, his brows tightly knit. "What're you doing?"

"You want me wearing it to our special place?" She shrugged, fighting to keep the choke of emotion tightening her chest from showing on her face. "If you want me to keep it on..."

She reached for the ring but stopped when Eddy touched her arm. "No. You're right. Leave it. I've got something way better anyway. Let's go. Remember, you scream or anything, the closest person to us pays for it."

Kate nodded then glanced one last time at Joe's ring, at the picture below and the poem written in Eddy's handwriting.

C'mon, Joe. Make the connection. And then they left.

Chapter Sixteen

"She's with Eddy."

"Where?" Clayton asked Ginny before Joe had a chance.

"In the office, I think. But seriously, he's a dweeb. Nothing to worry about."

Joe heard Ginny's last words from a distance as he stormed down the aisle toward Kate's office. His heart thumped in his throat, steady, choking. She was okay. *She's okay.*

He knew before he pushed open the door. The office was empty. His gaze fell on the desk, to the spark of sunlight off a band of gold. He walked to it, numb.

"Don't let your imagination get carried away." Clayton scanned the empty office from the door. "She's fine. Eddy's just a kid. She's safe with him. She's safe."

Joe knew Clayton was trying to convince himself as much as him. Good thing. His brain didn't have room to give a damn how Clayton was dealing with this.

"That your ring?" Clayton asked when Joe picked up his birthday gift to Kate.

Joe didn't answer. Didn't want to, didn't need to. He rolled his academy ring between his thumb and finger. She could've taken it off for any number of reasons. But why leave it on the desk? Even her tight little riding breeches had coin pockets. Joe's gaze fell to the framed glass the ring had sat on.

A photo, familiar in several ways. He shoved his ring into

his front jeans pocket and picked up the photo.

Clayton crossed the room to the desk. "Listen, I'm sure she liked the ring. I know she did. But women are complicated. Hard to know what they'll feel sentimental about...or not."

He was probably trying to be helpful. Joe just wanted him to shut up and for the constriction in his chest to ease. "What do you make of this?"

Clayton took the photo. "Looks like it's from her stalker. There were a ton of people here today. How the hell did he drop this off without anyone seeing him?"

"We all saw him," Joe said. "Just didn't know it."

Clayton blinked. "Shit. He was at the party."

"Right."

"You think he took her? We have to call the cops."

"No point. They won't come." Joe could almost hear Clayton's mind clicking. He didn't have time to wait. "Where's Eddy sleep?"

"Eddy? Why? I mean, the kid's got a crush but he's harmless."

Joe exhaled, slow, easy, trying to calm the apprehension coiling his muscles. He raked a hand through his hair, closed his eyes and tried to count to three. *One.* "Clayton. Where— does—he—sleep?"

"Boys cabin. Number two."

Joe pushed past him out the door. Clayton dropped the photo back on the desk and followed at his heels.

"You got a cell?" Joe asked, his feet crunching loud over the white gravel drive to the service road. The doors to the mess hall were open across the road in front of him. The lights were on, but the building was empty. Everyone was at Kate's birthday party. Everyone but Kate...and Eddy.

"Here." Clayton jogged to catch up. He shoved the phone into Joe's hand.

Joe figured he was probably the last person in the free

world not to own a cell phone. He hated the things. Too intrusive. Like a noisy neighbor following him around asking questions twenty-four-seven. If he wasn't near a phone, he didn't have time to talk.

He flipped it open as they walked and found the internal phonebook quick enough. Kate's number was number one on Clayton's speed dial. Would've bugged the hell out of him this morning. Now he'd counted on it. Joe pushed the button. The connection clicked. The phone rang. And rang. And rang. Clayton and Joe crunched across the service road and the phone rang again.

On the eighth ring Kate's voice mail picked up. The sound of her voice made his gut twist.

"Kate. It's me. Call back." Joe clicked it off and dialed again. This time the call went straight to her voice mail. Joe shut the phone and shoved it at Clayton.

"What?"

"Someone turned off her phone."

"Maybe she's just out of range."

"It'd keep ringing. Goes to voice mail when the phone's off." Joe didn't like cell phones. That didn't mean he didn't understand how the systems functioned. It was one of those things that came in handy in his line of work.

"Maybe she was calling you back at the same time."

Joe grabbed the phone again, trying not to let his hopes leap. He pushed the button. Her voice message picked up. He shoved the phone back to Clayton. *Dammit.*

They jogged the steps to the boys cabin side by side. Joe reached the door first and pushed it open.

"Where?" He scanned the large one-room cabin.

Left and right of the door were matching single beds with foot lockers at the ends, nightstands, shelves filled with personal items and a basic armoire each. Next to them following down both sidewalls were three sets of bunk beds, six total, with armoires in between.

Beyond the two lines of bunk beds were another set of single beds, one on each side, and the same setup of nightstand, shelf and armoire each. Directly opposite the door on the far wall was a large fireplace framed in river stone like the ones in his and Kate's cottages. Twelve campers and four counselors lived here, and there was no sign of Kate.

"Last on the left," Clayton said. "I think."

Joe threw a dark glance over his shoulder then marched down the aisle between the beds.

When he reached the end of the cabin he bent for the footlocker handle on the left. *Eddy Reynolds* was written in black marker on a strip of masking tape on top. "Locked."

"What're you looking for anyway?"

"Proof. Direction. Fuckin' anything."

Clayton swung past him and went to the nightstand. He rummaged through the little drawer and searched the shelves while Joe knelt beside the bed. Nothing more than gut instinct had him running his fingers along the underside of the bed frame. When he fumbled over the metal key his breath exploded out of him in a huff of relief.

He went to the locker and opened it. Clayton noticed when the lid clunked against the footboard of the bed, and came over.

"Looks normal enough," Clayton said.

Joe's quick scan took in the shallow tray on top, magazines, a deck of cards, flashlight, bug spray, spilled bottle of talcum powder, a couple pens and pencils and a pocket knife. He lifted the tray and set it on the floor. School books, sweatpants, a couple towels, but Joe shoved his hands beneath the obvious piles and felt a cool metal cylinder. He pulled it out.

"Damn, nice camera," Clayton said.

Joe turned it over and flipped it around, examining it. "High-powered lens."

He handed it to Clayton and focused on the locker again.

He shoved the clothes and books out onto the floor, uncovering a device about the size of a five-pound bag of sugar. "This one of those digital printers? Prints pictures straight off the camera?"

"Yeah," Clayton said, distracted.

Joe grabbed a white envelope peeking from under the little printer. He opened it as he stood, thumbing through the stack of photos. "These are all Kate."

Then he reached the last few. They were still of Kate, except Joe was always close by. He pulled out the last photo. It was dark, grainy, but there was no mistaking the image. Him and Kate in the lake. The black water hid their lower bodies, but Joe knew damn well they'd been in the middle of sex. *Son of a bitch.*

"Look at this." Clayton stared at the back of the camera.

Joe shoved the lake photo into his back pocket and traded Clayton the rest for the camera. The display window showed an image still on the memory card. "Same photo he left in the office."

Clayton snorted, more confused disbelief than humor. "So what's this mean? Eddy wouldn't let anything happen to Kate."

Joe shoved the camera back into Clayton's hands and headed for the door. "Eddy *is* what happened to Kate."

Clayton jogged after him. "What're you going to do?"

"Going after her."

"You know where he took her?"

"It helps." Joe shook off the attitude. The guy was just as worried as he was. "That's why he gave her the picture. Means something to him."

"I'm coming with you," Clayton said, finding Joe's stride and matching it.

"No. Call the cops." Joe crunched down the drive to the stables.

"You said they wouldn't come."

"That's when we *thought* she'd been kidnapped." Joe turned into the tack room. "Now we know."

"And that'll make a difference?" Clayton stopped at the door.

"Probably not. But throwing around her daddy's name might." Joe loaded his arms with his borrowed saddle and pad then headed down the aisle toward Sunshine's stall. He'd left her bridle on when he went looking for Kate.

"You want me to use her father's clout to pull strings?"

"Fuckin'eh. 'Bout time that name did her some good." Joe dropped the saddle and went into the stall to grab Sunshine. "If that doesn't work, call the man himself. Tell him Garity says his kid needs him."

"She's not gonna like this." Clayton watched while Joe threw the saddle and pad over the gray mare's back and tied the girth.

"She doesn't—"

"Get a vote. I know," Clayton said. "Hey, Garity."

With a foot in the stirrup, Joe pulled himself up then swung his leg over Sunshine's rump and sat. "Yeah?"

"You love her."

"Right."

"Prove it. Bring her home."

"I can do that." Joe yanked the reins and Sunshine spun around to face down the long aisle.

"Horse in the hole," Joe yelled and gave Sunshine one sharp kick to her ribs. The mare's weight shifted back then launched forward, thundering them down the aisle and out the far end like a bullet from a gun.

He cut the corner at the service road, laid the reins against her neck and shifted his weight to steer her between the cabins. He kicked her again when her hoofs hit the path to the river, once more as they traced the river's edge toward the bum slide.

Dammit, this was his fault. This is what happened when he let himself care about the principal. If he hadn't been worried about making Kate happy, about being too protective, too overbearing, Eddy wouldn't have gotten near her. It'd never happen again. He'd keep the necessary emotional distance between him and his principal from now on.

He'd nail Eddy to the wall, get Kate safe, then marry her. She wouldn't be his principal anymore, she'd be his wife. And pity the man who threatened his wife.

Sunshine galloped into the clearing near the waterfalls quicker than he'd expected. Joe threw his weight backward, pulling hard on the reins. The mare's weight shifted. She slid on the backs of her legs several feet. Joe jumped off before she'd found her footing again and ran toward the shoreline.

The river's edge was barred from sight by a thick wall of trees except through a narrow walking path. Joe ran blind, not knowing what he'd find when he breached the forest wall on the other side. If not for fast backpedaling footwork, he'd have tumbled right into the rushing water.

His left foot slid over the muddy edge and he dropped to his ass, his hands bracing behind him. Joe pulled his foot back, his sock sloshing inside his sneaker. "Shit."

A quick glance up and down the river revealed nothing. Maybe he was wrong. Maybe the picture of Kate at the bum slide had nothing do to with where Eddy had taken her.

No. Joe knew he was right. He felt it in his gut and trusting his gut had never steered him wrong. He exhaled, forced himself to shift gears, become the guard, the cop, and push the panicked lover to the back recesses of his mind. He scanned downriver, slower, dividing the search area in sections. Methodically his gaze searched background, then foreground then shifted to the next section.

He'd thoroughly covered a one-hundred-eighty-degree panorama and found nothing. Joe exhaled, closed his eyes, cursing under his breath. Where else could Eddy have taken her?

And then he heard it, above the rumble of water, like distant whispers, *voices.* Joe opened his eyes and narrowed his vision, using his best guess at which direction. *Movement*. Up on a higher outcropping of shoreline, near the cliff the counselors called the high dive, something caught his eye. He kept watching and within seconds he saw it again, only this time he recognized it as a thick braid of dark cinnamon hair.

His chest squeezed, muscles coiling, brain locking on to years of training. He kept low, made it back to the shelter of the trees. He gathered his pant leg above his ankle and pulled his gun. Clicked the safety off.

The weight of his weapon felt good in his hands. He practiced religiously, was a damn good shot, though he'd only drawn twice in his years as a cop. Never pulled the trigger on anyone. It was usually the first question people asked when they found out he used to be a cop. Ever shoot anyone? No, he hadn't, and that was a good thing, but it didn't mean he couldn't.

Crouching, Joe circled around through the trees, finding the path of least resistance. The roar of the waterfalls grew louder the farther upstream he traveled, keeping his approach silent. In minutes he'd closed the distance and followed the shoreline as it rose higher and higher above the river.

He stopped when he reached the clear patch of ground from the trail that led over the edge of the high-dive cliff. Eddy and Kate were another twenty or so yards farther upstream where the precipice jutted out thirty feet above the water.

Joe could only see Kate's back, but Eddy was facing in his direction. His shiny pock-scarred face was tense and reddened, his brow low, lips snarling back from his teeth as he spoke. Kate stood in front of him hugging her elbows, shaking her head. She was talking, but Joe couldn't hear. There was a backpack on the ground near Eddy's feet. It was open with a crumpled ball of wrapping paper next to it.

Joe had to get closer. If he kept low and moved quick, he could cross the open ground and find cover again in the small patch of forest that still separated them. His muscles tightened, ready to bolt, but then a flash of light froze him to the spot. The fuckin' little prick had a gun.

Sunlight glinted off the barrel when Eddy waved it to emphasize his words. His actions spoke volumes. Eddy had no concept of the damage a gun could do. Joe's mind clicked over the good and bad of it, weighed his options. The good, Eddy was likely a lousy shot with little or no experience, and the bad, he didn't know enough to be scared to pull the trigger.

Shit.

Joe rolled his head on his neck, loosened muscles and moved when Eddy turned away. He'd closed the distance by nearly half and come as close as he could in secret. Eddy and Kate stood beyond the tree line in the center of a fifteen-foot stretch of open ground to the edge of the cliff. Joe leaned behind the very last tree between them.

"Just stop it," Eddy said. "Everything's perfect. You're ruining it. Take your birthday present so we can be together. You have to accept it."

"That's not how it works and you know it." Kate took a small step closer and Joe's gut clenched. "You can't give a person an engagement ring as a gift unless you're already a couple."

"We are a couple."

"No. We're friends."

Joe held his ground, waiting to see if Kate could talk Eddy off the proverbial ledge—and the real one. His shoulder braced against the thick tree trunk, Joe raised his gun, lined the shot and waited. He'd take Eddy out in a heartbeat if it came to it. He wouldn't think twice. Not when Kate was involved.

"That's how the best marriages start. As friends." Eddy closed the distance between them. "I love you, Kate. I know you love me. You're just scared to admit it."

"No, Eddy."

"I understand that you think it's wrong. I mean, it was only a couple years ago I was camper here, a kid. But I'm a man now. I can be what you need." He reached for her, a gun in one hand a ring box in the other. He stroked her arms with his wrists and Joe watched how Kate's body tensed.

"I saw what you did with Joe, Kate. When you were naked. I saw the two of you screwing. I'm not mad." Eddy shrugged. "Well, I was. But I know you were just trying to make me jealous. I forgive you. Besides, once we're married you'll be in my bed. Forever."

Kate stepped back, her mouth lax. "What do you mean you saw? You said... When?"

"You know when. At the house, and before that at Bare Lake. I watched him fucking you. You looked straight at me."

"No. That's not true and you know it. Listen to me. I didn't want you to watch me. I didn't want you to take those horrible pictures. I don't want to marry you. I don't feel that way about you. I can't."

Eddy shook his head, blinking. "But you do. I can tell. The way you treat me, the way you talk to me, like, like I'm special."

"I talk to you like a friend, Eddy. That's all. Understand?"

"No. You're lying. You're just saying that 'cause Joe's poisoned you against me. You think he's the only one who can do those things to you. But I can do everything he can, Kate. I want to. I think about being with you, being inside you all the time." He glanced to the bulging ridge at his crotch. "See what you do to me?"

Eddy moved to grab her, but Kate stepped out of his reach and right in the line of Joe's sight.

Dammit.

"Don't run from me." Eddy's voice dropped, held the sharp edge of anger. "You don't know what it's like watching Joe shove his cock inside you. Listening to you call his name, listening to you moan like that. I've lain in bed night after night thinking about doing that to you. I won't wait any longer. You can't tease me like this."

Instinct raised the hairs at the back of Joe's neck. The

251

situation had just gone south. He couldn't shoot. Kate was still in the way.

He strode forward, cleared his sight, gun double fisted in front of him. "Don't move."

But Eddy was just as quick. He lunged for Kate, spun her around, jammed the barrel of his gun against her head hard enough to make her wince.

The world stopped. Time ticked by slow and heavy with each solid thud of Joe's heart. "Let her go."

"No. No, you just, just go away." Eddy's gun hand was shaking. He inched them backward, holding Kate tight to his chest by crossing her arm to her opposite shoulder, his hand strangling her wrist.

"Not gonna happen, kid." Joe sidestepped, trying to find an opening. He was a damn good shot, but with Kate's body in front of Eddy's and his head ducked low by hers, Joe wasn't ready to take the risk.

"Why not? No one invited you. You're not supposed to be here." Eddy squeezed Kate tighter, stepped farther back. "You're ruining everything."

"Don't wanna hurt you, kid. You keep this up, it's not gonna end pretty."

"Shut up." Eddy wagged the gun at Joe, then swung it back to Kate's temple. "Just shut up. She's mine now. She took off that stupid ring you gave her. I got her a better one. A diamond."

"I took it off to clue Joe in—" Kate stopped short when Eddy jerked his grip around her, made her wince. They stumbled backward several steps before Eddy caught his balance and steadied Kate.

Joe swallowed the flash of rage flooding behind his eyes— found the numbing calm honed from years of training. "I got this, dollface."

"No. You don't have anything," Eddy said, his face red, lips curled back from his teeth. "You shouldn't even be here. I just needed a few more minutes. A few more minutes and she was gonna say yes."

"Wrong, kid."

"Ya-huh. You ruined it. That's why I brought her here. This is our special place. Where we kissed for the first time."

Kate squirmed. "I never kissed you."

Eddy's gaze dropped to Kate and Joe inched closer.

"Yes you did," he said. "The other kids were teasing me 'cause I'm not a good swimmer. You sat with me and hugged me. Told me a lot of smart people don't waste time learning to swim well. Then you kissed me."

"I kissed your cheek."

"'Cause the rules wouldn't allow you to kiss me on the lips."

"No, Eddy. I was—"

"Give it up, kid. You're not winning her this way," Joe said.

Eddy's looked up, eyes widening when he saw how close Joe had come. He shuffled back, dragging Kate. "Stay back. I don't need your opinion. You just want her for yourself. I won't give up. I've waited too long. She's the only one. I'd rather, rather die."

Something flashed behind Eddy's eyes, some desperate rationalization.

"Easy, kid," Joe said, circling slow, trying to herd him back from the cliff's edge.

"What would you do if I shot her?" Eddy's voice was like ice, chillingly calm.

"You'll go down before your ears stopped ringing."

Eddy flinched at Joe's blunt response. "Figured you'd say that. But then we'd finally be together."

He seemed to lose himself in his thoughts for a second, then his eyes focused on Joe again, brows high. "You think it'll hurt? When you shoot me, will it hurt?"

"Yeah. It'll hurt like hell."

Anger rolled across his face like a storm cloud. "'Cause

you'll make sure of it, right?"

The scenario shifted in Joe's mind. He was playing this wrong. "'Cause you won't die from it. She'll be gone. You'll have killed her for nothing."

Eddy blinked at that for a moment. "Bullshit. I don't believe you. You love her too much. You'll kill me on reflex. Won't even think about it."

Joe liked to believe he had more control than that, but he'd never been in this position before, never cared so damn much. This wasn't working. Trying to force the kid was pushing him in the wrong direction, both physically and emotionally. He'd shoot her or take her over the edge of the cliff with him. Time for a new tactic.

"Alright." Joe held up his hands in surrender. "Okay. You win. I'm puttin' it down. Let's talk this out."

Joe clicked on the safety and tossed the gun—not so far he couldn't dive for if he had to. Eddy's shoulders relaxed, his choking grip around Kate eased.

"Good. Yeah." He exhaled, watching Joe's gun as it hit the dirt. "But there's nothing to talk about. You need to leave. Everything will be fine if you'd just leave."

"I'm not leaving without Kate."

"'Cause you love her?" he asked, his tone caustic.

"Yeah." Joe's gaze dropped to Kate's, held. "I love her."

A smile tried to flicker across her soft lips, but Eddy's tightening grip squeezed it away. "Well, I love her too. I love her more. And she was starting to love me back."

Eddy shook his head, a twisted sneer curling his mouth. "Now, what? 'Cause of you I'm gonna go to jail. Right? And you'll be around to help her get over it. To get over me. It's not fair. If it weren't for you distracting her we'd be together already. If it weren't for you..."

That same telling flicker he'd seen before in Eddy's bug eyes was Joe's only warning. Eddy swung the barrel of his gun.

"What was I thinking? I just have to get rid of you. Solves everything."

A flurry of sequences happened at once. Joe dove toward his gun. An explosion roared past his ear. Kate screamed. White-hot fire pierced his flesh at the shoulder and the hard ground slammed the air from his lungs.

He centered his vision on Kate the instant he could and saw her ram her elbow into Eddy's gut. The tall lanky young man doubled over and Kate stomped the toe of his sneaker with her hard boot heel.

"You ass..." Kate shoved from his grip.

Eddy dropped the gun and stumbled back, pain squeezing his eyes nearly shut.

Adrenaline, fear, rage, all of it thundered through Joe like a freight train. His muscles coiled so tight his flesh was hot from it. He launched to his feet. Charged, shoulder down. The distance between him and Eddy disappeared. Their bodies collided, the young man's thinner frame buckling over Joe's like a wet blanket to a wrecking ball. Eddy huffed when he hit the ground, crushed between the hard earth and Joe's solid muscled body.

Joe pushed up to his knees, fisted the front of Eddy's T-shirt and jerked him up. His glasses were gone and he blinked, squinting, his brows tight, face an ugly snarl. Joe made a fist, punched—clean and quick. Kate's stalker collapsed beneath him.

"You're bleeding," Kate said when Joe stumbled back to her.

He glanced at his shoulder. His T-shirt was dark, nearly black, with blood. His flesh burned the second he actually saw the evidence of his wound. He bit back the pain, reorganized his thoughts to more important things.

"You okay?" He cupped her face even as she nodded. He had to touch her, had to make sure. Her skin was warm. The dark hair behind her ear, moist from sweat, brushed his fingers.

"I'm good." She forced a smile that trembled the more she tried. "Thought the two of you were going over the edge for a minute. Long drop and the water's not deep enough here."

Her smile vanished, eyes glistening as she buried her face in his chest. "Gawd, I thought he killed you when he shot that gun."

Joe stroked the back of her head, holding her. "Naww. Saw it comin'. Used my Spidey sense. Can't kill Spiderman with bullets."

She snorted, her laugh shaking her shoulders and the sound did things for him no drug on earth could do. She was alive. She was safe. *Thank God.*

He straightened, tipped his head toward the sky and exhaled. Relief rippled through him. Adrenaline drained away and with it the ability to ignore his body. A flood of burns and stabs and aches swamped over him. His shoulder, the stitch in his side, the scream of his muscles, exhaustion taking the flipside of adrenaline.

She shifted in his arms, raised her head so her chin rested against his chest. He imagined she was smiling at him, could almost feel those greener than green eyes staring up at him, but he didn't have the chance to look.

"Joe, watch out!"

Joe swung his gaze around just as Eddy rammed shoulder first into his side, ripping him from Kate's embrace. Eddy had knocked the wind out of Joe, and they hit the ground hard. Pain roared through Joe's body, centering like a white-hot poker at his shoulder. They tumbled, one over the other, toward the edge.

Just as the ground fell away beneath them and the open air rushed past, one thought echoed through Joe's head.

The water's not deep enough here.

Chapter Seventeen

"It's for you," Clayton said behind her. Kate twisted her chin to her shoulder, tucking the scratchy gray ambulance blanket tighter across her body. She dropped her gaze to the phone he held.

She sniffled. "Who is it?"

"Your father."

She felt her brows float up but couldn't help it. "What's he want?"

"To talk to you."

"I don't want—" She bit her bottom lip on the reflexive response. She wiped a tear from her cheek and took the phone.

"Hello."

"Katharine?" Edward Mathers' voice hadn't changed in fourteen years, a warm tenor, crisp, assured. She liked that, never mind why.

"Yeah."

"I, ah…heard you had one hell of a birthday." He sounded nervous, the lightness forced.

"Uh-huh."

"I'm glad you're all right. I'd, I'd like to see you. If you want. Perhaps dinner?"

Her belly tightened. "I—"

"Just dinner. No strings. I, I miss you, sweetheart."

Kate's gaze swung to the two patrol cars and the

ambulance blocking the circle drive of the main house ten yards away. Red, white and blue strobe lights flashed in sequence off the trees and grass and house, making movements seem stunted and turning everything a muted unreal shade. She hunkered closer to her knees on the step below her, Clayton still hovering close behind on the grand porch.

"It's been so long," he said. "I know I wasn't the best father. I've got no excuse. But I'm getting old. Well, old-*er*, and I'm starting to see things differently. We're family, Katharine. Blood. You're all I've got."

"My family's here."

"I know, I know, and I'm not asking for you to walk away from them. I'm just asking...I'm just asking for a place in your life."

Two ambulance attendants struggled with their gurney over the white gravel drive. Their patient lay still as death, tucked beneath a gray blanket, neon orange straps across his chest, waist and thighs. Metal legs collapsed as they shoved the slim bed into the back of the truck, one of them jumping in behind to check his vitals.

Kate's stomach roiled. Her body shook despite the warmth of the blanket. She couldn't tear her eyes from the long stretch of that body on the bed, from the poke of his toes beneath the blanket, the steady rise and fall of his chest.

"Katharine?" Edward Mathers said. "If it'll help, you can bring that Garity fellow. When he called to quit the other day I got the feeling things had taken a decidedly personal turn for him. I'm guessing the feeling's mutual?"

Her chin trembled, emotions choking at the back of her throat, a knot she couldn't swallow away. Her hand went to her lips, tried to hold back a building sob.

"Katharine?"

The door on the closest police car opened. A uniformed state cop pushed out. He turned and opened the back door. Joe's wet leg and sodden sneaker fell out, followed quickly by the rest of him. He stood, soaked to the bone, bandage over the wound on his shoulder, but safe. The cops were finally done taking his statement.

Joe shook the officer's hand then swung his dark eyes to Kate. His ink black hair clung wet against his head and in drying waves down to the tops of his shoulders. His mouth curled in a crooked smile, the scar at the corner of his lip lost in his grin. He winked and Kate's heart skipped.

"Katharine, are you—"

"Okay," she said to her father.

"What?"

"Dinner. I'll be there. And I'm bringing Joe...my boyfriend."

"Really? That's, that's great. Excellent. I'll call later to set a date. Soon, right?"

"Sure."

"Excellent. Then I'll talk to you soon. And Katharine?"

"Yeah?"

"Happy birthday."

"Thanks." She pushed the off button and raised her hand, knowing Clayton was close enough to take the phone.

"Just like that?" he asked. "All's forgiven?"

"No. But it's a place to start. And I can do that."

"Least he's finally showing some real interest. Can't believe he was Frank's email contact," Clayton said. "You think he's genuine? Paid a pretty penny for a few tidbits of info and some snapshots."

"Don't know. But it's time I find out." She pushed to her feet when she saw Joe heading toward her.

"I'm proud of you, Kate," Clayton said. "You've really come into your own. I admire you."

She glanced over her shoulder and smiled. "Yeah? Thanks, big brother."

"And as much as I hate to admit it." Clayton tipped his chin toward Joe. "He's a good man. He's also an arrogant ass, and he sure as hell takes some getting used to. But you mean more to him than his own life and I like that about him."

"Yeah." Kate winked. "I like that about him."

She jogged down the steps and over the cobblestone path, throwing herself into Joe's arms. He caught her, winced when her arm brushed over the bandage on his shoulder and squeezed her tight to his chest.

"Hey, dollface." He nuzzled her neck.

She loosened her hold, sliding down his body until her feet touched the ground. "Ick, you're cold and wet."

"Go figure." He framed her face with his hands, stole a kiss and she gave him another. The warmth of his mouth, the soft strength of his lips, sent a simmering wave of pleasure through her body. Heat pooled low in her pelvis, muscles flexing. She pushed up to her toes, wanting more, loving the hot taste of him, completely forgetting about his wet clothes.

"Ah, excuse me." They parted, though Joe's hands never left her waist, and looked to the police officer suddenly beside them. "Thought you might want this back. Found it up at the scene."

Joe glanced at Eddy's ring box. "Belongs to the guy on the gurney. How's he doing?"

"Concussion, broken leg, broken arm, couple busted ribs and a busted nose. Surprised you didn't break anything," the uniformed officer said.

"He cushioned my fall. Nothing I could do about it. Happened fast."

"I bet. Lucky you both survived," the cop said. "He'll be getting a psych eval. Let you know where things go after that."

"Thanks, man. I appreciate it."

The officer gave a nod then headed for the ambulance tossing the ring box and catching it as he walked.

"Oh no. Your ring," Kate said.

Joe stepped back and dug into the wet pocket of his jeans.

He pulled out his academy ring and held it up for her to see. "You mean this ring?"

"You kept it with you? Yes." She held out her hand in the small space between them, fingers splayed. "Can I have it back?"

Joe wrinkled his chin, shook his head. "The kid was right. It's a stupid ring to give to a woman."

Kate's chest squeezed. "No. It's perfect. I love it."

He shrugged. "No diamond."

"So? What difference does that..." Her breath caught. "Wait. What're you saying?"

"Marry me."

"Wha? We've only known each other a couple of weeks."

"We'll make it a long engagement if it makes you feel better."

Goose bumps rushed over Kate's body, her heart a thundering gallop in her ears. Was this happening? The sweet comfort and sizzling chemistry she felt with Joe was different, but did it really mean he was the *one*? Her heart knew the answer, but years of heartache made her hesitant.

"Then why bother getting engaged now?" she asked, emotion clogging at the back of her throat.

His dark eyes held hers, intense. He gathered her close. He was trembling, barely, but she felt it. "I can't live like this. I have to know you're mine. I have to know you're not going anywhere."

"I'm not going anywhere."

"Then marry me, Kate. I love you."

Her heart suddenly found a steady beat as the world slipped into perfect rotation. She smiled and pointed to the ring he'd closed in his hand. "I want that."

"Marry me and it's yours."

"You gave it to me for my birthday. Technically, it's already mine." Warmth and love flooded through her. She smiled, bright, happy. "And I'm already yours."

She splayed her fingers between them again and Joe slipped his precious ring into place.

"Yes, I'll marry you," she said. "But I'm keeping the ring."

"You keep the ring and I'll keep you. Sounds fair."

"Right."

About the Author

Alison Paige is the pen name of multi-published author Paige Cuccaro. She writes as Alison Paige when her stories run hot and spicy—and as Paige Cuccaro when the fun in the bedroom is more of a sexy simmer. The romance is always key, whether it's between people of this world, or out of this world.

Alison (Paige) lives in Ohio with her husband, three daughters, three dogs, three cats and one parakeet and a bearded dragon named Rexy in an ever-shrinking house. When she's not writing she can be found doing the mom thing with a book in one hand and a notepad and pen in the other. Ideas come without warning and the best way to stimulate your imagination is to enjoy the imagination of someone else.

To learn more about Alison Paige, please visit www.AlisonPaige.com. Send an email to Alison Paige at Paige@Cuccaronet.com.

GREAT CHEAP FUN

Discover eBooks!

THE FASTEST WAY TO GET THE HOTTEST NAMES

Get your favorite authors on your favorite reader, long before they're out in print! Ebooks from Samhain go wherever you go, and work with whatever you carry—Palm, PDF, Mobi, and more.

SAMHAIN
PUBLISHING
LTD

WWW.SAMHAINPUBLISHING.COM